The Second Cup

SARAH MARIE GRAYE

the dissociated voice

Acknowledgements

Thanks to Elena Schweitzer, Helen Addyman, Karl Drinkwater, Rachel Gilbey, Leanne Marshall and Suzie Cairney. And a special thanks to all the book bloggers who have supported me. Book bloggers are awesome.

To Dr Helen Read, for my diagnosis,
and for a life that's starting to make sense.

Today's the day

Today's the day. I'm going to do this.

That's what I say to myself over and over in my head as I pull on my leathers, fasten the straps on my boots, and pull on my crash helmet and adjust the chin strap. Actually, I'm mumbling to myself, saying it out loud: "Today's the day. Today's the day." I take a quick look round to make sure there's nobody around to hear me. Not that it would make much difference. I'm so focused on today I have no space in my thoughts for other people.

I walk up to my bike. She's a beauty. I think bikes are female, as ships are. There's something enslaving about her curves, the way she calls me. I'm addicted to the buzz I get when I ride her. I don't even need to be going quickly. I like to think she responds to my every move, but I'm also conscious of the sliver of fear I get whenever I twitch the throttle and her engine growls.

I put the key in the ignition, climb over her, then put my gloves on, taking time to pull my jacket sleeves over the edges. There's nothing quite like the pain you feel deep in your bones from riding a bike in the cold when you've got a draught between your layers. I've got a patch of skin on my lower back that I believe has been damaged from my early days of riding when my trousers and jacket didn't zip together. The nerve endings on a 10in-by-2in stretch of skin have never fully recovered, not even after hour upon hour of hot baths.

Kicking up the stand, turning the key, pulling in the clutch, putting her in first, I'm a conductor in front of an orchestra playing his favourite piece of music, I know every move. I pull down my visor, my final move before I pull off from the kerb and join the living.

"Today's the day."

1 teapot

FAYE

I. Must. Not. Blink.

I must not blink. If I blink he might not be there when I open my eyes again. As I stare at his back, he grows in front of my eyes, his shoulders broadening, splitting the seams of his suit. The sounds around me becoming the dull bass of dance music in a passing car. Other people merely debris collecting around the doorway to my right and gathering in piles of trash outside restaurants diagonally opposite. I'm not sophisticated enough for this end of town. But the independent boutiques and quaint shabby chic cafes morph into gaudy shops and chain restaurants before my eyes. It's embarrassingly bland now Jack's here.

What does he think about how Manchester has changed? It's not on his mind right now. He's listening intently to the man facing him, dressed in an identikit suit to the one he is wearing, who is talking animatedly about something, struggling to gesture with both hands when one of them holds a heavy laptop bag and the other contains a carry-out coffee cup. They look like they're heading to an important business lunch, their coffees the fuel to keep them going through three courses of meeting and maybe to help combat the bottle of beer they will have as a nod to the fake freedom these trips out of the office afford them. I always thought Jack would end up the sort of person who attended important business lunches. I always worried he would be.

I swallow awkwardly to push down the lump that has formed in my throat. The skin reaching down below the back of my tongue and into my oesophagus is too dry to cope with my desperate gulping. The sides stick together as my throat constricts. It is painful but, like the traffic and the people causing an irritating hubbub around me, I ignore it and stare at his back. My blink creeps up the inside of my eyelids. The whites of my eyes ache and tingle, pricked by a thousand pins no thicker than the hairs of a newborn. I have to blink; I have no choice. I surrender to the fogginess of the inside of my eyelids then wrench my eyes open again. I want to kiss the man Jack is talking to for rooting him to the spot just 30 yards in front of me, for holding him there longer than my blink. There's a jiggle in my hips – what my Mum called my ants-in-my-pants-dance. I could never stand still as a kid.

Ants. In. My. Pants.

Fate has brought Jack to me today. I'd cursed when I'd laddered my favourite sparkly green tights. Footless ones so my toes didn't get pinched by the seams. Ones I could wear with socks. My outfit wouldn't work then, so I'd had to strip off to my smalls and start again. I'd cursed again – and this time out loud – when Waterstone's in the Arndale only had a hardback of *Everything You Need You Have* in stock. I had to traipse over to the branch on Deansgate for the paperback. But now, when I'm just yards from reaching the Deansgate store, I realise it was meant to be.

If it hadn't been for the Machiavellian splinter sticking out at the bottom of the bannister, my tights would have escaped ladder-free, allowing my legs to get me into town earlier and maybe in time to buy the last paperback copy of the book in the Arndale. I hadn't asked when the last one was sold, but it's feasible that it was earlier today – and I hope it was because it made bumping into Jack all the more fragile and all the more delicious. I need ants in my pants now. I'm tense. I relax my jaw and shake out the stiffness consuming my body by jiggling my arms and hopping from foot to foot. I blow out air a few times, filling my aching cheeks. I need to be ready if he turns around.

If. He. Ever. Does.

Not that I'm leaving this up to his actions. I can't risk Jack and his companion walking the other way. Nope, I'm grasping this with both of my typically paint-splattered hands. I notice a green man flashing to my left. Perfect. I cross Deansgate in a few purposeful strides. I've got my fake Ugg boots on. They're moon boots because they're so bouncy. I've got socks on plus slipper socks inside my boots to keep my feet warm. And I have memory foam insoles that, although they have gone a bit lumpy, still give me that extra lift with each step. They may not take me to Jack by a single click of a red sequined heel, but they're the fastest footwear I own.

A few glances down the side of House of Fraser and I'm across to the busy restaurant corner. The human mass outside is a mix of the office crowd, foreign students attempting to experience the tastes of England, and bewildered OAPs harking back to how different it was when they popped in for a pre-theatre dinner. The group is the perfect camouflage and I can stare at Jack without causing

3

strangers on the street to stumble away from me in panic. I try to get a good look at his hands. They were one of my favourite parts of him because they were so huge and would consume my dainty ones in one gulp. He always claimed to love my hands too, but it's a compliment I found hard to believe at the time.

PAINT-SPLATTERED HANDS

It was coming up to the end of the first term and it seemed like Jack was holding Faye's hand at every available moment to compensate for the time he wouldn't be able to over the Christmas break. Although Jack's home in Preston wasn't that far away, Jack and Faye were still too young to consider visits to each other's parents. It would be another 18 months before Faye graced the front step of Jack's parents' house – at Faye's insistence – and it would be her one and only visit there.

Faye's hands were always a mess of overly dried and paint-streaked skin, her nails always a rainbow of the flecks of paint that worked their way underneath her nails, and sometimes within the splitting layers, refusing to be budged by the spinning hook on the inside of her set of nail clippers no matter how much she scraped. Her dry, cracked skin got worse as her course continued, no matter how much Nivea she slapped on.

Her final year work was in acrylics and she loved using rich blacks and deep, oppressive blues. Limiting her colour palette had positive financial implications too. Her work contained sweeping arcs that were reminiscent of Georgia O'Keeffe's flowers, but less overtly sexual and more aggressive. That's what Faye liked to think anyway, although for her tutors there was "an understanding" missing from her work that couldn't be learned: that she needed to go out and live life and experience sorrow before she could transfer it successfully into the canvas. One of them even yearned for a life where only mature students studied fine art so that those inexperienced in the ways of the world were forced to go out and live in it first. Another believed Faye shouldn't just be reading books about the artist that influenced her work, but heading to places such as Santa Fe – where O'Keeffe's museum was and where she spent much of her working life – and to walk down the same streets the painter had walked, to experience the painter's life from a range of different angles.

Jack loved holding Faye's hand. It wasn't an issue of ownership, more of showing her off as a prize, as if he'd been the only one clever enough to leave the confines of Manchester University and venture into the creative belly of Manchester Metropolitan University to seek out an unusual beauty of translucent skin and burnt curls, of a figurine who could have stepped out of a Pre-Raphaelite painting herself. Why she could almost be Jane Morris – the artists' muse, model and encapsulator of all things from that era. Except Faye was born 140 years later, so her narrower jaw, wider eyes, thinner lips and altogether more "feminine" face of modern day tastes were never captured by Dante Rossetti's sleight of hand and manipulation of brush.

What Jack usually left out of the telling of this story is that they met at a walk-in centre, being typical students who had not only not listened to their parents when they were told to register with a GP as soon as they arrived, but who also ended up ill in Freshers' week. It had been an usually hot and muggy week for late September, especially in Manchester. The main job of the doctors was looking out for cases of meningitis, and handing out the usual doses of antibiotics needed to keep glandular fever at bay. That particular year, their tasks also included handing inhalers out like sweeties to anyone who might have smog-induced asthma. Jack and Faye had queued for matching drugs in the pharmacy afterwards, while he joked she had caused his breathlessness.

Since leaving university, Faye had lived to understand what her tutors meant. She had felt the pain, loss and anger they thought she needed to feel to grow as an artist. Although her newer work contained far less black paint, it was very much darker, harder and colder – far bleaker than anything she could have imagined herself producing within the walls of the university and the constraints of a degree.

Faye had lost her life when she lost Jack. He stopped holding her tiny, fragile hands in his boulderous ones; he turned and walked away. She was made of amorphous solid and as each of his footsteps vibrated through the paving stones heading away from her, they reverberated through her glasslike structure, fracturing her life, her body, her soul into too many tiny slithers. No matter how many pieces of herself she picked up and fused back together, there were always more pieces missing, more pieces to be found. And after seven years of hunting, Faye had stopped looking, deciding to live with the cracks hidden under her clothes in an attempt to get on with her life. It was a decent attempt too because while she didn't think of him, she was able to construct a new version of herself where she stopped seeing the spider's web of fissures that crawled across her body. She filled the gaps in her life with reading and meditation, and with yoga. She eventually reached the stage where she could speak his name and although her heart would pound, it wouldn't pulse out of her chest, splintering her fragile frame once again.

She became able to think of him in abstract terms and talk about the life they'd lived together as undergraduates, telling the story up until the point where he left, just after she attended his graduation ceremony with his parents, fighting for one of the few extra tickets, brushing over the fact that he didn't attend hers, even though her Mum needed only one of the two tickets automatically issued to her. The tiny chinks in their relationship had already begun to appear by the time Jack upped sticks and moved to London without her. It's just that Faye hadn't been able to see them (or made excuses for them) until afterwards, when she was looking back. Then she saw all of them, magnified in their new significance and she started to doubt the very core, the very foundations on which their relationship had been built. Mostly though, she just had unanswered questions.

She longed to see him, to talk to him. But she couldn't. Ethan kept her grounded and attempted to keep her sane, but he also kept her stuck in Manchester for long enough that she lost her chance to follow Jack. It was the time before Facebook, and Jack was able to easily slip between the layers of life in the capital and effectively become one of the ghosts locked up in the Tower of London.

But as she painted, Faye grew stronger, and with each stroke she started to heal herself. The canvas became her therapy and she became more complete with each composition. Faye stopped needing Jack. She moved on.

FAYE

I catch a glimpse of one of his hands. They're not as big as I remember, but then I'm not as birdlike, so all things are relative. I stare down at my hands. They are aching. My fingers, my arms, my chest and down into my boots, I ache for the person I got over years ago. I'm hit with a sudden and severe case of dystonia, my whole frame seizing up. I freeze: every muscle stiffens and cramps, every ligament tightens, every tendon contracts. Pulled by my marionette strings, my limbs jerk as I weave in and out of oncoming pedestrians. I reach the next layer of human coverage outside another neon and plastic eatery. Here I'm hidden by a collection of buses at the bus stop too, their engines trundling like the curmudgeonly musings of impatient old men too arthritic to get moving, but who take great pleasure in their grumblings.

I use this cover to cross back over. Jack and his companion are now ahead of me once again, but this time I have Jack facing me, half hidden behind the boulder of shoulder of the man mountain he's talking to. His coffee is from Subway. I want to run up and smash the textured paper cup out of his hand. As much as I don't want Jack to be a city boy, I would rather that than a failed attempt. Why not a rich cup of Illy? But he does have his back to Patisserie Valerie. Maybe it is his companion who doesn't want to spend money on coffee, who doesn't see it as an everyday luxury to treat oneself to.

Beth refuses to fall in love with coffee. She is obedient to all that is old-fashioned tea with milk. I long for her to be with me right now so we can face this together. I could lean on her confidence and her conversational skills. "Jack," she could say, "Long time no see" she could say, even though she's never met him. But he would recognise her and crush her with one of his hugs. And then she would refer to me. "Remember Faye?" she would ask, with enough of a question in her voice to not sound arrogant that of course he would. But it would be evident that he did from the shyness in his smile and the way he would glance down at the space between our feet.

I look from his coffee cup to his face.

A. Mono. Brow.

His eyes are too close together and between them a

smattering of rebellious hairs that have crossed over the bridge of his nose. A nose that surely should be more bulbous too? His broad chin and slight ears are the right shape, but his top lip is too thin and disappears all at once too soon to meet the edge of his bottom one. Someone has rearranged all his features. He no longer looks like himself. I have to find out what has happened to him.

"Jack?"

He looks up at me, straight at me, in fact. He knows his name. His companion turns to look too.

"Hello?"

It is his companion who answers for him. Why doesn't Jack speak for himself?

"Do I know you?" His companion asks.

"Jack, do you know this woman?" Jack asks his companion, calling him Jack, which is rather strange. The companion shakes his head a little, attempting to answer "No" to Jack without offending me.

"It's not you I know," I tell the companion, "It's Jack," I say, nodding in the direction of Jack.

Jack stares back at me, his face becoming even less familiar as it is flooded with a mix of bemusement and confusion.

"I'm not Jack."

I look hard at him, blinking. And I blink again. Now I can't blink enough. The windscreen wipers of my eyelids wash away the blurriness to help me to see clearly. But the swimming features in front of me won't form into the face I remember.

"I'm not Jack," he says again, this time softer as if recognising the absolute importance to me that he is.

Warm vomit rises in my throat, flooding my once-dry

skin with too much wetness. I have to get away from Jack and NOT-Jack before the contents of my throat works its way into my mouth, through the hairline cracks between my clamped lips, and over onto the paving stones and their shined leather shoes. I stumble away from them, raising a palm to them to tell them that I'm okay, that it's a case of mistaken identity, that it's not their fault that the wrong one of them is called Jack – and that I'm just fine dealing with this news on my own. As I walk backwards, I receive an aggressive shoulder barge from someone who thinks I should have turned around before trying to make my escape. The bang jolts the vomit into my mouth and I turn and throw my face forwards, sending the warm greeny-yellow liquid down the concrete blocks that separate Subway from its neighbour. I stare at the sick in shock, realising I can identify the worms of noodles I had for lunch.

There. Are. No. Carrots.

Suddenly this NOT-Jack person has his arms round my shoulders and is leading me into St Anne's Square and over to a bench where he can sit me down. He sits down next to me, one arm limp around my shoulders, unsure of what to do next: whether to take a firm grip on my shoulders, or to rub my back, or to sit there in silence, or maybe get up and leave. He chooses silence. So we sit there in silence together, with the real-but-not-the-right-Jack standing watching from just a few feet away.

This. Is. Not. What. I. Laddered. My. Tights. For.

2 teabags

BITE MARKS

"Brrrrm. Brrrrrrrm. Brrrrrrrrrrm."

Beth makes the noises for the toy motorbike as she takes it careering round the edge of the window ledge, pretending the bite marks along the edge of the wood are tyre treads. Except they aren't bite marks, they're scars left by a family of woodworms marching their way through Beth's house. But Beth's parents don't know that yet. And because Beth is the naughty one the assumption is made that the teeth marks are hers. Beth can no longer remember they aren't hers because she's heard the story so many times it now sounds like the truth. But then who questions their parents when they're five years old?

BETH

The world around me is changing. Am I changing with it? I'm no good at change. I know that nobody is, not really, but I'm worse than most. Boredom suits me better than the pounding in my chest and in my ears that comes with anxiety and stress. But this time is going to be different. I'm embracing change: because of Faye.

There are days when I wake up with a fire crackling inside me so loud I can achieve anything. On those days I still own a motorbike and take it down the roads out to Buxton, the wind howling, making me shiver but also warming me. But I can no longer get to ride along the famous biking roads into the Derbyshire Dales to the Cat and Fiddle Inn, no longer park up alongside the other two-wheeled grown-up toys, and no longer head inside to warm myself up with a mug of hot chocolate or a decent brew. I sold my bike before I moved back up to Manchester.

I bought it as a graduation present to myself – a second-hand Yamaha TZR 125cc, the £600 price tag added onto my graduate loan. But within weeks of buying it I started having terrifying dreams. Riding my motorbike along narrow country lanes, the wind whipping at me, the hedges seeming only inches from me. The front wheel starts to give way and the screeching bike slides from under me. I travel one way the bike another, totally out of control. That's when I wake up, crying out, coated in sweat. Or I'm on a motorway with high concrete walls either side and when the road corners slightly I can't go with it because my steering is locked. I have to let the bike go from underneath me in an attempt to save myself or crash along with my bike headlong into the concrete embankment. It's like a dream where you're falling, but I wake up just before my body smashes into the wall, my skin wet and clammy. Once these dreams became frequent travellers in my sleep, I stopped enjoying riding, fearing that I'd become a red stripe along tarmac or an ugly mosaic on a concrete wall. My fate was visiting me in my slumber and being played out before my closed eyes. But it wasn't the fear of death that consumed me, but the fear of the pain I'd be left in if I survived. And what if I ended up paralysed? Worse than pain, I feared being out of control.

I sold my bike within six months of buying it. My parents were thrilled, so thrilled in fact that it didn't occur to them to tread carefully on the subject. My parents would refer to my "crazy motorbike purchase", mocking me not only for buying one but also not being "crazy enough" to want to ride it. On a couple of occasions, I was close to telling them I sold it because I was worried I'd decorate a stretch of road with grisly fragments of my brain. But I didn't bother, knowing my parents would see it as me being melodramatic and not take me seriously. If there's one thing that's going to push you to kill yourself, it's your parents mocking you for it. They were often my final straw. I'd also have to hear the story, yet again, about how I'd only bought a motorbike because my Mum had taken a toy one off me as a child because I was making too much noise. Everything was about me making too much noise. I don't even remember having a toy motorbike. Would my parents let me have such a toy?

The days where I wake up with purpose and hope are flanked by many other days where there seems little point in going through the motions because the only reward is sleep, simply an intermission to waking up and doing it all over again. I've tried to keep the fire burning by living recklessly, as the orange hues of the flames are the only colours flanking the edges of my life. But how can you choose this? How do you live recklessly if you're not reckless by nature? I am sometimes impulsive, but if there's any preparation involved, it's not recklessness. When I forget feigned spontaneity doesn't work, I fill my life with dares, often private ones I share with no-one but myself, pacts with my mind that make me seem defiant of the natural order of things. My friends don't understand I'm just keeping the kindling burning; they believe I am a force of nature for pushing myself ever further towards the edges of my own achievements.

Faye understands my love of dares because she too loves filling her life with "mini adventures" – although for different reasons. She is the person most likely to head to Manchester Piccadilly station and jump on the next train about to leave to see where it will take her. It's why I've been to Marple, Faye meeting me at the departures board with a picnic hastily bought from Sainsbury's. The plan was to pick a random train from the board – although we'd limit ourselves to £5 a ticket. We chose to head to New Mills Central, but by the time we'd got to the front of the queue to buy tickets, we'd missed the train. The guy behind the counter looked more than a little confused at Faye's request to list other stopping trains so we could pick one, Faye declaring Marple sounded best out of the choices, the glint in her eye, the smile flickering over her lips, enjoying a moment of harmless abandon.

We got on the rickety old two-carriage train that had spluttered as it pulled into Piccadilly. It couldn't manage as far as the end-of-line bumpers at the platform, never mind Marple. The man who climbed out of the driver's carriage to take up his seat at the opposite end of the train looked like the human version of the train, old and past his best. Hunched slightly, he struggled along the length of the two carriages, resting his hand on the side of the train to catch his breath before hauling himself up into the driver's carriage at the opposite end. The guard, who'd opened the doors for the dozen or so passengers getting off, was slightly more spritely in his step but still looked like he'd be heading off to a care home at the end of his shift. Somehow these two old men managed to get the train to leave on time – a grand feat in today's cacophony of National Rail and a myriad of multicoloured franchises. The sharp pinks of First Transpennine's new trains competed with the splash of red on Virgin trains and the cool elegant aquamarine of Arriva Trains Wales, each vying for a platform, and each fighting for the next green light. Our purple and blue Northern Rail train rasped along, giving views mainly of the backs of houses with glimpses of half-hearted rural landscapes. We chatted non-stop about nothing of any substance, talking over each other and finishing each other's sentences like we were siblings maybe, or an old married couple. We chatted over the simple food choices Faye had made: cheese sandwiches, cheese'n'onion crisps and cloudy lemonade.

Each time we pulled into a tin-pot little station that was little more than slabs of concrete by the side of the track, the train would hiss and wheeze to get itself going again. I had no idea if we'd make it to Marple but I understood the joy Faye got from escaping somewhere new on a train: getting a kick out of the journey itself, watching other people's versions of the world go by. Getting on a train just for the hell of it was the perfect planned and purposeful escapism.

I'd met Faye when I'd gone for another one of my long walks – in an attempt to clear my head – meandering in and out of streets, exploring little sections of the city I didn't know between the main roads that I did. I found myself by a row of shops in West Didsbury, back when it was still the unfashionable part of the neighbourhood, and before it became recognised as the uber-cool bohemian quarter. I'd wandered along, so lost in my thoughts, that I hadn't noticed I was getting tired and hungry. I wasn't sure of the closest park, but my plan was to find somewhere to buy something to eat then hunt for the signs of one, a huddle of treetops, in every direction, to have an impromptu picnic. First though: food. A newsagent, a grubby Chinese takeaway, and a deli. I chose the deli – the best choice for finding something that made my insides feel good. The delicious smells hit me as I walked in. I wasn't hungry; I was starving. My mouth salivated and I had to fight the urge to dive on the food the other side of the raised glass counter and gorge myself.

"What would you recommend?" I asked the girl the other side of the counter.

"Well," she said, obviously well versed in answering this question. "It depends whether you're looking for, something hot or cold, whether or not you're a meat eater or a vegetarian…"

"Both," I said. "To both questions."

She frowned at me, confused.

"Want both hot and cold, eat both meat and veggies."

She saw the look of hunger in my eyes and smiled.

"I'd recommend our pasties: they're homemade," she said. "Not by me," she added hastily, as if I might think that and then discover she was a fraud.

I nodded, and she put one in a bag for me.

"I'll take that now, while I think about what else I want."

"£1.25," she said, handing me the bag while I fought around in my pocket for some change.

I took a huge bite of the pasty and let the pastry melt on my tongue while I chomped through the meat and potato filling. After gulping it down and before taking the next bite, I asked: "What else?"

That's when she offered me the chance to try a scorchingly hot chilli. And somehow, we ended up sitting in the back of the shop, chatting as we both ate, her picking at her food and doing most of the talking, me nodding along while I gulped down milk to help my mouth recover from the chilli challenge.

At the end of her shift, the pair of us left the shop – the owner giving us both Paddington Bear hard stares, wondering why Faye had allowed me to be in the back of the shop on the fold-down chairs reserved for staff. I don't know if he ever grilled her about it, but he was always a bit gruff with me whenever I went in the deli after that, even though I always bought loads of food.

"I must be one of his best customers," I'd once said to her, but she shook her head, laughing.

"All the regulars think that: that the place would struggle if the money they spent here was suddenly withdrawn. The food is fantastic and my job is to make sure every customer thinks they're the only one who's cleverly discovered it."

I hadn't only discovered the food; I'd discovered Faye too: the girl who could open her emotional floodgates on a whim, who rarely left anything bottled up. The opposite of me.

THE SLOW TRAIN

When they get to Marple, they head downhill first, discovering a ridiculously perfect high street of boutique shops with a high-end gastropub next to a river, where they treat themselves to bottles of posh organic ginger beer. They then head up the hill, beyond the station, sniggering in the shock and bewilderment to discover that Marple's centre is a typical small-town mish-mash of red brick, brown brick, glass and concrete slabs that culminated in a soulless and characterless pedestrianised street of chain shops. It was a mix that would seem inoffensive anywhere else but is jarring after their picture postcard morning. Although it's the drabness that helps jerk Beth back to reality and makes her journey back to Piccadilly and her own colourless existence a slightly less painful one.

They visit New Mills a few months later and it's like visiting Royston Vasey from *The League of Gentlemen*, where the shops are "local shops for local people". They return to the station early, sitting on a bench trying to swing their feet like kids do, even though their legs are long enough to smack against the tarmac. For Beth, swinging her feet is an attempt to stay in the moment. Staying in the moment stops her coming back down to earth with such a bump that she bruises her coccyx and her bones and teeth rattle. But even if Beth stays in the moment at the time, afterwards there's a longing for something to fill the space the adventure leaves. During an adventure, she can carry an atlas stone in each hand and pull a 5-ton truck with her little finger. Afterwards she's a dead moth's wing, all dried up, crumbling to a whisper.

There are days when to find herself so parched would be a blessing as she's filled with the tears from every injustice anyone has ever faced and all the injustices there are to come. Worse still though, is when she needs to cry but finds there's a dam behind her eyes, when even the normal fluid coating each pupil, iris and sclera is soaked up by her body. Blinking and dry-eyed on the outside; drowning on the inside.

BETH

I'd been expecting an uneventful end to an ordinary Friday: a few drinks after work before heading home. The only thing strange about the day had been the weather: the sun was shining. I'd been back in Manchester for about two years after being down south for eight, and every time I'd visited in those eight years – in winter or in summer – it had rained. Yes, it was a typically cold January day, but what little snow had fallen had now melted, the rain hadn't replaced it, and there wasn't a cloud in the sky. Anyone who wonders why the English talk about the weather should come to Manchester. Even a rare true summer treat of vest top and flip-flops will be accompanied by a sneakily hidden umbrella.

Unruly weather pleases me. It refuses to be monitored or controlled, sometimes waning towards the day's weather report only to abandon it abruptly a few hours later. It's so honest about who is in charge: the world is, not the people. So much happens outside of our authority, yet we kid ourselves that we are in control of our fate. Tell that to someone killed by a lightning strike, or by a tree crushing their car in high winds. And if we don't control our own deaths, what control do we have over our lives? Except that right now, after this week's Friday drinks, I'm strong enough to beat at my chest, give an ululating cry, and swing between trees, from vine to vine. This all-consuming strength grew from the tiniest molecules of fortitude forming in the hippocampus and is now pulsing from my every pore like a cymbal-crashing, drum-rolling crescendo. Like the Gorilla from the Cadbury's Dairy Milk advert.

I'd been sitting in The Blue Pig with Olivia and Abbie, in our favourite booth in the corner by the window, underneath one of the bar's absurdly large chandeliers. We'd been swapping stories of the day when Faye had arrived, taken a big gulp out of her pint before slamming it down on the table, making all three of us jump.

"Right, now I have your attention," Faye said. "I have some news." She paused for effect. "I've just not met Jack."

"What?"

I was the first to speak. I usually am. My sensitivity cog works far slower than my curiosity cog, so I often put my foot in it. But you can't really go wrong with a simple question like "What?" – especially when it's the reaction your audience is looking for.

Sitting next to me, Faye took centre stage, embellishing her story with theatrical twists and turns, pausing in all the right places to allow us to respond with the appreciative "ooh" and "ah" noises she expected. She took her story beyond the point of the taxi home, telling us about the old shoeboxes underneath her bed that she searched through to find photos where his features were in the right places. Faye wasn't over Jack. That's what this boiled down to. She had no choice but to find him to see if he thought them splitting was the same terrible mistake she did.

I'd heard the story of Jack so many times I'd forgotten it wasn't mine; that it had happened to someone else, was part of someone else's life. When Jack first got himself a job down in London, Faye had eagerly talked to him about living in London together. She was a few days into making plans – choosing areas to visit, deciding whether or not to go for a larger flat or a nicer area – when she noticed discomfort spread up from Jack's body and across his face. The more she talked about plans, the more uncomfortable he looked until he broke down and told her that he'd found a room in a shared house in Hackney – that he wasn't inviting her to join him. She was meant to be the love of his life and she was being replaced by a life in the capital and a posh new job. Faye was demoted to a life of singledom.

That was seven years ago, and in so many ways Faye had moved on. She'd thrown herself into her painting, her grief oozing out of her fingers through the brush and onto the canvas, every stroke painful, every painting hauntingly beautiful. Deep down I knew her heart remained out in the wilderness, never fully coming to terms with the future she would now never have. But the wilderness brings with it a certain freedom, and Faye's feelings had been released into each rich and flourished composition. Now she wanted to give up that freedom, to return from the wilderness, and looking for Jack would give her an action plan, a future laid out, a point on the horizon to aim for.

I felt a stab of jealousy, which jabbed me in the ribs, the blade clashing against bone, knocking the breath out of me. But the hot jealousy was quickly stomped out by a rush of shame crawling over me like an army of centipedes, their tiny feet stomping my skin into itchy red tracks. Wanting it for myself would mean taking it from Faye. We couldn't both have the same happy ending.

"I think you should seize the moment too," she said to me. Then, casting her eyes around the group, she'd added: "All of you."

"But I've already got a man," Olivia said, a look of nervous indignance on her face.

Did Matt count as a man? I'm sure if you stripped him off he'd have the same dangly bits as any other bloke, but there was something about him that made him seem very much not like a real man at all. If you peeled off his skin would he reveal himself to be a lizard-like creature? Was it lizards who would have no compunction as to how they treated their girlfriends? Olivia looked at me for support, but Abbie beat me to it, which is good because I had nothing good to say about the guy at all.

"Faye isn't talking about us all seeking out new men; she's talking about us all seizing what we want out of life rather than living out our lives in the half-existence she 'thinks' we occupy now."

Faye nodded enthusiastically, not noticing the stress Abbie put on the word "thinks".

"I mean we should be grabbing our lives with both hands and making something of the opportunities in front of us,"

Faye said. "Happiness is within our grasp – we just have to be willing to reach out."

Olivia looked down at her shoes, her thin blonde hair falling and forming a self-preservation force field across her face, wishing she'd never spoken. She's a timid thing at the best of times and hiding behind her hair is her intuitive way of protecting herself from possible bullying. Livvy didn't want to grab the world with both hands; she wanted to move through it as painlessly as possible. Actually, no, she wanted to sit as still as possible and have the world leave her alone, Faye included.

First jealousy, then shame, and now guilt. I was the one who brought Faye's friendship into the mix. Before that my friendship had been a much safer place for Olivia. Abbie and I were counterbalances, each of us stepping in when the other one pushed Olivia too much – which usually meant Abbie sorting out the mess after I'd opened my sizable mouth once or twice too often.

Faye turned her attention back to Abbie.

"Thinks," Abbie said. "The half-existence you 'think' we occupy."

Standing up, Abbie shook her hair away from her face in response to Olivia's cloaking, and took the tactical response of heading to the ladies and removing herself from the equation entirely. Abbie has a great career that drains the life out of her; a beautiful house that drains her finances; and is on her second husband, who drains her emotionally. She has more than enough life slipping through her fingers but maybe didn't want to grab it to stop it from slipping away.

So that just left me.

The champagne of teas

A black tea from India, Darjeeling is known as the "champagne of teas". Grown in lush green tea plantations on the foothills of the Himalayas, the large-leafed plant produces a delicate and fragrant flavour.

Olivia loved to go for afternoon tea with Beth – the Edwardian glamour of the Rosylee tearooms, the vintage quirkiness of Sugar Junction, the thrill of somewhere new. Knowing the tea's nickname, she would always choose a pot of Darjeeling for herself to secretly toast the unexpected success of her friendship with Beth.

3 teacups

OLIVIA

When Faye talked about each of us making changes to our lives there were three sets of eyes on me. Maybe only fleetingly, but I still felt them. And if I sniffed I could almost smell the wafts of pity. Every day I'm alive is a day I'm judged. What the others didn't understand, and what Beth forgot, is that Matt rescued me first.

I used to work for a large consultancy, probably a lot like the one Abbie works for. It sounds impressive – enough to impress my Mum and have her telling all of the neighbours – but I worked in an open-plan office full of typists and admin girls, and was like being back in the school playground. I was the girl who didn't wear lashings of mascara and huge hoop earrings; the one who wore neat ankle socks instead of long socks pushed down into choreographed wrinkles; the one who wore her school tie with the thick end in front and who didn't pick the stripes out. I had "bully me" tattooed on my forehead.

THE PIT

It can't be as bad as school, Olivia tells herself. But she is wrong. And although she tries to get on with them, she is the outsider once again. Very soon she stops trying to be part of their gang, thinking they will leave her alone and concentrate on their other victims. But this only seems to make things worse. They are angry she believes she is above their opinions of her. Every time the door to "the pit" – as she has not-so-fondly named the basement office – opens Olivia hopes it's a bloke, any bloke, because the girls will forget about her long enough to preen themselves and flirt with whoever it is. It's pathetic to witness, but it's also a relief. She watches them simper and giggle, and in return watches the men become absorbed.

Sophie is the queen bee of the group. She wears her dark brown hair as a backcombed and smoothed mountain upon her head with clipped in extensions forming rivers down her back. Her mascara is so thick her eyelashes are spider legs and her foundation so heavy her skin takes on the texture of suede. She keeps the rest of the girls, her flock, in check with her mood swings: mischievous and fun one minute, moody and cold the next. The only time her mood is stable is when the pit door swings open. The sneer that curls at Sophie's top lip turns into a pout: she lowers her defiant chin into a more submissive pose. And the eyes that were narrowed at Olivia now gaze at the new arrival briefly, before flitting away and back again as the intended receiver of her attention returns her glance. Although she would love to fit in, to be accepted, Olivia doesn't understand why men flirt with Sophie and why the other girls want to be just like her.

The only bloke Sophie isn't interested in is the post boy, Matt. Olivia knows it's him coming into the pit long before she sees him because Sophie's face distorts in his presence, her mask slipping and her features contorting into the Bride of Chucky. Unfortunately for Olivia, while Sophie's gang are purposefully ignoring Matt, they have time on their hands to make stinging comments to her – and occasionally to the other outcasts, who have distanced themselves from Olivia in an act of self-defence. Matt always tells them to shut up and stop being so nasty, but they respond with comments like "Can you hear something? No? It must be my imagination." – and then dissolve into giggles.

Matt can brush off comments aimed at him because he can quickly escape the pit after his short, twice daily visits. It is the nasty comments fired at the "shy blonde girl" he finds difficult. He is unable to watch Olivia cowering in the corner fighting for her life as Sophie's scorpion tail thrashes around, her extended telson piercing Olivia's flesh with a level of intensity and urgency that he never sees aimed at anyone else. For Matt, the final straw is when they make her cry.

OLIVIA

I desperately try to wipe the eyeshadow off with tissue, using the tears collecting in the corners of my eyes as make-up remover. One tear managed to work its way down my cheek, taking glittery green sweet-smelling clumps with it. Sophie gasps with a heady mixture of delight and feigned shock, covering her mouth with her hands, showcasing her bejewelled false nails in the process. Her sheep re-enact her stance; all nails and slack jaws.

My tears are from the frustrations of my own stupidity as much as they are from the girls' cruelty. I was stupid enough to be persuaded to try on eyeshadow that came free with a magazine, wanting too much to believe the compliment that the mid-green shade would suit me. I failed to grasp they were setting me up for a heady mixture of "scally" comments and cackles of laughter. Not even hiding behind my hair is going to save me this time.

"Oh-em-gee! She's actually crying," Sophie exclaims, not even attempting to conceal her delight. "She's crying because she realises how ugly she is."

Matt leaves his trolley mid-round and storms out of the office. The girls make jokes about him being my superhero, but their nervous laughs betray them. Images of the Virginia Tech massacre fill my mind as I wonder if Matt somehow has access to a gun and is going to shoot them all down in a spray of bullets. I know nothing about him other than he pushes the post trolley round the building. Maybe he's as unhinged as Seung-Hui Cho and is ready to slaughter the bitches of the pit before turning the gun on himself. Sophie would be the first one down, her face blown off, the blood splattering her fan club, them huddling together and crying, begging for Matt to forgive them, to spare them.

The pit door is pushed open again, this time by one of the managers from HR. She holds the door open with the tips of her fingers, as if not wanting to come into contact with anything to do with our office, not wanting to breathe in the stench of cloying perfume and cheap hairspray. She scans the space disapprovingly, her cropped bob swishing left and right, but always falling perfectly back into place. She looks behind her and Matt steps into the room, first pointing at Sophie, then at me. Two stern hand gestures later and we both rise from our seats and follow her out of the office, leaving Sophie's entourage whispering and leaving Matt to collect his deserted cart.

The three of us travel up in the lift together to the HR department on the top floor. Sophie positions herself next to the manager and opposite me in the lift so she can scowl at me without the manager seeing. Thankfully, we don't stop at any other floors and the uncomfortable journey is over almost as soon as it begins. More hand signals result in me sitting in a chair in the corridor outside the office while Sophie is escorted in. I'm sitting outside the headmaster's office. It's the first year of secondary school again when I scrapped with a girl who said my Dad wasn't around because my Mum was a whore and nobody knew who my Dad was.

Either 10 minutes or two hours later, Sophie comes out of the office with two streams of mud down her cheeks from her eyes. Her eyelashes are clumped together in peaks, framing her puffy sockets. I stare straight at her, shocked that she is capable of crying, but she doesn't dare look at me in return. This is when I realise that she's the one in trouble here and not me. I'm faint with relief. I try to keep my head centred on my shoulders and not lolling to one side as I offer up a shaky smile to the HR manager in return for my "promotion" to HR. There are many sets of eyes that scan me as they pass me in my new seat by the fire exit on the top floor, but I don't have to hold my breath every time I hear the life signs of another human being behind me. I've been pulled free of the cackling masses in the pit.

The work is a mind-numbingly bland blend of photocopying, stapling and filing, and it's not long before my new desk takes on the persona of a Japanese "banishing room", where the loneliness and boredom of an empty existence are used to force people to quit their jobs. I know I was effectively alone in the pit, but they couldn't pick on me every minute of every day, and when they weren't doing, their general chatter of all things celebrity and television helped the day pass. Left with just my thoughts, the minutes morph into hours, and I finish every day exhausted and utterly demoralised.

The Second Cup

Even though my new job in HR is no better than the one I left behind, I still need to thank Matt for what he's done. I've tried to speak to him on his rounds, but he always stumbles away from me, and I'm never quite brave enough to go after him. Hoping he'll feel safer in the confines of his own kingdom, I cautiously head down to the post room. A simple "Thank you" and Matt blushes from his neck to his hairline, the colour burning up his skin at a rate of knots. When his post room colleagues start jeering, I realise what hasn't occurred to me all along: that he fancies me. He wasn't some knight in shining armour that had done this out of the goodness of his heart – it was because he liked me.

"Ask her out then" – from one of the post room lads.

"Erm…" Matt manages. And I realise it's my turn to come to his rescue.

"I'd love to," I say, smiling.

Our first date is a bit awkward because neither of us has much to say, but when he holds my hand on the way to the bus stop my heart soars and I don't care if he isn't much of a conversationalist. It takes very little to convince him to get the bus home to my place rather than the one back to his. And he never heads home after that, except to pack up his things so he can move them into mine.

I'm too grateful to the HR manager for my new job to leave until Beth helps me see it's nothing but a snub – as a way to keep the pit girls happy and to stop any further complaints, rather than to think about my needs. Deep down I know I need another job because I'm worried my brain might seize up from the monotony of it all and never work properly again. Thankfully, being stuck in the corner away from everyone else is the perfect place to work on my CV.

When I hand in my notice to the HR manager, I get flashes of a saccharine-smile that doesn't reach the eyes. It's like she's had Botox to the whites of her eyes. It's so creepy it burns itself onto my retina and stays with me for months, popping into my head at random moments when I have my eyes closed. I've tried smiling without it reaching my eyes, but can't do it. I even practise in front of the mirror. I think it must be a skill you're born with, like being able to curl your tongue – or curl your lip the way Sophie did. I got a leaving present of some smelly stuff from Boots, and all the girls in HR signed my card. The pots of lotions and potions are still in their cellophane, sitting in their wicker tray, making my bathroom shelf look pretty. It reminds every morning, when I'm having a shower and brushing my teeth, how lucky I am to work where I do now.

I also got another card, which came up through the internal post, delivered to the HR post hatch by Matt, who always saluted me on his rounds. It had my name on the front in the curly, childish handwriting that I recognised as Sophie's. Inside it just said "Glad you're finally leaving" and the words were surrounded by lipstick kisses in clashing shades. When I showed Beth, we talked about setting fire to the edges of the card and then reposting it to Sophie, faking her childish handwriting on the front, or spelling it out with letters cut from a newspaper like in a ransom note, or taking the card to the police so the girls have to have their lip prints taken instead of their fingerprints. Having someone to snigger with made me realise why the pit girls hung off Sophie's every word – because it feels good to belong, to have someone on your side.

Ironically, it's because of Sophie that I have both Matt and Beth.

I had been sitting at a bus stop, waiting for my bus home from work when I met Beth. Although Sophie drove to work, some of her cronies didn't and got the bus just before mine. I used to wait until they'd gone before I went to the bus stop, so if their bus were late, I'd miss mine and have a half-hour wait. Matt's shifts in the post room started and ended before my office hours, so I didn't get the chance to commute home with him at my side for protection – not that I'm sure it would have helped. They may have just seen us as a double target. That evening was another evening where I had to let my bus go and had a wait on my hands. I was painfully aware that every minute I was standing waiting was another minute I could be closer to home and every tiny bit of serotonin in my brain had to work overtime to stop me from crying.

A girl came along and, slouching against the shelter, took a fag out of a packet and lit up. The motions of hand-to-pocket followed by open-packet-to-fag-to-lighter-then-to-pocket-again were so fluid I knew she was smoking a cigarette for habit's sake and not for the craving. I was about to sigh loudly in the hope she'd notice the smoke was heading straight for me, when the girl caught my eye, gave me sheepish half-smile and said "Sorry". She then attempted to get her packet of cigarettes back out of her pocket, this time fumbling, losing her grace along with her autopilot. She held her fag packet out, offering me one. I realised the sorry wasn't for smoking near me; it was for not offering me one. I shook my head but smiled, grateful for her act of kindness, even though I'd been cursing her only seconds before. Her offer of a cigarette, a small but seemingly selfless act, stopped my brain from going into automatic implode.

"You okay?" she asked. I nodded, this time without the smile. I closed my eyes, the tears suddenly threatening the insides of my lids again.

"Hmm," she said, in a voice that said she did not believe me. I didn't open my eyes because I didn't want to see pity on her face. I waited for the sigh and the "Cheer up it could be worse" comment or something equally useless to be thrown my way without any real thought. But she didn't say anything, and when I eventually opened my eyes I saw concern, genuine concern, not pity.

Behind the bus stop was a scruffy little cafe. I'd never gone in, but I'd noticed it because it had a front door that didn't shut properly: it used to swing violently each time someone entered or left, but stop about half an inch away from the door frame. I'm sure it was because the door was damaged, but I liked to think it was the owner's way of telling people they were always welcome, that the door wasn't closed on them. The girl saw me glance at the door as it swung from another customer leaving.

"Let's go for a brew," she said, standing up straight.

Lounging against the side of the shelter she'd seemed fluid, like mercury, but now, staring at me, waiting for me to stand up so we could head into the cafe together, she was half matron, half sergeant major. Strangely unintimidated by someone so forthright, I got up and followed her into the cafe, sitting down opposite her at a table by the window. I watched her take a few long, hungry drags before burying her cigarette stub into the sea of discarded butts, each with a dark orangey-black circle at the end of it as evidence that someone had sucked the life out of it. I watched her grind it down with her fingers before flicking away the ash that clung to her skin. I shrunk away, watching. I knew they called smoking a dirty habit because of what it did to your insides, but what grossed me out more was the idea of putting my fingers in a glass bowl full of grubby filters other people had puckered their lips around, leaving traces of dried spit on them.

The ashtray wasn't the only dirty part of the cafe. The

smoke from everyone's cigarettes clung in the air, being wafted back and forth by the air stream created by the rocking door. It was just before the smoking ban in 2007 and everyone it seemed, except for me, was puffing on one, making the most of the last few months of being allowed to have a smoke with their brew. The table we were sitting at had recently been wiped clean, but grease still gleamed in the trails of water which had not yet dried on the plastic top.

I much preferred the anonymity of somewhere like McDonald's, where my tea would be served to me in a coated paper cup that I knew no-one else had drunk out of. But I still sipped at the tea plonked down in front of me, even though I guessed the drips round the top of the mug were there from someone else's slurping. I was not going to snub the friendship this girl seemed to be offering, whoever she was. With my first sip, a trickle of tea ran over the lip of the mug and I used its heat and its wetness to wash off the dried drips with my thumb. It was very cathartic: I was washing away the day and starting afresh. I took my next sip with more gusto, watching the asbestos-mouthed girl opposite tackle her tea in big gulps. We'd talked for ages about nothing in particular while she smoked her way through another cigarette and we drank our way through another round of teas.

As soon as the smoking ban came into force, Beth quit, but the smell of the thick smoke mixed in with the strong scent of the Thierry Mugler "Angel" perfume has stayed with me as strongly as the memory of that day. Even though I didn't get anything off my chest about work that evening, I felt a lot better afterwards. I didn't know much about friendships, but I knew this girl was offering me hers and I wasn't going to hesitate and give her time to change her mind.

And now I don't just have Matt and Beth. I have Toby too.

The job I get after leaving the consultancy is for a small legal firm called Cruthers. I'm an administration assistant and PA. The work suits me down to the ground because it's all about organising people or things. I like order and lists and everything in its place. The firm I work for is so small I'm the tea maker, receptionist and all-round dog's body rolled into one. But I'd say the tea making is probably the most important part of my job because Toby, the boss, likes builders' tea – strong, milky, with two sugars – and I'm the only person in the office who gets it right. I don't mind though because Toby appreciates everything I do and a good boss means I can face going to work every day. I talk about Toby so fondly, Beth thinks I have a crush on him. I don't. To me he's like an uncle, being there for me when things get tough. I only wish he were my uncle because then I could go to him for strong, comforting hugs.

People who have someone to give them regular hugs don't realise how painful it is for everyone else. Before Beth's frequent hugs, I could easily go six months, 12 months, without a proper hug. My Mum's hugs are a pathetic arm-round-my-shoulders squeeze, the type that don't require much commitment by the hugger and that are difficult to reciprocate by the huggee. And Matt is too manly to do hugs. I think Toby's hugs would be the best in the world.

As well as frequently praising my work, Toby is regular with the pay rises to make sure I don't even think about leaving. Not that I would. Sometimes it's as if Toby is the only one who believes in me anymore. Beth used to.

That evening at the bus stop, she noticed the locket round my neck, but looked through it and saw into my chest, saw how empty I was inside. She used to tell me that she couldn't believe how alike we were, that finding me made her less alone, that she needed my friendship as much as I needed hers. But she doesn't like Matt, even though I think he's hollow inside too. She tried to hide it at first, but she was angry with herself for not coming into my life sooner when she discovered I'd been with Matt just a few months. "I could have stopped you from saying 'Yes'," she'd say to me, over and over, as if repeating it could turn back the clock. She doesn't say it anymore though. She used to tell me that she felt alive when she was in my company, but now it's Faye that makes her giddy with laughter. And although he's never been one for hugs, Matt used to hold my hand and tell me he loved me, but now his hands are too busy holding his Xbox controller.

Beth claims she and Matt are nothing alike, but to me they are the same: they are both getting ready to leave me – and I'm left holding my breath, waiting for the day to arrive.

4 teaspoons

ABBIE

I traipse down Thomas Street, away from The Blue Pig, the girls and the promise of better lives, stopping to look behind me every minute or so in the hope of flagging down a taxi, slowly getting soaked by Manchester's evil drizzle. The rain, which begins as soon as I leave the pub, suits my mood, but it's turning my hair to frizz. I want to stomp home, but the faster I walk along the uneven paving stones and random patches of cobbles, the more likely I am to rip the dainty fabric on my favourite Ralph Lauren shoes. So I take each step carefully, knowing at least my hair can be fixed when I get home.

I can't stop to wait for a taxi. I have to keep walking. I have to get away before the pain I feel over the potential of someone else's life devours me. It isn't jealousy of Faye's fortunes, far from it: but the notion that she has an opportunity never to befall me is too much to bear. At first, I join in musing over whether or not Faye should sidestep a day at work and head to Jack's parents' house, or whether she should cross the Rubicon and head down to London. But it is too tortuous, so I wrap myself up in the cotton wool folds of three, maybe four, glasses of Riesling, the sweet scent reminding me of my favourite Squirrel floral gums from my Gran's kitchen cupboard, the perfumed taste reminding me of the overwhelming wafts of Anais Anais that came with childhood hugs from her as I nuzzled myself into the soft folds of her ageing skin.

The wine slips coolly down my throat, warming my being and blurring the edges of my vision so it's as if I am watching my own personal sitcom from the 70s. But wine can only do so much and it isn't enough to soothe the assault of enthusiasm coming from Faye, so I feign a headache and leave the others to their drinks. I schlep as far as Piccadilly Gardens before managing to wave a black cab down. As I allow the rumbling of the taxi engine to lull me, I wonder if Faye is right: if I need to seize my life by the scruff of the neck and give it a good shake, as the alternative is to sleepwalk through the rest of it.

I sit up with a jolt. Yes, she's right. I need to leave my husband.

The realisation fills my head to bursting, sloshing around my intoxicated brain, as the taxi-meter spins round feverishly and the taxi itself flies down the A56 towards Sale. I know I should have phoned for a private hire rather than taking the £30 hit of a black cab but I just want to be home. As I watch the various buildings – Victorian terraces, new builds, smart office blocks and warehouse-style businesses – fly by, the realisation that I need to leave my husband grows in my head until it's throbbing like the headache I'd claimed to have. I have other worries in the recesses of my mind, but I can't quite reach them through the carousel of ideation and ethanol. The taxi can't get me home soon enough.

By the time we reach home, my thoughts are back with Faye. She's such a strong person, but that is no excuse for deserting her at the pub. And after seeing her like that about Jack, I'm starting to wonder if she's just strong on the outside and weak on the inside – as weak as the rest of us. I'm hot with shame. If she's not the strong person I thought she was, she needed my support, not my desertion. In a vain attempt to right the scales, I tip the taxi driver a fiver. Outside the house I compose myself. I scan for any signs of life but all the lights are off. I married an early bird when I was a night owl – something I now find ridiculously funny, my choked laughs escaping as unfeminine, unwieldy snorts.

I put my key in the lock. And stop. What exactly am I going to say to him, to the early bird? I can't believe it had totally slipped my mind to think about how Dominic would feel, how he would react. He's the reason I kept the pretence going, yet in my drunken state I could forget him completely. It was the second time I was being selfish tonight – first with Faye and now with Dominic. I turn the key slowly, holding my breath as if that would mean I'm less likely to wake Dominic up. I let myself into the dark hall, feel my way through to the lounge without putting a light on and collapse onto the sofa.

Sleep comes up to meet me as my body sinks into the corded fabric. I will deal with Dominic in the morning. Hopefully by then, my mind will be clear enough for me to have formulated an idea of what words to use. I don't know how well I sleep or whether I toss and turn in the night, but by the time I'm woken by male coughing I've become one with the sofa, fabric grooves carving Maori warrior markings into the skin around my right eye, across my right cheekbone, and on the right side of my forehead.

Dominic is a smoker and he noisily hacks up the contents

of his lungs every morning. I'm not quite sure how I ended up with a smoker either, but then Dominic wasn't right for me in so many ways, so what was one more incompatibility? I stumble up from my impromptu bed and lurch lazily towards the kitchen where the sound of half-hearted choking is coming from. I rub my eyes, not caring that I'm smudging what's left of last night's make-up across my face and into the temporary grooves in my skin. I instantly feel guilty, knowing how much care I should give my eyesight. A memory of standing on the toilet seat, reaching for perfume, flashes before me.

Dominic looks up from his position half crouched over the kitchen sink and smiles at me, his blonde fringe hanging down the same way Paul's unruly curls use to. I try not to think of Paul. I also try not to think about the greeny-brown glop that has just freed itself from Dominic's lungs and is now making its way down the kitchen plumbing.

"I was worried when you didn't text," Dominic says to me, gently reminding me that I usually let him know if I'm going out with the girls. "But you made such a racket letting yourself in that I knew you were home safe. Too drunk to make it up the stairs, were you?"

Dominic smiles such a genuine smile that I feel guilty about wanting to leave him. But then he spoils it by leaning over to kiss me, the image of his phlegm still burning in my mind. As his kiss burns into my lips, I wonder if he can taste any trace of my mental betrayal on my skin. I open my eyes as he pulls away. No, he can't – I know it because Dominic has that look on his face that says he wants sex, not that he's hurt or shocked, or even relieved. I have no idea what his genuine reaction would be.

"I'm off to bed," I tell him. He winks at me.

"Please don't want sex," my eyes plead with him.

"I'd join you" – he pauses for effect – "but I've got work."

He grins at me as he watches my comprehension struggle through my hangover fug to the front of my brain. Work. Oh buggeration. That's what those alarm bells in my head had been for. As a retail manager, Dominic works every Saturday, so I hadn't minded too much when my latest project called for Saturday working too. What the hell was I playing at drinking so much on what was effectively a school night?

But I'm not the type to take sickies. Instead, I schlomp up the stairs and into the bathroom, hoping a cool shower will wake me up enough to tussle with a day of practise presentations. I stare at myself in the mirror. Thankfully, my temporary sofa scars are already fading, as are the skin creases around my nose from where my face had crumpled into itself as I slept. I long to keep my face make-up free but refuse to let the world see the true horrors of my hangover so, shower done, I put on the minimum I can get away with, and attempt to stumble through the day. My boss is sympathetic to my fever, never once assuming that I'd be someone who'd consume her body weight in lady-petrol at such a key point in our project delivery. I am grateful for his concern and make sure I am drinking lots of Lemsip when he's looking and inhaling double espressos when he isn't.

THE LETTER "A"

Abbie has a habit of jangling her car keys when she gets out of the car. Right now, she's jangling something that doesn't look like a real key, it's more a plastic and metal key fob, and it's what gets her into her BMW 3 Series. She used to jangle the keys to her second-hand VW Golf with far more spirit, a set of keys where a homemade letter "A" took pride of place, a present made by Paul. Now when she locks her car outside her home, she digs around in her bag and clips on the tacky photo keyring Dominic gave her. It holds a photo from their wedding day. In between the homemade "A" and the wedding pic, Abbie's keys carried a heavy metal keyring that spelt out her name in scroll font. Ebbs had joked that he'd splashed out on her full name – a dig at Paul and his "A", which had initially made Abbie laugh out loud, but which irritated her more and more with each telling.

ABBIE

By the time I finish work, the skin on my face is screaming to be scraped clean of make-up. I don't care that the aftereffects of drinking give a ghostlike look. I used to wish I were prettier, but poor Olivia is cursed by her looks. Before meeting her, the equation in my head had been "pretty equals confident and successful". But when it doesn't, it's crippling. Other people expect you to be everything good and positive – and so see Olivia's shyness as aloofness. As I look like what my father would call "standard stock" others don't expect anything other than "ordinary" from me. So when I deliver, at the very least they are impressed, if not blown away, and let me have what I want. At 21, I was happily married to Paul, we'd both just graduated – me in Business Management and him in Law – and I was slowly working my way up the career ladder and wondering when it would be the right time to take a break to have a child. I wasn't sure if I should have one straight away and risk stalling my career before it began or wait until I had a few good years behind me but risk being an older mother and not having enough energy for my Son or Daughter. So I decided to let fate decide and came off the pill – it would either happen quickly or it wouldn't.

I didn't get pregnant – and was very relieved because, by

29, I knew I'd made a mistake: Paul wasn't the one for me, baby or no. I hadn't stopped being attracted to him: you don't stop desiring someone who is 6ft 3in tall, with broad shoulders, muscly frame, unruly dark fringe and chocolate eyes. Like me, he wasn't typical silver screen fare, but his comely face came alive whenever he spoke to me, hands gesticulating, the skin around his eyes crinkling. He was someone who should never be photographed because it wouldn't capture his spirit and do him justice. Yes, I still fancied him, but Paul's magic had stopped working on me. My knees no longer turned to jelly when I saw him; I no longer found the hiccupy noise he made each time he took his first sip of Prosecco endearing. And while it hadn't got to the point where it was like nails down a blackboard to me, I had no intention of waiting until it was. The sex was still good and I even initiated it at least every three weeks or so to ensure he didn't feel he was doing all the work. I still managed to find enough strength within me to laugh at his corny jokes, while he still put up with me shaving my legs in the bath even though I never remembered to rinse the tub out afterwards.

We changed in different ways during those years. When we first got together, we had to watch every penny. I didn't want to ask my parents for help – I wanted to live free of their conditional love – and his family wasn't in any position to help us financially anyway. As we both earned more, we were able to relax and splash out a bit, but Paul never seemed to want to. He wasn't a miser exactly, but he'd buy me a potted plant rather than flowers because the plant would carry on living and the flowers would be dead within a week. In the beginning, I'd found it quirky and loveable, but towards the end I wished he'd occasionally buy me a bouquet of my favourite peonies just for the hell of it.

When Paul suggested we go our separate ways I was horrified. I'd accepted being in a "loveless" marriage for the rest of my life and the idea of being single made my blood not just run cold but freeze in my veins. I accused him of meeting someone else, of having an affair, but he said he just felt tired of always trying to meet my standards and forever falling short. I couldn't believe that's how he saw our marriage. I was so angered by it I had to leave him, even if it did mean being single again. And I made sure he took all his damned potted plants with him. And all his stupid homemade letter "A"s.

EVERYDAY HONEYMOON

As she was going through the motions of ending her marriage to Paul, Abbie met Ebbs. He seemed fun and adventurous where Paul had been dependable and reliable – and he knocked her off her feet. Ebbs wasn't flashy, but Abbie was thrilled to have any amount of money spent on her without having to listen to witterings about depreciation values. They had a whirlwind romance followed by a fairly straightforward break-up when they both realised they weren't over their exes. A number of months after Abbie realised the relationship was falling apart at the seams and shortly before they split, she met Dominic. It was perfect timing, as finding Mr Right before letting go of Mr Okay seemed rather prudent to her.

Her second marriage was also Dominic's second, but he treated it with the puppy dog buoyancy of someone naively entering into their first. When he produced a stunning engagement ring on their third date, it was the perfect meal, the perfect ring and, were he the perfect man, it would have been a perfect day to say "Yes". Abbie knew he wasn't her perfect man, but didn't have it within her to say "No", not when he was looking at her with so much love tinged desperation. So she said "Yes" with every intention to let him down gently later. But when he started planning the details, Abbie got caught up in the excitement and started to believe it could work. And when she found herself standing in the glass atrium of Manchester Art Gallery wearing a Kate Halfpenny vintage dress, stunning low-heeled Jimmy Choos and with a bouquet of lilies, stephanotis and baby's breath in her hands, the butterflies she had in her stomach were good ones. The Malmaison Hotel spoiled them – champagne on ice, chocolate-dipped strawberries, candles and the most amazing Egyptian cotton sheets. Abbie's skin sizzling where it made contact with Dominic, who insisted on lying there with their legs intertwined. They couldn't take a proper honeymoon because Abbie was so busy at work – putting in extra hours at Schmitt Thomas Smith, her eyes focused on her next promotion – but two nights in the honeymoon suite was all she needed because life with Dominic was going to be like a honeymoon every day.

ABBIE

When I'm not with him, I can convince myself that my marriage with Dominic is worth working at, but the minute I'm in his company, any resolve I had just dissolves away. The times we still have sex, I aim for early morning, not only so it has to be a quickie, but because I can rush into the shower straight afterwards, scrubbing away the invisible bruises, the mucky residue he leaves on my skin. But now my frontal lobe has finally accepted what I've known all along – that my marriage is a sham – I am cheating on Dominic for every second that I don't tell him. I'm still going through the motions with my body, but not giving him any part of my brain, I am cheating. Cheating doesn't require another person. Now my decision is made, any delay in telling him is cruel.

Is this where Jack was in his head when he deserted Faye before the ink on his degree certificate was dry? Was he just trying to save her more pain? Did he do so because delaying the decision to leave Faye, letting her move down to London with him, would have been even more cruel?

5 teapots

BETH'S HEAD

Beth's head is filled with noise. It's the coarse revving of a 750cc engine or the roar of a 50,000-strong football crowd at Old Trafford or the Etihad. A noise with no discernible reason or message. Beth's head is packed full of polystyrene and cotton wool. So full that a pin dropping would make only a dull thud. She takes deep breaths but the air is thin and hot and her lungs become vacuum-sealed, sponge-like alveoli squashed flat. She doesn't want to be here. She wants it to be 20 minutes ago, when she was heading up Tib Street, turning left onto Thomas Street, heading towards the huddle of Northern Quarter bars, feeling alive in her favourite part of the city.

BETH

I reach The Blue Pig slightly earlier than usual. As I push the heavy door to the bar open by leaning all my weight on it, I'm unnerved by the emptiness of the place. Something is happening somewhere else and I am missing it. What am I missing? I shake the question from my head. Even if something were going on somewhere else, I hadn't been invited and probably wouldn't enjoy it anyway. With big events, I find myself standing on the periphery, watching other people lose themselves in the moment. I have to ask myself afterwards whether I enjoyed the occasion or not.

I survey the room as I stand at the bar, watching people shrug off their work lives along with their jackets and ties. A group of young lads transform from a clan of suit wearers into a mishmash collection of wide boys, likely lads and home-grown mummies' boys – a group that only have the thirst for an after-work pint in common. I don't know whether to feel sorry for them or jealous of them. They have no idea that they are a motley crew with no real connections among them. But then again if they have no idea they are surely enveloped in blissful ignorance.

I order half a Leffe Blonde and allow myself a happy sigh as I watch the barman perform the ritual of squeezing pieces of lime and lemon over a fat, chunky, chiselled glass, then dropping them in before filling the glass with pale liquid. It's only the first mouthfuls that bring contentment to my chest, but I am willing to spend the rest of the evening a little hazy in return for being momentarily buoyed up, allowing to drift along the surface of life, a brief respite from the exhaustion of forever treading water.

I take my first few sips, smiling to myself as I experience the initial lift from my struggle against the tide. I smile as I picture myself lying on the surface of the sea, looking upwards, with the troubles of the world below me. As I scan the bar to see if our favourite seats are free, those around me are fish swimming together in shoals, not sure if they're hunting or being hunted, as dolphins bumping noses in pre-mating sessions, as whales spraying their audience with self-important squirts of water. I claim the large table – our large table – in the corner by the window with comfy leather sofas. It's often empty, the sea life preferring to perform mating circles by the bar.

I like to arrive earlier than the others because it gives me a few minutes to clear my head. I slouch back and let the cool liquid pour down my throat, sighing as it flows through my veins, down my limbs, washing through my head, soothing my brain. I also people-watch, searching for those stripping away their scales, comfortable in their own skin, but usually finding myself transfixed by a hipster instead, attempting to be cool in red skinny jeans and a handlebar moustache, or a guy in a too-shiny suit and footballers' haircut trying to casually pull someone he obviously has a thing for. As I lounge back on the sofa, staring out of the window, watching the world go by and allowing my thoughts to meander round my head, I notice a familiar figure walking towards the bar, taking small hurried steps, head down like she is battling against a strong wind. It's Livvy.

I watch her approach. She should be breathtakingly beautiful. With her high cheekbones, naturally pouty lips, eyes as clear as glass and skin as smooth as marble, she is a stunning creature. She wears natural make-up and is jewellery-free except for a simple locket that hangs around her neck. She casts a striking shadow. People are wary of Olivia though because something is missing from her face. Not a feature, as such, more an expression. She usually wears a haunted look that distorts her features. It's what initially drew me to her. As I try so hard to hide my unhappiness, I can't help but be curious about a girl who so obviously wears hers across her face.

The sun bounces off the large glass windows of the bar, forcing Olivia to shield her eyes from the sun, her raised hand turning into an enthusiastic wave when she spots me. Relief floods her face. She's been worried we wouldn't show. That relief removes every shadow of pain from her face and she transforms from cygnet to swan before my eyes. She arrives at the entrance to the bar as someone is leaving, which is fortuitous, as her tiny frame would struggle against such a heavy door. I was already getting up and out of my seat to help, so I stay standing to greet her properly, knowing she will hug me as if we haven't seen each other in months. Dumping her bag on the sofa opposite me to free up her arms, she gives me a hug tight enough to squeeze the life out of me. The warmth of her friendship flows out of her body and into mine where we touch, and I'm strangely at peace in the company of this girl who is so different from me in so many ways but has a better understanding of who I am than anyone else. We share a moment of real happiness, extending the hug with a squeeze of arms and shoulders, simultaneously allowing our barriers down and allowing reciprocal smiles to spread across our faces. In that moment, Livvy is the most beautiful human being.

Livvy gives my arms one final squeeze and then heads to the bar, head down, almost colliding with Abbie – and there's quite a bit of Abbie to collide with. She's one of those lucky girls who has extra pounds in all the right places – enough to make skinnymalinks like me look like gangly stick insects. I used to assume girls like Abbie were jealous of my thin frame, confident that I had been blessed with something they wanted. But I'm less sure of myself as I get older and often feel like skin stretched over a bag of bones in Abbie's company.

Once they've been served, they plonk themselves down on the sofa opposite me, Livvy nestling into the corner, shoes off, feet pulled up underneath her, Abbie smoothing her perfect bob and stretching herself out elegantly. Abbie starts off with good intentions, sipping at a white wine and lemonade. Livvy fiddles with the chunk of lime sticking out of her as yet untouched bottle of Sol, obliterating the piece of fruit first before taking a single sip, as if psyching herself up to drink. She'd be much happier sipping at a dainty cup of Darjeeling and annihilating a too-thick, too-rich wedge of cake. Abbie is perfectly dressed, as always: expensive skirt suit with an almost-low-cut-but-not-quite silky top. The only imperfection is how tired her eyes look. She isn't sleeping well again. I wonder whether it is work or home life that is draining her energy this time.

While we chat, Faye sneaks into the bar behind us and is served her usual pint; a habit picked up from the days of cheap drinks in the students' union bar. She walks up to our table, takes a gulp of beer and slams her glass down to get our attention. Faye is looking at me but a sideways glance tells me that both Livvy and Abbie are rolling their eyes. Faye has a habit of making everything a big deal, so we're used to her dramatic entrances. I shuffle across the sofa so she can sit down. She launches herself, dive-bombing into the space next to me, almost knocking me out the other side. It's only a week since we were sitting at this very table hearing all about NOT-Jack, but I'm wondering if this particular pint-slamming episode is justified, as the years have gone by on Faye's face.

"I've found Jack," she says.

I gasp – and hear the gasp echo around the table as Livvy and Abbie join in.

"I found him so stupidly easily I wish I'd tried ages ago. Anyway, I'm far too late, but at least I know that now."

Too late? I struggle to picture Jack married with blonde-haired squealing kids running up and down the hall as he opened the door to Faye, his similarly golden-haired wife coming out of the kitchen to see who it was, bringing wafts of her expert cooking with her. It doesn't quite seem real, so I look to Faye to fill me in on the story.

"You're definitely, definitely too late?" I ask.

She takes a deep breath. "He's dead."

My world stops. Not in the same way Jack's has, but figuratively. I think about death every day. What the world would be like without me on it. Whether there'd be an actual gap, like a vacuum, or if it would just fill up with air, particulate matter and exhaust fumes. Sometimes I walk into pockets of air that feel like a different current has just hit me. The light is different, maybe hazy, and the air tastes bitter, almost metallic. It's a little like when a shiver goes down your back and you are temporarily not a part of this world. If that shiver can be caused by someone walking over your grave, then it's feasible that the pockets are air are caused by the voids left by people who have departed this life.

"How?"

I instantly regret letting the single syllable loose as soon as it leaves my lips. Six disapproving eyes. Three shocked looks. No social skills. When did everyone else learn to engage their brains before speaking? It wasn't a lesson I remember from school and it certainly wasn't one I learned at home, surrounded by keen intellectuals with a penchant for highbrow conversation and academic one-upmanship, where confrontation was king. I often didn't realise what I was saying or doing wasn't acceptable until it was said or done – and then I'd watch a road crash of reactions collide in front of my face.

"He killed himself."

My mouth starts to form other words, to attempt other sentences, but I can't get them out, still paralysed by the horror that met my previous utterance. Instead I put my arms around Faye and pull her into me. The soft felt lapels of her jacket against my skin. The same mix of felt and chunky buttons that banged against me when she threw herself onto the sofa. Was that forced glee? And why? Why not be sombre and help prepare us for the grief? I picture the blonde-haired kids again, sobbing this time, huddled into their mother's slim legs, the three of them standing at a perfectly dug grave surrounded by luscious grass: the wife wearing waterproof mascara and crying dainty tears.

"What about his wife? His kids?"

The confusion I'm feeling about Faye's inappropriate entrance is now mirrored on her face. I've asked yet another ill-timed question.

"He wasn't married. He didn't have kids."

I roll my eyes to the top of their sockets, as if I'm rolling them at myself. With so few words I can be so, so dangerous.

"I should stop talking."

Faye squeezes me, returning my sideways hug, and I know I'm instantly forgiven: "There was an inquest into what happened and the police say it's unequivocal, because of the tyre marks on the road, that he planned to ride his motorbike into the wall. But it doesn't matter now, because…"

But Faye's words are lost on me. A motorbike. The sepsis from the disease – the disease of death – is spreading through my veins, curdling with my blood, reaching boiling point inside my head, but sending cold chills down into my hands and feet. The lights in the pub are too bright for me, but my neck has stiffened and I struggle to protect myself from the streams of fluorescence hitting my eyes. My pounding head mirrors the rhythm of my pounding heart and echoes in my ears and throat.

The Second Cup

Can someone take your suicide if you don't use it? Is this how Jack took his life because I didn't take mine? Many bikers die, but for most of them it's at the hands of careless car drivers, not of their own volition. I can't help thinking that it should have been me. I attempt to inhale again and again, gasping at the lack of oxygen entering my lungs. I feel my consciousness hang in the air as my body slithers off the front of the sofa, sinking down towards oblivion. I feel a set of hands on me, supporting me, and I give into them, allowing them to guide me to the floor. My body goes into shock. My head fills with noise. The noise of a motorbike engine.

BETH

It's dark around me. The winter days are short, but the streetlamp that usually shines through the thin curtain fabric and into my bedroom hasn't come on yet. It's dark inside me too.

Someone is here. I can hear the essence of someone moving around in the kitchen. Sounds that are both alien and familiar, as someone does things they are used to doing, but in my kitchen not their own. The kitchen door opens and footsteps make their way along the hall. The door opens to my bedroom, bringing with it the low glow of the energy-saving light bulb behind it. As the minutes pass, the bulb will get brighter, but when you first switch it on it is sluggish to respond. I'm also sluggish to respond. It takes me a few seconds to register that Olivia has come in and is holding out a mug of steaming liquid towards me.

"Tea," she says when I don't take the mug from her. My arms seem too heavy to lift to take the cup from her. I half shrug my shoulders. In response, she holds the mug to my lips, tipping it gently so that I can take sips. Before I taste it, I can tell from the faint sweet, almost floral, fragrance that it is the perfect brew. Olivia prides herself on them. She likes to make tea in the pot I keep in the corner of my kitchen – a pot that turns into an ornament collecting dust between her visits. My parents drink pots of tea, their lives seemingly revolving around whether or not they've drunk the second cup from the pot.

Dad: "Have we had the second cup?"

Mum: "Yes we did, I'll put the kettle back on."

Dad: "Have we had the second cup?"

Mum: "No we didn't, I'll pour it out now."

Dad: "Have we had the second cup?"

Mum: "I made that pot hours ago; it'll be stewed now. I'll put the kettle back on."

Dad: "Have we had the second cup?"

THE GREY SHEEP

Beth looked down at her brown cord dungarees and orange T-shirt. She had splashes of blue paint on her arms and grass stains on her knees, but no sign of any grey. How on earth could she be a grey sheep? That's what her Dad had said. That she wasn't a black one, just dark grey. He'd found it really funny. Grace and Charlotte had laughed too, but Beth could tell that neither of them understood.

"What colour am I, Daddy?"

"What colour am I?"

They'd both sung their questions, dancing round his feet. He'd scooped up Charlotte, tickling her as he did. No longer the baby of the family, Grace waited patiently for her turn. Beth made puking noises.

"Enough of that, thank you, Elizabeth." The voice was

without a body, but Beth knew from the elongated version of her name that it didn't matter which adult had spoken, she was in trouble.

"Can I be a sparkly sheep?" Charlotte asked, wriggling free of her Dad's arms and spinning round so the sequins on her Barbie tutu caught the sun's rays.

"What colour are sheep in real life?" asked Grace, taking a serious tone.

"They're beige," Beth said getting one final comment in before she was dragged inside the house for being insolent, and even though she knew the question was for their father. "Beige. Perfect for you."

THE DAVID BOWIE LEOTARD

They were practising long-arms. Running up, two feet together on the board, two hands placed together on the vault, two legs up in the air and over, like a whirling handstand. It was Beth's turn. Beth looked down at her red leotard, smoothing down the material where it bobbled near the seams where the shiny red fabric met with a splash of blue zigzagging across her chest. Her Mum called it her David Bowie leotard.

The only grey was on the soles of her feet from the dirty floor.

She focused her mind, planted her left foot down, the first foot of her run. Head bowed slightly, but eyes locked forward, she sprinted towards the wall of wood and leather. Feet pushed firmly down on the felt top of the board: hands planted firmly on top of the shiny brown leather. But not so firmly at all. Suddenly palms slipping, arms banging, chest winded. The vault hardly moved. But in Beth's dreams that night, the apparatus takes on a life of its own. She runs up to the vault, the air whipping at her. She jumps up, aiming her outstretched hands at the centre, where the leather has become darkened with years of adolescent sweat. But her hands start to give way and the rocking vault slides from under her. Beth travels one way the vault another, totally out of control. That's when she wakes up, crying out, coated in sweat.

Try as she might, Beth couldn't get herself over the vault again. Training sessions became a frustrating game of running up and stopping on the springboard or powering into the vault. Although the bruises from the latter were more immediate, the repeated sudden stopping took its toll on her right quadriceps. Beth's Mum is taken to one side. The David Bowie leotard is given to charity.

THE PAPER ROUND

Beth looked down at her ripped jeans with haphazard patches sewn onto them and her blue-and-white striped off-the-shoulder T-shirt. She knew she had splashes of blue eyeshadow on – and definitely no signs of any grey. The only item ruining her perfect outfit was the bright orange bag full of newspapers she pulled around behind her in rusted pushchair frame. She hated the smell of the coated PVC, but loved it too because it signified independence – including spending 48p a fortnight on *Smash Hits* to get copies of the lyrics to her favourite songs, the ones she recorded from the Top 40 onto TDK tapes. Then it was 97p on 10 Silk Cut. Well, she'd tried being fit and healthy and that hadn't paid off.

Charlotte and Grace didn't get paper rounds when they were old enough, even though Beth had paved the way by fighting for the right to earn pocket money. They didn't get any sort of part-time job, not even at university. They decided to be home students so they could concentrate fully on their studies, their gargantuan brains throbbing to escape the confines of their skulls. They both came out with firsts, the pictures of them holding ribbon-tied tubes of cardboard taking pride of place on the mantelpiece, positioned to leave a prominent space where Beth's photo should have been.

The Japanese tea ceremony

The Japanese tea ceremony is more than just drinking tea. It is a performance, a solemn event, which embodies one's connection with the spiritual world.

The Japanese tea ceremony – which was passed down through families and through generations – can take years to master, with Geishas dedicating their lives to learning these and other traditional skills.

The tea rituals Beth's parents follow are almost religious or cult-like in their fervour. However, these liturgical actions won't be passed down from generation to generation – not as far as Beth is concerned.

6 teabags

OLIVIA

I can't talk to Beth about Jack. I need to, but not now. She's not ready. In fact she's not fully here, as if she's hiding behind voile curtains like those that float from her bedroom window. She's been a ghost since her body collapsed like a rag doll and she slid forward off the sofa and to the floor, struggling to catch her breath, gasping and heaving, rocking on her heels. We'd tried to hold onto her, to stop her falling, but we just couldn't catch her in time. It had taken all my physical strength, and Faye's too, to pull her up and back onto the sofa. We could have done with another pair of hands, but Abbie had vanished.

Making tea for Beth resonates with me. It is a seemingly easy task that takes great skill and preparation. When Toby told me I made him the perfect brew on my first day at Cruthers, I knew I'd found where I wanted to work. I had a boss who appreciated simple things done well. I have to remove a layer of dust and cobwebs from Beth's teapot before I can use it. It's become part of the tea ritual I follow when I visit, and it pleases me to wipe away the old and see the pot gleaming again.

Beth has never met Jack, only knowing him from the stories Faye told all of us, but the news of his death has affected her as profoundly as if it were a poison that could spread through her body, stopping her limbs from working properly. Beth is refusing food, but still gratefully drinking cups of hot tea. Beth drinks her tea ridiculously hot. To wash the poison away maybe. She can't hold the mug for herself, her arms languishing beside her body as she decomposes against the haphazard wall of pillows I've built up behind her. I hold each brew to her lips, her mouth gulping on autopilot as the fluid touched the desert skin of her lips.

Jack died in a motorcycle accident. Except it wasn't an accident: he'd purposely aimed his bike at the concrete wall running down the side of the motorway and ploughed into it. An inspection of the crash site showed no skid marks, no usual signs of someone desperately trying to stop. The police, the pathologist, everyone involved, they all believed he'd intentionally crashed his bike into the concrete cliffs that rose up from the road on the M602. He'd been in Manchester for a Monday business meeting and had decided to ride up on his bike the day before, a way of clearing the cobwebs – that's what he'd told his friends. Wiping away the old.

Faye seems strangely calm about the whole event. It's too soon for her to have been through the cycle of denial, anger and guilt, and found a place of acceptance. It would have taken me a lot longer than a few days. Does Faye's brain work the same way as mine? If it does, there's a good chance she may be just about to break the spell only for Jack's hocus pocus to take hold again in the form of everlasting guilt. In her shoes, I'd be blaming myself for being the last straw. Mulling over his past as he rode down familiar roads, the carefree life he had before whatever it was that made him kill himself happened to him. He'd been a mere few miles away but didn't give Faye a chance to clear her cobwebs. So maybe it wasn't about her at all. Whatever she's thinking, she now has Ethan to lean on and I'm very grateful for that because I need to focus on Beth.

Picking us up from a pub, the taxi driver assumed Beth was comatose with drink and spent the journey making unhelpful jokes about lightweights. I'd just been relieved he was willing to take us: the first two black cabs I'd tried to hail had pulled away as soon as they'd seen Beth's limp body leaning against mine. That was Friday night and it's now late Saturday afternoon. I honestly expected Abbie and Faye to have both been round by now. I didn't want to have to leave Beth alone to pick up some of my things from home, but it looked like I didn't have any choice, as both of their mobiles were ringing out or going straight to voicemail. Abbie has a habit of working late and working most weekends, but it's unusual for her not to have her phone switched on.

I wish I could call Matt and ask him to bring a bag of my things over. I wish Matt were more like Toby. They've both rescued me – although Toby doesn't realise it on his part. For some reason I can't see Toby as boyfriend material. It's not an age thing, even though Toby is years older than me; it's because I took an instant liking to Toby and don't want to throw that away. I felt I had nothing to lose with Matt as I didn't know him. If anything, I rushed through the bit where Matt and I got to know each other so we could settle into the normality of a relationship. I desperately wanted a boyfriend and Matt got the job on a first come, first served basis.

I sometimes wonder why I'm still with him. I know I hate the thought of being alone again and I feel guilty about how I behave behind his back, but surely there must be more to it than that? I'm certainly not with Matt for his heroic side. He's not done anything erring on the side of brave since the day he rescued me. In fact, sometimes he's more like those girls from the pit than he realises. He's still working there in the post room and occasionally makes comments about the fact he works for an international firm while I work for a small "family" company – which is meant to sound like a swear word. I get paid more than him and do a harder job, but that doesn't seem to figure in his version of the world. It's almost like him rescuing me gives him the right to be the next person who picks on me.

Part of me wonders if this is the way long-term relationships go, where you niggle each other until your little habits end up baiting the other person. I'm good at holding my tongue and offering him sex as a way to appease him, quietly letting his comments pass over me as if they didn't cut deep into my flesh every time. I've stopped telling my story of how Matt rescued me in front of Beth because she sighs and says: "And you went for a drink to say thanks. End of." The last time I told it, for Faye's benefit, Beth pointed out the story was from over five years ago. It horrified me that I'd spent half a decade in a stale relationship, but was also secretly thrilled that someone wanted to be with me that long. I wish Beth understood that I needed to be in a relationship as much as she seemed to need to be single.

Beth, Abbie and Faye are the first in-crowd I've ever belonged to and every Friday night part of me holds my breath and hopes they don't notice that I shouldn't be part of it. When Beth first brought Abbie along I honestly thought my days were numbered. I cursed myself for letting that happen, them only meeting because I was too busy protecting Matt's feelings to go out for Bonfire Night. Then Faye joined and I realised that made Abbie's situation as precarious as mine had been, although for me it's worse again – as Abbie slips down the rankings, so do I.

I'm waiting for them to turn round and say "Sorry, but we don't want you to hang around with us anymore" – like my so-called friends did at school. That school crowd still hangs around together and occasionally I see one or two of them when I pop round to my Mum's. They ask me if I want to join them at the pub, but I always politely decline. They seem to have forgotten the way they treated me, but I can't, not unless I get an apology. Even if you're a kid and too young or too stupid to know what you're doing, when you get older, you should be able to look back and realise – and to try and make amends. "I was just a kid back then" doesn't wash with me. People should take responsibility for their own actions. Part of me longs to join them though, to get away from the routine of my life which is long stretches of evenings with Matt broken up by glimmers of fun on Friday nights and aerobics classes with Abbie on a Tuesday.

When I spend an evening watching Matt charge round a virtual castle killing virtual aliens before watching repeats of *CSI* and *CSI: Miami* on 5USA I know there's more to life than this. But then Matt will do well at his game or notice a big clue and spot the killer and, with him in a good mood, things won't seem so bad after all. But then Matt will use me as his verbal punch bag, a left-hook of an insult flying at me, quickly followed by a few nasty put-downs below the belt. On those days I'm trapped a personal *Groundhog Day* of Xbox games, telly repeats and contempt.

So I escape the only way I know how, by getting drunk. But the alcohol replaces the niggling doubts with an emotional aching that threatens to tear my body in two and I look for comfort, for belonging, anywhere and with anyone. I end up snogging some random bloke, hugging, touching, only to wake up the next morning filled with loathing and eaten up with guilt. I have to pretend I'm too hungover for Matt to touch me, scared that he will be able to tell that my skin, my lips have been touched by someone else. Then I spend the next few days or weeks trying to make it up to him until he snaps at me again, I drown my feelings in beer and so the dance begins again.

Beth thinks I deserve better, but she's wrong. I'm the one who cheats on him, not the other way round. I hate to admit it to myself, but in many ways I'm worse than the pit girls. They were horrible to me, but at least it was to my face. I'm horrible to Matt behind his back. Beth says it's my lack of self-esteem, but I don't understand how that works. Surely if I had no self-esteem I wouldn't think I was worth it and wouldn't have a long-term boyfriend let alone mucky fumbles with random blokes. No, if I had no self-esteem I wouldn't think I deserved to feel wanted. So Beth is wrong about that – I'm just incredibly selfish and hate myself for it. I've had to come to terms with the fact that I'm not a very nice person, which makes me cry into my pillow each time I cheat. But it doesn't stop me doing it again.

But I'm being a nice person right now, being there for Beth as she's been there for me. For some reason, even though she sees how I behave, she's on my side not Matt's and won't let the others say a bad word about me. The time Abbie tried to get me to tell the truth by wrenching my hair back from my face it felt like she'd slapped me. Beth didn't speak, but the look she gave Abbie said everything. Abbie stalked out of the pub that night so angry she didn't even down the last of her wine first. It took a couple of weeks of her licking her wounds before she came back and we weren't sure if we were going to see her again. She's seemingly not very good at conflict because, true to form, Abbie has disappeared again.

I bin the cold, uneaten toast and wash the plate it was sitting on, along with the two mugs and various items of cutlery I've used, plus the bowl I guiltily filled with three portions of breakfast cereal to keep me going through the day. Then I go into the bedroom to explain to Beth that I'm popping home to get some things. She seems to be frowning the way I do when I've got a headache coming on, so I check her bedside cabinet, the top of her dressing table and finally the mirrored cupboard in the bathroom before finding a tub of painkillers.

The white plastic tub is so light I'm pretty sure it's empty, but a quick shake and forlorn rattle corrects my presumption – there's one tablet left. I line up the lid arrows but struggle to pop the top off, cursing the manufacturers of childproof containers for making them adultproof too. The single Paracetamol I tip out onto my hand looks so large it is of cartoon-like proportions. There is no way Beth can swallow this as it is, so I pop back into the kitchen to carefully cut it into quarters using the only sharp knife I can find in the cutlery drawer. Taking the pieces of tablet and a glass of water back with me to the bedroom, I carefully feed Beth the quarters of tablet. Her face reacts to the bitter taste, but she dutifully swallows the pieces down.

I sweep Beth's hair off her face, tucking it behind her ears and smoothing it down her shoulders, in a gesture that's antithetical to Abbie's aggressive affront on my hair. I talk to her slowly, like she's a small child, explaining that I won't be gone very long and that I'll be back as soon as I can. I then call a cab from Beth's landline, hoping to save a little bit of money in the way of phone credit to balance out the funds I'm splurging on taxis I can't afford. Thankfully, the taxi driver is willing to travel in silence after my "Yes/No" answers make it clear I'm not in the mood for inane chatter.

I open the door to the block of flats, jiggling the key in a way that is now second nature. I push the door open to the strange mix of mildew, people's bodies and random cooking smells, plus the faint smell of bleach. I take the two flights of stairs slowly, rather than my usual two-at-a-time. Standing outside the front door of my own flat, I realise I don't want to go in. I stare at the Yale key on my fob, its jagged edges staring back at me angrily. We don't bother with the deadlock. It's really stiff and I never got the knack of unlocking it as I have with the main door. When Matt moved in, I just got the Yale key cut for him. Deadlock keys are so expensive. I take a few deep breaths and compose myself before pushing the Yale key into the lock and slowly turning it. I can already see the disdain on Matt's face as he looks up from his Xbox, ready to pick a fight with me about where I've been and why I haven't called or texted – something that's only just occurred to me to do as I'm standing in the communal hallway.

I hear the phone ring and Matt jump up and run across the flat to answer it, probably assuming it's me. I let myself in quietly and stay standing in the hall, waiting for his phone call to finish, ready to tell him piously what happened the night before and how Beth needed me. But when he heads back out of the bedroom and into the hall, it's as if he doesn't see me. The mixture of shock and horror on his face would suggest he's just taken a call about me being the one in the road accident instead of Jack. He walks across into the lounge silently. I prod myself in the belly to make sure I'm real, and not a projection from beyond the grave. Realising I'm being stupid, I follow him into the lounge. Matt is sitting on the sofa staring into space.

"Matt, are you okay?" I use the same voice I used earlier

with Beth, wondering if there's an alien on the loose from one of Matt's games zapping the "grown-upness" out of the adults around me. I try to catch his eye, wait for him to launch into his rant about how he was there for me and how I shouldn't need anyone else. He usually loves this argument, which always ends with me telling him he lives for his Xbox and him sniggering, never denying it. But this time Matt carries on staring. Exhausted from 24 hours looking after Beth, and the tension from Jack's death tight in my shoulders, I snap.

"What?!" I shout at him. "I'm not dead you know – I'm standing here, waiting for you to notice me. What is it this time?"

He doesn't react, so I go over to him, bend down and touch his shoulder gently. He recoils as if I've burned him, but it snaps him out of his gaze and he turns to look at me.

"It's Maggie," he whispers. "She's dead."

His body buckles into a heap on the sofa, shaking as he sobs. I sit there, gently rocking him as I comfort him, horrified that I'd been thinking such awful things when his Nan has just died. He sniffs and wipes his face with his hands.

"Can we go and see her?" he asks calmly, almost emotionless, when he eventually runs out of tears. "Now?"

I nod, going into the bedroom to get changed, quickly throwing off yesterday's work outfit, wiping myself down with face wipes and changing into my usual home comforts of black linen trousers and a greying T-shirt. My words "I'm not dead you know" reverberate around my head and I wish I could take them back.

"My Nan not worth the outfit then?"

I ignore him, noticing he's wearing jeans that have seen better days and a T-shirt that looks like it has never seen a wash, never mind an iron. I refuse to argue with him, as it seems disrespectful to Maggie. We walk silently to the taxi I have waiting on a meter ready for my return journey to Beth's.

Beth.

Except for giving the driver the address of Maggie's care home and telling Matt to wear a seat belt, I don't speak to either them for the whole journey. Instead I leave long, awkward messages for Abbie and Faye, curtly asking them what they think they're playing at and insisting they get their arses round to Beth's place. I tell each of them I haven't managed to get hold of the other in the hope that neither of them relies on the other to step up to the plate. I spend the rest of the journey staring at my phone for any signs of life, grateful that I hadn't taken the phone call from the nursing home. Breaking the news to Matt would have been too difficult, too painful. I'm glad it had been the job of a stranger: that it fell to someone who'd probably done the job a million times before. People go into nursing homes to die, don't they, so the staff would be trained to deal with it.

Maggie hadn't been looking after herself properly for the last four years and when Social Services had moved her from her small council flat into a care home she seemed to shrink from the sparkly person she had been into a tiny, frail old lady, so her passing shouldn't seem like a shock. But it did. The thought of her dying filled me with a sense of sadness far sharper than I'd felt before. First Jack, now Maggie. And maybe Beth too: she seemed dead on the inside.

I remember eating sponge cake and drinking tea made in a pot – something I only did with Beth – and hearing stories about what a rascal Matt was when he was a kid. From the careful way she cut the cake, I'd say she'd gone out especially to buy it for my visit. Matt seemed half proud of her interest in him and half embarrassed that I was there to hear the stories, especially the ones about how her Son, Matt's Dad, was useless with him. It made me realise that you could have parents worse than mine. My Mum didn't mean to get pregnant by her married boss and she cared about me even though she couldn't cope, whereas Matt's parents didn't give a damn from day one. He used to tell me how he didn't care about them either, but he protested a little too much and I realised the cuts must have run deep. It's another reason why I'm still with him I guess: I knew if I left him I'd be labelled as a deserter, along with his parents.

When we get to the nursing home, it looks like it's closed, as if there is no life left inside the building now that Maggie's gone. I try to turn the handles on the forbidding front door, but there is no give. I then try to push one of them open using the full force of my body weight. They are definitely locked. So I ring the pearl doorbell that takes pride of place inside circular grooves carved into the brickwork. I hear nothing – no ringing, no footsteps. There's no way of knowing if the bell has sounded deep inside the building or if it's broken. With an agitated Matt pacing up and down beside me, threatening to put a brick through the window, I call them up. It rings and rings until a member of staff eventually answers. She is very short with me, explaining that evening visiting hours don't start until after the residents had finished their tea and biscuits. When I can finally get a word in edgeways, I explain why we're here. The line goes dead. About a minute later the front door opens and we are ushered inside.

I stop in the hallway as I do every time we come for visiting hours, each time forgetting just how bleak the building is on the inside. The care home is an old hospital, and the sense of decay in the air isn't only from the elderly people: it's as if the building is struggling with its last breaths too. Matt pushes past the nurse without a word and heads up to Maggie's room. I mutter an apology to her and start to head up the stairs after him.

"Excuse me miss," the nurse calls after me, "but we have paperwork that needs to be signed."

I sigh, turn on my heel, and follow her into the office. Matt is sitting alone with Maggie while the nurse slowly goes through a pile of coded forms, reading everything out in a monotonous tone, marking where I need to sign with a cross and stamping each of the forms with great relish. I am relieved to hear that Maggie's care at the home has been paid for by the council, so there are no bills to settle. I feel instantly guilty for thinking it, but then I feel guilty about most things. Beth often jokes that I must have been Catholic in a former life. She talks about Catholic guilt as if it's a particularly special type of guilt. No matter how independent of her parents her life becomes, she never seems to get beyond the guilt her life choices make her feel.

Once all the paperwork is signed, I head up to join Matt. As I enter Maggie's room he shoots me a dirty look. He is sitting in the armchair by the side of her bed, his hands clasped in front of him.

"Nice for you to join us."

"I was filling out the paperwork," I explain, whispering even though Maggie couldn't be woken.

"Yeah, whatever. Any excuse."

Anger wells up inside me: "It's not an excuse. I was trying to save you from having to do anything other than grieve."

He stands up, the bedside lamp casting his shadow high on the ceiling like he's a bad guy in a cartoon.

"I'm not having an argument with you while she's lying here dead," he says. "So why don't you just leave."

The Second Cup

My anger drains from my body as quickly as it flourished and I realise I don't have the strength to fight with him. Instead I share the news the nurse had asked me to pass on to him about Maggie's funeral.

"You need to speak to the nurse downstairs. Either your parents can pay for it or the local council can cover it as a public health funeral," I explain, the words that we can't afford to pay hanging unsaid in the air. In the extended pause that follows, I nod a goodbye to Matt and leave the room, heading downstairs and walking through the now-open front doors and out into the fresh air.

I wonder if Matt's parents will do the decent thing for once and foot the bill for the funeral. I'm relieved it's not "them or him" because I'd end up paying for it and I know he wouldn't be grateful. I'd worked out long ago that if someone doesn't understand money, they never truly appreciate your financial sacrifices. At least that's what I told myself every time Matt didn't say "Thank you". He had a job so he knew what the value of money was, but before we got together he'd lived at the limit of his credit card – "It's my credit card, so it's my money" – as if he didn't understand the concept of debt. The guilt makes my head heavy, but I lie to him about how much I earn so he can't spend all my money for me.

When we started going out he still lived with his Nan, and would probably still be there if she hadn't ended up in a home, her over-55s council flat going back on the housing list. With Matt never officially living there, rehousing him wasn't a council priority. So he moved in with me – about four weeks before Maggie moved in here. I sometimes wonder about how convenient it was that I came along at the right time, and if I'd somehow been duped by his master plan. Had he chosen to defend me all those months ago as part of a scheme to get himself a girlfriend to move in with? I hoped not, but I couldn't shake the uneasy feeling I had about it.

I know I should call another taxi and head back to my flat, gather up some essentials and then head back to Beth's, but I can't face it, not just yet. I need to clear my head a bit more first, or there won't be any space in there for Beth and her worries. I check my phone to see if either Faye or Abbie has gotten back to me. There are text messages and a voicemail from Abbie. Nothing from Faye. I am just about to listen to Abbie's message when the phone rings, making me jump out of my skin and nearly drop my phone.

"Hello?" I answer.

"Is this Olivia Banks?" a voice I don't recognise asks.

"Yes. Yes, it is."

"Can you please come to the Accident and Emergency department at Manchester Royal Infirmary. A Beth Adams has been brought in."

7 teacups

FAYE

I listen to the message again. Olivia is asking nicely but her tone of voice says it all. She. Is. Not. Happy. But I can't go round to Beth's. Just the thought of it makes me feel I have a fist in my throat choking me from the inside. Watching Beth collapse in the pub was like seeing myself curled up in the shop doorway after meeting NOT-Jack. I'd tried to tell Beth about that, but I couldn't cope with her eyes widening into two too-deep pools of pity. So I built up my story from a pile of higgledy untruths, claiming I was proud of myself for not being the pathetic cowering creature that I had actually been, and how I'd got a taxi straight home instead.

I'd been happy to lie because I didn't want to be that person. I didn't want to grow up to be just like my Mum. I was 14 when my Dad finally left. I thought it would be for the best and that I'd be relieved because I'd no longer have to turn a blind eye to his sneaking around behind Mum's back. I didn't know Mum knew all about his cheating and was so terrified he'd leave her if she issued him with an ultimatum that she pretended to be ignorant. I understand now that he was very unhappy, trapped in a marriage he'd only gone into because my Mum was pregnant with me, and that he was going to leave my Mum at some point – that the only question was "when", not "if" – and that my Mum knew all this and still did everything she could to hold onto him for as long as possible.

So. It. Wasn't. For. The. Best.

Instead of bouncing back, my Mum became a shadow of herself, spending her day in her slippers and dressing gown, drinking tea. When I got in from school, one of my jobs would be the washing up. But except for my breakfast bowl, there'd rarely be anything other than mugs, scattered round the house with the half-drunk remains. I'd scrub at them for ages, but the dark rings where the surface of the thick liquid had clung to the mug were a nightmare to wash off. It's a habit of hers I picked up, but my own clutter of half-drunk brews served as a reminder to never let my life become as desperate as hers. Instead I filled my life with positive things, focusing on my creative and adventurous sides.

Getting into university and meeting Jack had seemed like just rewards for all my efforts. But then Jack had left and I'd become a shadow of a person, just like my Mum. It took every fibre of my being to move forward from that point, and I just don't have the energy to go through it again with Beth, not while I'm trying to come to terms with Jack's death myself – and especially as I went to such great lengths to find him.

THE GLOBE

After meeting NOT-Jack all Faye could think about was finding the real Jack. This was before Beth collapsed: when everything was still about Faye and Jack. Back when what mattered was the shoeboxes of memories under her bed.

Faye meant to keep just the important stuff. But what's important one day is another day's junk. A tangled river of homemade friendship bracelets, a selection of keys with no locks to fit into and ticket stubs for gigs she only vaguely remembers going to. No matter what these items meant when they were first given pride of place in the shoebox mountain, they were now sneaky, villainous barriers whose only job was to hide the address of Jack's parents – an address she can picture written on the underside of a brown envelope in Jack's lazy scrawl.

In one of the boxes Faye finds her globe, the one that used to sit on her windowsill. She used to spin it, randomly planning where she'd travel with Jack (once they'd both graduated) by where it stopped. But her symbol of post-university freedom became one of torment after Jack moved 185 miles, 2.99 degrees south and 1.82 degrees east from her. On the globe, the gap between them was just 2.5mm.

FAYE

I shove the globe back in the box I found it in and carry on searching for more scraps of paper. I'm rewarded 10 minutes later when I discover the mug-rim-stained envelope between a red gas bill and an unopened packet of Christmas present labels of cute hand-drawn dogs with snow moustaches and beards.

Jack's parents live in an area called Larches. It sounds nice, but I'd been shocked to find myself in a rundown council estate the only time I visited. Jack's parents had seemed lovely, but Jack had the anger towards his parents that many teenagers have. It was anger that didn't seem to be fading as he spent his university years in Manchester – if anything it was getting worse. His anger made me uncomfortable: it seemed out of place in the Jack I knew. Part of the reason why Jack had headed down to London was to finally break free of his "shitty past" as he put it. Manchester just wasn't far enough away. I wasn't sure if turning up to their house unannounced was okay, so I spent hours putting a letter together to his folks.

Dear Ted & Sylvie,

I'm not sure if you remember me, but my name is Faye Simmons and I dated your Son Jack while he was at university in Manchester. I recently caught up with an old friend from his course, we ended up talking about old times and it got me thinking about getting in touch with other friends from the time.

I'd like to see Jack again and find out what he's been up to and how he's doing. I'd really appreciate it if you could pass this letter onto him so he has my address or, better still, send me his address so I can surprise him with a letter of his own.

Wishing you both well.
Love, Faye

The bit about bumping into an old friend was a white lie. I could hardly say I was wondering, so many years after leaving me, if he could help me finally bury the ghost of our relationship that still haunted me. And my plan to surprise him with a letter was a fib too – if I got hold of his address I had every intention of turning up on his doorstep. I put a first-class stamp on the letter, which seemed a bit reckless, but I had to restrain myself from going and posting it by hand and waiting outside their front door for their response.

I manage nine mornings – not including the day I sent

the letter – of checking the post for a letter from them before skipping work and getting the train to Preston. I wish I'd thought of suggesting a quick visit in my letter, because now me turning up would look like I was forcing myself on them unannounced, either because I was too impatient to wait for a reply or (worse) because they didn't want to have anything to do with me. But my star sign for the day had said: "Carpe diem – seize the day. Otherwise an opportunity might pass you by forever."

If Beth were here she'd point out how that could mean almost anything, but it was enough for me to find myself on Piccadilly station concourse buying a saver return to Preston. I stare at the miniscule amount of change I get in return for my tenner and decide to skip grabbing myself a gorgeous "Breakie to GoGo" from Boost Juice Bar. I put my train tickets away in my purse to stop my nervous fingers turning them into all kinds of strange origami creatures, and head up the long travelator to platforms 13 and 14. All the trains to Preston go from 14, out through Deansgate and Salford. It had been a long time since I'd made this train journey, Jack's strong hand firmly grasping my sweaty one, him grinning at me with a look that said he knew his parents would love me. And they'd seemed to; they'd welcomed me into the family. But I hadn't seen them since our split. I had his parents' phone number but, for some reason, calling them up out of the blue seemed far more terrifying than arriving on their doorstep unannounced. Maybe it was because I was used to jumping on trains.

The Preston train I get on is the stopping train. Chewing my hair as we trundle along, I remove split ends with my teeth so I can justify leaving it another month before I go to the dreaded hairdressers. I am always fascinated by stations like Lostock and Blackrod, which seemed to be in the middle of nowhere, houses dotted in fields and maybe the occasional business nearby. I wonder how these people live away from the bustle of a big city. I know we're all meant to crave living in the country, but I can't personally see the attraction of having cows and sheep for neighbours and no 24-hour garage within walking distance.

When I arrive in Preston it is raining. I get out my trusty, if slightly rusty, brolly. I head up the road to get the bus, cursing the town planners for not putting the train and bus stations closer together. The bus station is cleverly hidden behind the shops and market, making it a nightmare for any newcomer to find it. I don't blame them for trying to hide it though because it's an ugly bugger of a building. I head for the 27 bus bay to Larches, but the routes have been renumbered and rearranged. Now it's Stagecoach and not the Preston Bus Company; I need the number 89 instead. This is the sort of change that unnerves me. How much else has changed in the years since Jack headed down to London? I get on and sit by the window so I can watch the almost-familiar scenery go by. I get off in the centre of Larches and meander down the typically curved roads of the council estate.

Every second or third house has a different front door or a fence out the front instead of a hedge – the owner's way of marking the fact they have bought their council house and are now on the property ladder, of saying "I'm better than you because I own mine now". I wonder what the burglary rates are like and whether those with fancy doors get broken into more often. I'm bemused by the number of concrete slablike drains that decorate the pavement here, and particularly the frequency with which they are in sets of three. Whoever planned the facilities for this council estate either didn't know the negative associations connected to three drains, or thought the residents of such an estate were already deemed unlucky and so didn't matter.

I turn up outside Ted and Sylvie's house, surprised to see a newish front door and block-paved front, the front hedge removed so what was the garden could now be used as a parking space. This is not what I expect from the staunch Labour voters and proud council tenants I remember them to be – and I wonder if this is what Jack has chosen to spend his money on. I have no idea how long I'm standing there before I'm jolted back into reality by the pizza delivery moped almost running me over, cutting across the pavement dangerously close to me in order to pull into the block-paved path. I watch the teenage lad get off the scooter, ring the doorbell and then start faffing about with pizza boxes. The door opens and a man in his 20s I don't recognise appears at the door. At least two or three other similar-aged people are hovering in the background.

"That's £22.95 please mate."

Money and pizza boxes change hands.

"Cheers. Keep the change."

I watch in a daze as the pizza delivery lad gets back on his scooter, the front door of the house slams shut, and the scooter revs its hair-dryer engine before making another death-defying manoeuvre past me and tearing down the road at an almost respectable 28mph.

They. Don't. Live. Here.

All the way up on the train I'd been working through in my head how this meeting would go, but it hadn't occurred to me at any point that his parents might have moved. I'm falling, my arms outstretched, but with no-one there to catch me. I have one last sliver of hope to cling to: that the occupants of the house in front of me have a forwarding address. Holding myself together, I tentatively walk up to the door and ring the bell.

"Go away!" one voice shouts.

"Yeah, go away, we're eating pizza!" adds another.

I hear laughing and whooping noises coming from inside.

It is enough to make me crumple and I find myself crouched down by the doorstep, crying.

"Faye?"

I stop my tears.

"Faye is that you?"

I look up and around in the direction the voice comes from and see an elderly man with a concerned look on his face staring down at me from the other side of the fence. It was Ted and Sylvie's old next-door neighbour, the one who joked with Jack that he'd have me if Jack ever got bored. I'd offered to walk his dog for him when he wasn't feeling up to it, something I'd done just to be nice. But it meant he remembered me and, all these years later, my kind act was about to be repaid.

"If you're looking for Ted and Sylvie you won't find them here; they've moved."

I sigh.

"Yes, I'd worked that one out, thanks."

I give him a watery smile, realising I may have sounded rude when all he was doing was making conversation.

"I've got their new address over in Frenchwood if you're interested."

My face cracks into a relieved, overjoyed smile.

"Yes please!"

The neighbour disappears inside. I want to jump for joy, but my legs are rooted to the floor, almost as if they are afraid that moving from their spot will break the spell and he won't come back out again. He reappears a moment later with a piece of paper torn from the corner of a newspaper, one line of an address scrawled in old man's handwriting. I'm just about to ask where Frenchwood is when he speaks.

"It's a bit of a trek, mind. It's the other side of the town centre. You'll have to get a bus into town and one back out again. It's off London Road, on the way down to Walton-le-Dale. It's lovely down there, near the river. Well it was until they built one of those new-fangled out-of-town centres. Ruined it, if you ask me."

I grin at him again until I twig he might think I'm not taking his comments about new-fangled centres seriously. But I can't contain my happiness when "a bit of a trek" turns out to be just getting a bus back into town and then one going out the other side of Preston. My feet tingle with impatience and the paper burns in my hand, as I listen impatiently to the neighbour reminisce about his old neighbours.

"I remember the day Jack turned up here. He was a little lad, even though he was four, he was small for it."

"He was four?" I'd always assumed this home was where Jack had grown up. First the number 89 bus, now this.

"Well Ted and Sylvie were here, they'd been here forever by then. But they finally got the go-ahead to get a little one. And there he was, bright as a button from the moment he moved in."

"Jack was adopted?" He'd never told me. What else didn't I know?

"Yes, he was – although you must never mention it to him because they never told him." He looks worried. "Promise me?"

"I promise," I say, holding up the piece of paper. "Without you, I wouldn't get a chance to catch up with him."

With a half-convinced nod, the neighbour heads back inside his house. I shout "Thanks" at his back as he disappears inside and closes the door. Was our conversation a dream? No, I have the piece of paper in my hand with the address on, and it is taking me on the next leg of my journey. Two buses later, via a trip to a scruffy-looking sandwich shop, I get off the bus near an equally shabby-looking garage. I can see the river and the two pubs either side of the road sitting next to it and agree that it's a lovely looking little area. Soon I find myself standing outside another council house just up the road from the river, staring at another unfamiliar front door.

I knock as confidently as I can muster, then step back from the door. It is only after I knock that I twig they won't have received my letter and so they won't be expecting me at all. I can't decide if that's a good thing or not. But I stand my ground, refusing to run away when I'm this close – even though there is a group of young teens nearby who could easily be blamed for playing knock-a-door-run. I hear the typical sounds of someone older shuffling along in the hallway and psyche myself up for the door opening. When it does, I see Ted, dressed smarter than I've ever seen him and looking far older than I ever thought he would.

When I first met Ted, I'd been startled by how much like Jack he looked – the same immense jawline, the same extensive nose, the same strong facial frame to carry off both features. Now I knew this was a fluke, and not because Jack took after his father. And I wonder if Jack didn't tell me he was adopted because the neighbour was right and he didn't still know. Why would he question his life when he looked so much like his Dad? When I look at Ted this time, it isn't the similarities that strike me, but how lost he looks. He carries the same haunted look Olivia usually wears.

"Oh my God, what do you want?" he asks, almost accusingly.

"Who is it dear?" I hear Sylvie's voice from the lounge. But she isn't willing to wait for a reply from Ted and is already on her feet and into the hall. She gasps when she sees me, then runs to the back of the house, into what I guess is the kitchen.

"It's too little too late!" she shouts, her voice trailing behind her.

"W-what?" I stutter. "I don't understand."

But Ted just sighs and uses what looks like his last bit of energy to shut the door in my face. My half-dream is turning into a waking nightmare. Am I just meant to walk away? I'm not sure. I knock again and, for the second time that day, "Go away" is shouted at me through a closed front door.

I want to scream "NO!" back at them, but the word catches my larynx as I try to spit it out. I have to swallow down the bile that is bubbling up and burning the back of my throat. I have no idea what to do next, either in reality or in my quest to find Jack. I count my breaths, in and out, in and out, like counting sheep, but to calm myself rather than sending myself to sleep. I refuse to find myself rocking in yet another doorway, especially with the youths nearby now showing more interest in me than they are their battered football and stickered skateboards.

I unglue my feet from the path, slowly turn myself round and walk sluggishly through the quicksand pavement that leads me back down to the main road and the bus back to the station. A bus flies passed when I'm moments from the stop and I have a flash of understanding as to why Beth struggles to wait for buses. When other things are going badly, a missed bus is the tipping point, the last straw, the straw that breaks the camel's back so badly that the creature is paralysed for life and unable to function normally ever again. I see this in Beth and I'm starting to see it in myself now too. You can keep your life in order and under control to a certain point, but when something pushes you over the edge, you free fall. And now I'm falling.

8 teaspoons

ABBIE

I sit myself down at what is quickly becoming our regular table with a large glass of white wine. No foolish lemonade for me, because when I have something to celebrate I do it in style. Faye is late again but I can't hold it in any longer. I'm going to share my news just with Olivia and Beth instead.

"I've done it," I tell them. "I've filed for divorce."

Beth and Olivia stare back at me in shock. For a moment, none of us moves. Then Beth jumps up and hugs me so tightly I can feel my extra layers being compressed.

"That's fantastic news!" she squeals.

Her buoyant comment kick-starts Olivia into action, who joins in with the hugs and celebratory comments. When it was Beth's turn to hug me again, I can see she is already desperate to ask the first of her questions. So I gesture for us all to sit down again and wait for her to speak, mentally preparing myself for the onslaught. But her first totally flummoxes me.

"So," she asks, "how did Dominic take it?"

I look at her, horrified: "He, erm, doesn't know yet."

And that's when Faye decides to walk up to the table and slam her pint down again, stealing the limelight, leaving me to ponder my situation alone. There's something uncomfortably familiar about Faye. Not her personality or her mannerisms, just the way she looks. As soon as she's animated, the feeling dissipates, but if I catch her still, like in a photograph, it's a bit like having a ghost at the table. Nobody else seems to notice, so I keep it to myself, waiting until I work out who she reminds me of – probably someone off a TV show.

I allow myself to drop back whenever she takes centre stage, to take a breather. So when Beth collapses at Faye's news, I let Olivia take charge: I take a few steps back from the table. I can't be the one to help Beth anyway because I need to be with Dominic. I can't let him find out by being served the papers – that's far too harsh. I need to explain everything to him. Well, I will be leaving out the details of how he repulses me, but I should at least try to get him to understand that I married him on a whim and that I need to take my life back and make it my own. While Olivia holds onto Beth, I down my wine, and find myself out the door and heading home.

Looking back, finishing my drink was a strange thing to do, but I was on autopilot. And the Dutch courage was going to come in handy. On my way home on the tram, I think about the mess my life is in. Well, I'm not being fair to myself: it's my romantic life that's a mess: the rest of my life was fine. I already feel like I'm cheating on Dominic mentally by not wanting to be with him anymore, but I have a growing realisation that, in some ways, my treatment of Dominic is on the same level as the nasty way in which Jack treated Faye, in which Matt treats Olivia – and in the way she treated him too. I need to be a better person than that.

Since I accepted that my marriage with Dominic was a sham I'd just been going through the motions. Well now at least Dominic deserved me to say things out loud to him too, rather than me burying my head in the sand and pretending there wasn't anything wrong until the documents arrived. What had I been thinking? My solicitor had looked at me very strangely when I'd given her my own address as the one to send the papers to. I guess she thought it was strange that I was divorcing someone I still shared a house with. I keep my fingers crossed the whole journey, hoping that Dominic wants to be freed too, that he might be angry and embarrassed about me making the decision without him, but that he'll be happy with the outcome. I have no plans to stay with him even if he doesn't want a divorce, but at the same time I don't have any reason to hurt him just for the sake of it.

Dominic meets me in the hallway of my house – and it is my house thank God, as there was only my name on the mortgage. I couldn't afford to buy Paul out of the house when we split, so it meant the double upheaval of being single and homeless. This time round poor Dominic would be facing both, but I push the guilt I feel to the back of my mind as I know any short-term pain I cause him would be better in the long run.

"I heard your key in the door," he says by way of explanation. He looks at me concerned as I'm home early for a Friday night. "Fall out with Beth?"

That's the usual reason I'm home early. Every once in a while her opinions go too close to the bone for me – and the only way to get her to apologise is to make her realise just how far along "too far" she's gone. That would take me storming out of the bar while shouting back at her something along the lines of "You know where I am when you're ready to apologise" – and I wouldn't check my phone on the journey home, to giving myself time to calm down. Once I got in the house, I'd check, and there'd usually be a voicemail from her, apologising, although it would occasionally take until the next day. I hadn't stormed out since Faye had come along.

I look at Dominic looking back at me concerned and feel the tears welling up in my eyes. Then his arms are around me and he is giving me a big bear hug and saying soothing words over and over in hushed tones. I let him lead me to the sofa, sit me down and pass me a tissue. Then he moves to the relative safety of the opposite sofa and I am reassured I am doing the right thing. He's given me his maximum amount of affection: and for me it is the minimum required. It was just never meant to work between us.

I like tactile men, except when it comes to sex – that's when I didn't like Dominic's hands all over me. I know I was sending out mixed signals. You can't say to your husband: "I love hugs and curling up on the sofa together, but only when we're fully clothed and I prefer sex with as little skin contact as possible." Or maybe you can if you're with the right person, but I couldn't say it to Dominic. So he didn't know whether or not to sit with me; he didn't know me at all.

As if reading my mind, Dominic clears his throat to get my attention: "This isn't about Beth, is it?"

I shake my head, my hair swishing round my face.

Dominic sighs, already out of patience where my emotional outburst was concerned: "Come on then, spill."

I take a deep breath in, hoping it would stop my voice from cracking: "I want a divorce."

Dominic looks shocked but quickly composes himself.

"I knew it wasn't working. I just wasn't expecting you to

confront the situation. I thought I'd be the one ending it," he says.

"We can tell everyone you split with me if you want," I tell him graciously.

"What?" he asks, incredulously. "And make out like I'm the bad guy?"

I'm confused – does he want to be the dumper or dumpee? He can't be both. But I decide not to press him about it because I no longer need to make any attempts to understand him! That thought brought a smile to my brain that I had to fight to keep off my face. I'm glad Dominic and I can still be civil to each other though.

He looks at me – he knows it's not everything: "And?"

"I've already filed the paperwork."

When I explain to him it's why I left town early, not mentioning the Beth situation, just that she and Olivia had been horrified I'd filed for divorce without telling him, he cracks up laughing. By the time we're both a large glass into the bottle of wine we're sharing to toast our divorce with, Dominic is relaxed enough to revisit the funny side again and again. He loves that I'd been ready to celebrate with the girls and that they'd sent me packing for being so thoughtless, although he was slightly less amused that the paperwork was already on its way.

"Well there's the final example of how little we do together," he says, his voice tinged with sadness. "We never made any decisions together. Lots of couples discuss the decision to get a divorce before going ahead. We didn't even make a joint decision about getting married – I was all for it and I knew even back then that you were just going along with it."

Unlike mine, Dominic's first marriage had worked and it'd been cruelly stolen from him when his wife died from a

SARAH MARIE GRAYE

brain tumour. They'd given her 14 weeks to live and she'd made just six of them. On top of losing her, Dominic felt very angry about missing out on those final eight weeks. I hadn't known at the time of our marriage, but he'd proposed to me on their wedding anniversary. When I'd found out later and confessed to the girls I thought it was creepy, Beth had agreed. And Faye had asked me how I could feel ready to marry a guy when I didn't know something as important as the date of his first marriage. She had a valid point.

"I'm sorry Dominic, so very sorry."

He met my eyes and must have been able to tell I meant those words because he bear-hugged me one last time (hugs I know I will miss, even from him) before agreeing to take the spare room, leaving a very grateful me with the master bedroom. About an hour later, I hear the front door slam quietly, which is what your door does if someone wants to leave quietly but the door sticks. With Dominic gone, the air feels lighter. I'm so glad I have the house – my house – to myself.

ABBIE

I'm lounging in bed, enjoying the freedom of a lie in, of the king size to myself, my hangover strangely missing, when Olivia rings. I've been ignoring her texts, partly because I needed this time for myself and partly because my eyes didn't seem to want to focus on the glowing screen of my iPhone. But I feel bad about ignoring her call, so I call my voicemail service. As I listen to her message, I catch myself absentmindedly checking the ceiling for spiders. I have no idea why I do that, but if I've gone to bed without doing it, I have to switch my side light back on again to check – otherwise I can't settle down to sleep. Dominic doesn't know about my weird habit because he's always in bed and asleep by the time I come up to bed, but it's something Ebbs used to mock me about. I can't remember it happening back when I was with Paul.

I'm annoyed to hear Olivia is putting Matt before Beth – it's bad enough that I had to do that with Dominic. But she must have her reasons for deserting Beth and I'm pretty sure Faye can't be relied on to pick up the slack – an assumption that is confirmed six minutes later with a text from Faye. I smell my breath by breathing into the palm of my hand and then sniffing. I reek of wine. I look around me at the two – no, three – empty wine bottles discarded on the floor. Well I'd certainly celebrated in style, just not the way I'd planned. I wonder how many of the bottles I shared with Dominic and how many are my own. If I'm still drunk it would explain the lack of hangover.

There's no way I'm fit to drive. But I have to. So I wash my face, throw on some clean clothes, gulp down a whole French press of absurdly strong coffee, brush my teeth, pick up my car keys and head out of the house – my house – and drive painfully slowly and carefully in the direction of Beth's place, taking a convoluted route of back roads in an attempt to avoid any strategically positioned police cars out to catch any weekend boy racers. It would seem that inept blokes in uniform get a kick out of stopping my X3. When I get to Beth's I realise I have no way to get in as I don't have a spare key. I have no idea what the people in the other flats in her block are like so I don't know if I can risk buzzing any of them to let me in. I stand there a couple of minutes, reciting the lyrics to Bob Marley's *Everything's Going to Be Alright* to soothe my ragged nerves. I didn't even know I knew the words beyond the chorus, but I manage to drag them from the very outskirts of my brain.

I stand there whispering the words to myself until

someone leaving the flats holds the door open for me and I'm in. I get as far as Beth's front door before realising my position is now equally as futile. Even with my extra pounds, I'm not going to be heavy enough to bust her door down. And even if I were, what then? I'd have destroyed the lock – and maybe even the door and its hinges – and her flat would be unsecured. I'd be too busy trying to get an emergency locksmith to spend any time looking after Beth, so I might as well not be here.

I consider walking away, telling Olivia where to go with her trips to rescue people. But before I get back in my car and crawl home, at least I can call Olivia first and tell her. Except I can't face listening to her, hearing her barely concealed disappointment, so I decide to text her instead. I open my messages folder and scroll through the long thread of texts Olivia has sent in the last 24 hours to get to the point where I can start typing. The texts include instructions on where to find the spare key. Of course they do. Olivia is one of the most organised people I know – so much so that I'd love to steal her from the amazing Toby to have as my PA, except I couldn't cope with her self-esteem issues every day.

I head back outside the front door, shimmy down the side of the building by the hedge and feel for the key and front door fob along the top edge of the window frame of her bathroom. A slightly more bedraggled version of me makes it back to the front door and in through both doors to check on Beth. I catch myself in the long mirror in Beth's hall. I look like an overgrown Shih Tzu very much in need of a groom. All the lights in the flat are off and I don't want to wake Beth if she's sleeping, so I navigate through the flat using the light from my phone screen. My eyes appreciate the darkness too. I'd struggled with the lurid streetlamps and glaring traffic lights on the way here and was grateful to give my photoreceptors a break. I slowly turn the door handle on Beth's bedroom, open the door and tiptoe in. I can see the outline of Beth in bed and that of a chair positioned next to it. I'm guessing it's been placed here by Olivia, who probably spent hour after hour here alone with Beth, waiting for one of us to take over so she could go and do whatever it is that useless Matt wanted.

The room is quiet. Too quiet. I can't hear Beth's breathing. I lean over her face and a weak puff of breath hits my cheek. But it's not enough for me to feel comfortable about the situation at all. Hoping it will wake Beth so I can see she is okay, I reach over to the bedside light and turn it on. She doesn't even stir. I look around me for other signs of life and my eye catches a small white pot in the wastebasket. My heart is in my mouth as I lean down to pick it up. Paracetamol. I don't need to shake it to know it is empty. I frantically search my pockets for my phone and can't find it. Did I leave it in the car? I'm standing up to go and get it when I hear the thud as it falls from my knee. Of course, I used it as a torch. I pick it up and dial 999. Then double-check I've dialled the right number because it seems all wrong.

"Emergency. Which service do you require?"

"Ambulance. My friend has taken an overdose."

I'm quickly put through to the ambulance service to explain the situation, the fact that I found Beth alone, the empty tablet bottle in the bin, the address of Beth's flat. I'm then given a list of instructions to follow, things to check, that she is still breathing – I check again, even though I've only just checked – that I can feel her pulse, that her legs and arms are free and not trapped underneath her. I'm then assured that the ambulance will be there soon, but they ask me to stay on the line in case her situation changes.

Having to tell the emergency staff that Beth had been here alone makes me a very bad friend. Poor Olivia had tried to get hold of me, but in the end she'd had to leave – and Beth had taken the situation into her own hands. If I'd taken Olivia's call, if I'd left home straight away, would I have got here in time to stop Beth taking an overdose? Although should that role fall to her friends? Yes, I've failed Beth, but it should be Beth's parents waiting with her for the ambulance, not one of her friends. But then what would happen if this happened to me? Who would know to call my parents? No, it would be Beth or Olivia, or maybe even Faye, who would be sitting with me now, stroking the cold skin on the back of my hand, waiting for me to be saved.

The generation before ours bemoans the fall of family values, but they are the very cause of it. I don't know any friends or anyone in my social circle at work who regularly sees or hears from their parents. I hear the occasional conversation about the burden of an elderly parent, but it's usually someone from my parents' generation whinging about their parents. How can our parents blame us for having no connection with them when they struggle to find time for their own parents in their lives? They've brought us up to be exactly the same as that. If our grandparents whinge, then fair enough: their children have failed them. That's where the rot started.

The Mad Hatter's tea party

The Mad Hatter's tea party is a misquote from "Alice in Wonderland". Lewis Carroll in fact never refers to such an event, although he does have a Hatter character who exists continuously at 6 o'clock on the dot as a way to prevent his own execution.

A Mad Hatter's Tea Party is not the kind of tea party that Abbie would expect Beth to have. To Abbie, Beth has always seemed perfectly sane. Maybe even too sane. No, all this pill-popping nonsense should be left to Alice and the stupid book she was forced to read for GCSE.

Although Abbie was perfectly aware that she could be accused of following Alice's preoccupation with any bottle that even hinted at saying "drink me".

9 teapots

BETH

Whoever chose this club has got a lot to answer for. I loathe repetitive dance music, especially the type that sounds like some sort of siren constantly whirring and bleeping. Is it jungle? Or drum'n'bass? I lost interest in mainstream music before acid house infiltrated it, only knowing of its existence when all the older kids in school started wearing fluorescent pin badges with mad-happy faces on. It seemed strange that wearing badges was cool again for the crowd that had mocked those five years younger just months before for wearing Bros patches on their bomber jackets and bottle tops on their shoes.

I got into Depeche Mode and The Cure, via Human League and Eurythmics, wearing too much dark eyeliner to ever get away with, and often being sent to the girls' toilets to face the indignity of washing it off. I'd stand at the sinks next to someone whose understanding of make-up was as basic as mine, whose job it was to remove the thick coating of orange foundation that left a ring mark round her chin. I'd been sent to the loos for the same reason as one of the popular girls, but all they could see was how different we were. So why would I ever want to embrace anything they liked? They were as bad as my family: only considering those like them as worthy, while believing that those they rejected really want to be part of the in-crowd, when they're quite happy being exactly who they are, thank you very much.

I know I'm showing my age when I start whinging about the music, but it's on far too loud too – and my head is killing me. The disco lights aren't much to talk about either. Just blue flashing lights swishing round. I need to find whoever I came here with and let them know I'm going home. I normally love clubbing – always have done – but this venue is worse than the ones I used to frequent aged 16, where the place was so empty the doormen didn't care if your fake ID looked as dodgy as they did, with their cheap Burton suits and fat arms and bellies pretending to be muscle. I accepted pretty quickly that if I wanted to go out drinking underage, I'd have to err on the side of cheesy music and 70s and 80s nights because that's the closest I could get to dancing to anything I liked.

I can remember in my teen years, which were pre-Primark years, having to hunt through the sales racks in New Look and Mark-One to find potential clubbing bargains. I'd mix my shop finds with similar deals from the Arndale Centre's market before slipping out into the womblike bus station underneath the shopping centre to get the bus home. The bus would wind its way round the labyrinth of the bus station roadways before bursting out onto the street and my eyes would water from the first flares of natural light they'd been assaulted with in hours. The journey home would be a mix of sadness and impatience: sadness because I'd be heading home to a vitriolic attack about what I was wasting my money on; impatience because I knew it was only a few hours before I could escape to a friend's house for a "sleepover" (and a night out in Fallowfield).

Although nobody died in the 1996 IRA bombing of Manchester, the Arndale Centre bus station was one of the many structural fatalities that occurred in the resulting regeneration project. The centre of Manchester is now hailed a success, but I can't help but miss some of the supposed monstrosities that came before; those buildings that did a good job but whose faces didn't fit. They weren't in the in-crowd.

The clubbing buzz stayed with me long after I'd left home and in my early 20s I'd have described myself as an addict, needing to go out two or three times a week just to get my fix. I used to love big nights out, dressing up, the works, the ritual starting the minute you got home from university or from work. When I was younger I took a long time to get ready because I wasn't practised at putting make-up on, my Mum never owning any for me to steal and me never getting beyond lipstick and eyeliner with my paper round money. As I got older, the time doing my make-up was just replaced with an extra-long soak in the bath with the radio on followed by time dancing round my bedroom.

In those years, I wouldn't need much alcohol to loosen up and I'd spend most of the night on the dance floor, losing myself in the music, my whole body moving in time to the pulse of each track. When I stopped going out regularly I had to join a gym in its place, belatedly realising that I'd removed my main form of strenuous exercise only once I'd put on half a stone in just six weeks.

Now big nights out were usually pooh-poohed in favour of a night trawling bars in the Northern Quarter, sniggering at the occasional handlebar-moustachioed hipster who'd taken the sculpting of his facial hair a step too far. But every once in a while I'd get my way and we'd go on a big night out. First stop was usually Chaophraya, to line our stomachs, where we gorged ourselves on Yam-something-or-other and Pad-something-else, while I regaled the others with the story of the first time I tried Thai. On the first few visits there I hadn't realised that's what I did, but once the girls started saying my lines with me and giggling, I accepted the joke as my own: the tale of my first taste of Thai food becoming more outrageous with each telling.

ALL OVER AGAIN

With food in their bellies to protect them from the onslaught of alcohol, the four-strong clan partied the night away in Tiger Tiger – traipsing up and down the stairs after Beth, each knowing they'd end up on the top floor each time where the cheesy music was. Then exhibitionists Beth and Olivia would take over the dance floor in the Raffles Bar while Faye kept a dance-phobic Abbie company in the adjacent Loft Bar, the two of them finding a table by the door so they could alternate between watching the "Beth and Olivia show" in the other room and chatting to each other for entertainment.

Dressed in her usual uniform of everything black, but with everything skimpier or more tightly fitting than usual, Olivia would jiggle and jump about in time to the music opposite Beth. An ex-gymnast, Beth had an almost animalistic way of moving her body that was completely natural to her, but that would look ludicrous on anyone who tried to emulate her moves. Everyone expected Beth to be a confident dancer, but the transformation in Olivia would always catch Abbie off guard. She couldn't decide whether alcohol brought out the real Olivia who usually hid from sight through shyness, or if alcohol swamped the real Olivia, bringing out a faked confidence. What Abbie knew is that she didn't feel like the real her until she'd had her first glass of wine, so either version of Olivia was possible.

Faye would be jealous of both of them as she watched, but accepted that her artistic talents started and stopped with a paintbrush and that, except for her hands, she had no creativity in her at all. Abbie would also get a twinge of jealousy, but not enough to wish her childhood had been filled with anything other than recorder lessons. She wasn't at all musical but tried incredibly hard to play every sheet of music she was given, grateful that her Mum hadn't forced her podgy little body into a leotard.

She had curves now, but as a kid Abbie had just been plump, and PE at school was torture, the other kids taunting her because she had dimples on her knees. They say "out of the mouths of babes" and that's never truer than in the classroom or in the playground – or the office pit. Given enough alcohol, all four of them could regale the others with an amusing story of childhood persecution: humour being the chosen medicine to stop the memory hurting as if it were yesterday's tale.

Using Strawberry Cloud cocktails as her fuel, Olivia would be dancing until some arbitrary bloke hit on her, whereupon she would allow herself to be whisked off the dance area and into a darkened corner for a snog and fumble. Then the others would have to spend the rest of the night listening to her talk about how guilty she felt for cheating on Matt – although she'd behave exactly the same way on the next night out. The dancing would be over once Olivia had done the deed as Beth would be needed to prop her up and tell her it was a sign that she needed to leave her useless boyfriend. The pseudo-psychologist of the group,

Faye would always try and tease out of Olivia whatever it was in her childhood that made her behave the way she did, but she would have consumed far too much alcohol at this point to make any sense out of the answers she got.

They would all play their parts as the puppets in a play of inevitability until it was time to head back to Beth's. And the discussions over breakfast the next morning and the plans in the days and months that followed would revolve around nights out in the Northern Quarter, where floor space was scarce and the music wasn't conducive to fluid movements. Until time passed and memories faded, and then Beth would convince them to do it all over again.

BETH

It was only big nights out that began at Chaophraya. Our other traditions were Nando's in town or a Domino's delivery at mine while we all got ready – although half the time we did that we'd be too stuffed with Tuna Delight and Meatilious to leave my flat, slouching around and getting slowly drunk while sniggering at whichever romcom we'd decided to watch on Netflix.

The only event that could top a night out clubbing for me was a firework display. There was something quite spectacular about the flashes and bangs that the mini-bombs made and how planning and timings could transform these individual spectacles into waltzes in the sky. The more sophisticated shows, like New Year celebrations on the River Thames, were set to music, but the banging and crackling alone was music to my ears.

The best time for fireworks in Manchester was around Bonfire Night. The different parks around Manchester had their displays on different nights, so I could follow them round, fitting in five or six shows in one week. I met Abbie at the Bonfire Night firework display at Platt Fields.

It was a large park with a man-made lake which had rowing boats and paddleboats on in the summer – boats that were usually filled with teenagers in their first blossom of love, who didn't see the curved concrete edge of the lake and recoiled in disgust, and instead thought going on a boat together was a rather romantic gesture. Their version of a gondola, but with the rancid smell of stale water rather than the stench of Venice.

I was trying to enjoy the atmosphere when actually all I could feel was how lonely I was. I'd gone to events like this by myself so many times because that's how my life had been between groups of friends, and it had always been just fine before. But after getting to know Livvy, I was used to having a friend around to do things with. This particular night, and after she'd accompanied me to shows at two other parks, I hadn't been able to convince her to leave Matt and join me, so I found myself wandering round the park at a bit of a loose end.

I'd tried to enjoy watching groups of teens use the confidence given by the semi-darkness to practise flirting and to see the wide-eyed wonder of children using sparklers for the first time. But I felt too much on the periphery. I decided to try and cheer myself up the old-fashioned way: with sugar. I'd queued in front of Abbie for candyfloss. I can remember refusing to buy it in a bag because getting it all over your face when you eat it was part of the fun. The woman at the serving hatch wasn't having any of it because she didn't want to make fresh batches on sticks when there were bags made up.

I'd turned to the girl behind me for support, throwing her a "Don't you dare not back me up" look and she'd quickly agreed with me, anxiously nodding her head, even though I could tell she was the sort of person who'd buy it in the bag, pulling off tiny amounts so it didn't get stuck in her hair or make her perfectly made-up face sticky. The lady serving saw she wasn't going to get anywhere with me and gave in, making us both fresh sticks. We ended up chatting as we ate – Abbie still trying to pull ladylike amounts off with her fingers, even though it's more difficult to do that when the floss is hot and fresh. We both confessed why we'd both ended up there alone: out of necessity – her because her husband thought fireworks were childish. That's when Abbie told me she thought eating candyfloss on a stick with someone was better than in a bag by herself.

Abbie explained she was celebrating her birthday, which fell the day after Bonfire Night. As a kid she'd thought the fireworks were for her, not grasping how strange it would be for so many strangers to celebrate her birthday until she was old enough for the slow realisation to make her blush. I knew she felt being deserted by her husband all the more keenly as it was her birthday – and that the disclosure was her way of rewarding me for being her friend that evening.

The firework display was amazing. I always hold my breath when a display is happening, only half enjoying it in the moment in case it's rubbish, waiting until it has finished before truly assessing it for its greatness. At the first break in the show, I glanced over at my newfound friend and, seeing the childlike wonder spreading across her face, I knew I was allowed to start breathing again, enjoying the rest of the show properly for the first time.

I even agreed to stay for the bonfire to be lit. I find the fire itself to be a bit boring and would rather be on the rides. But it was her birthday and I wasn't going to do anything that might earn me a comparison to her husband! It also gave us the chance to chat more, brain dumping the main stories of our lives onto each other, the way you can with another female you click with. I'd usually go on the twister and the waltzers whenever there was a funfair, but Abbie didn't have the stomach for them, so instead we found ourselves on the teacup ride, giggling back at the children who giggled at Abbie every time she squealed. It was the best funfair ride ever.

CHRISTMAS TREE LIGHTS

As well as being fascinated by fireworks, Beth loved flashing lights of any kind. Just before Christmas, after they'd broken up from school for the holidays, the rules of the house relaxed slightly. Beth would attempt to lie in what her Mum would refer to as the "living room" – though the kids at school called it the "front room" – with the main light off and the Christmas tree lights on. They weren't fancy ones that flashed, but if she closed her eyes slightly she could make the tiny coloured dots blur into streaks of light between her eyelashes.

At some point she'd be interrupted, usually by her Mum insisting the main light was on because "normal people don't lounge around in the dark" or by her sisters who would decide their game just had to be played downstairs. Grace and Charlotte's favourite game took on many guises but would always end with them discovering they were long-lost sisters.

Beth failed to understand this game as, in her fantasies, she was discovered to have been switched at birth with another baby and was whisked away to a different family where the *TV Times* and *Radio Times* weren't kept shut away in a plastic folder. Beth and her sisters only got to watch whatever was on BBC1 up until and including *John Craven's Newsround* and then the TV was snapped off – except for

Mondays and Thursdays when they got to watch *Blue Peter* as well. The TV didn't go back on again until their Dad wanted to watch the news or their Mum wanted to see a documentary about ill or deformed children in some faraway country.

Not being allowed to watch any more telly made Beth all the more curious about magazines that told you what was on. If you read the magazines it was almost as good as watching the shows because you'd find out what happened that way. It's the *TV Times* she loved the most because it covers the forbidden channels. As well as all the shows for grown-ups, she'd get to read about the kids' TV she wasn't allowed to watch on BBC3 because of the "evil adverts trying to bankrupt hard-working families". Well, she thought it was called BBC3 because it's channel 3 and comes after BBC1 and BBC2, but when she called it BBC3 at school some of the kids laughed at her and told her it was "Ice TV". It doesn't look very cold from the pictures in the guide.

Beth was sure Grace and Charlotte had watched grown-up TV at a friend's house because they always played games with atrocious American accents and the only time she had heard accents like that was when Grandma watched *Dallas* on the small TV in the kitchen while she did the washing up – and they'd both tucked up in bed by then.

In the latest version of the game that interrupted Beth's peace, Charlotte and Grace had both survived living in the jungle by eating berries and drinking rainwater after a plane crash. There was always fierce competition over who would get to exclaim: "Oh golly gosh, we're sisters!" with Grace usually winning on account of being the older of the two. If Charlotte got the line out early, Grace would point out they hadn't been through the conversation where she could realise that and she'd make them go back and jump through the correct hoops before saying the triumphant line herself.

THE HOSPITAL CORRIDOR

The trolley Beth is on is pushed down a corridor where a snake of strip lights slithered along the narrow ceiling. Beth is thinking the white strobe light in this club is far better than the blue lights in the one before.

The trolley takes Beth through swinging doors with "Resus" written above them. As Abbie tries to follow, a member of staff steps across in front of her to stop her, and she is guided towards a jungle of plastic chairs in the waiting room.

The fairground ride

The Teacups ride – a set of between six and 18 spinning teacups on a multi-turntable system – has become synonymous with fairgrounds across the world, in part because of its prominence in all five Disneyland theme parks due to its links with the Walt Disney 1951 film "Alice in Wonderland".

But even those who have never left the UK will have had the chance to come across them – as the ride closest to the entrance at Alton Towers, or nestled underneath the frame of the Revolution white-knuckle ride in Blackpool since they were moved from their home in Beaver Creek in 2010.

They can also be spotted at many travelling funfairs across the country, just like the one where Abbie met Beth.

10 teabags

ANOTHER SLOW TRAIN

After seeing Jack's parents, Faye can't breathe properly. She needs gulps of oxygen and the air at Preston station is too tight. She hears a train for Blackpool South being announced and decides to get on it, as a walk along the beach will clear her head. It's a stopping service, but she doesn't care for the tiny stations along the single line route. She doesn't even notice the one called Moss Side. This would usually be something that would make Faye smile to herself and wonder if the people there got sick of hearing stories about Manchester gun crime. But as she doesn't notice, it's a thought that never happens.

FAYE

Blackpool any time outside the height of summer is not recommended, but today the beach looks particularly uninviting: the sand a rusty mud colour, the grey sea merging almost imperceptibly with the grey sky. The beach is empty except for the occasional dog sniffing for treasure followed a few metres behind by a faithful owner. With my brolly open against the drizzle, I stick to the safety of the promenade, running my hand along rusted railings, the paint and metal being constantly eaten away by the salty spray. The salt air feels good in my lungs and I breathe in gallons of the stuff.

The three piers crawl out into the sea like centipedes. Gaudy lights and buildings stop the eye from noticing how empty they are of visitors. It's quite sad now to think the "South Jetty" was built just six years after the North Pier because of overcrowding. I can remember Granddad calling it the South Jetty and thinking he meant the South Pier, not the Central one, which didn't come along until some years later. When I asked wouldn't it have made more sense to build all three at the same time and join them up at the ends, he laughed so hard he had one of his coughing fits that used to worry Grandma. She would stroke his back, and he would flap his hand at her to shoo her away. When I told Beth about the three piers story, and the laughing, she gave me the fiercest of hugs.

Then I spot it, in between a chippy and a shop selling rock and sparkly cowboy hats – Flavia's Fortunes.

It. Has. To. Be. Fate.

I dart across the tramlines and two lanes of traffic, swapping the mineral smell of the cold air for the hot scent of incense, which fills my nostrils and makes my eyes water. As I blink to clear my eyes, I find myself in a tiny space covered in silk scarves, ostrich feathers, candles and other standard fortune-teller fare. The lady behind the desk, who I assume is Flavia, but looks far too young to tell fortunes, looks up at me, sees the money in my hand, and smiles. She's playing what looks to be a strange form of Patience with her Tarot cards. She quickly tidies them away, shuffling them into a neat pile, but rather than paying me any attention, she shuffles into the back, behind layers of beaded curtains. hear the sounds of a kettle boiling and cups clattering, bu I'm still surprised when she returns with a pot of tea and two dainty china teacups with matching saucers.

She puts the tray down, sits herself down, and motions for me to take the chair on the other side of the table. She pours a little milk into both cups while I sit down. She then offers to take the money from my hand, squirrelling it away in her pocket. She then proceeds to make two cups of tea, pouring mine first.

"Only the first cup from the pot can be read," she says "– but the second cup is still good for drinking," she adds with a wink, as if she's only just thought of it. But I'm pretty sure that it's part of her act: that she makes "second cup" quips with every customer. For a split-second I wonder if I missed a conversation where I'd asked for a tealeaf reading instead of a palm reading as I'd planned. Seeing the look of confusion on my face, Flavia speaks again.

"Tea leaves are much better for matters of the heart. I always use Keemun tea as the leaves are a good size and they're not at all uniform in shape. None of that Ceylon and Assam nonsense – the leaves are far too small to deal with life's larger events."

The tea she has made with the fresh tea leaves smells amazing and I can't quite help but feel melancholic for all the life lessons trapped in teabags, sitting on the shelves of anonymous supermarkets – maybe even in boxes Beth has designed, which makes me feel more sad.

She tells me to drink my tea slowly while thinking of the issue at hand, but to stop short of drinking the final mouthful. She then stops talking, settles down and sips at her own cup. I'm curious to ask her how she knew why I was there and why tea leaves were best, but there was something about the way she sits so resolutely still except for the tilting of her cup that makes me do the same.

When I finish all but the final gulp, Flavia takes my cup and saucer and places them carefully in the middle of the table. She then turns the cup three times – I think it's anticlockwise – and turns the cup upside down onto the saucer, humming to herself while she does so. She then turns the cup back up again and leans down towards the cup to have a good look at any emerging patterns.

"See this," she says, pointing to the bottom of the cup, smiling, "it's empty. It means there's no extended future to your question – it is almost upon you. It's terrible when the bottom is clogged full of leaves because it means people have months, years even, to wait for the answer."

She pauses.

"It also looks like you could have quite an abrupt end to your search, so best prepare yourself for that."

She pats my hand then points to the clump of leaves by the handle.

"This hook shape means someone has got under your skin."

I look again at the clump, trying and failing to see any sort of hook shape.

"The area by the handle reflects our emotions. So that means there's a hook in your emotions," she explains, reading my dubious expression as being unsure why it's about my emotions, rather than why it's supposedly a hook.

But Jack has got under my skin. The leaves are right.

"It's also very much like a sword, which is where you've been betrayed."

"Which is it?" I ask.

"It can be both dear, if they're connected. You fee betrayed by this person."

I did feel betrayed by Jack. She's right again.

She starts to work her way round the edge of the cup jus below the rim, explaining that any leaves here signa activities over the next few days.

"Is that a triangle?" I ask, pointing to the next clump which looks nothing like a triangle but has three definite corners poking out at odd angles.

She smiles at me again: "You're a natural."

Apparently this triangle represents a three-way relationship, which is ludicrous because it was only ever me and Jack. But, unperturbed, she continues, explaining the triangle is also a hat, which means this person wants to reconnect with me.

"Is there someone else from your past, dear? Someone i could be?"

I shake my head, feeling disappointed that the reading i failing me.

"Well whoever this third person is, they're running out o time to find you," she says, pointing at the third clump which is allegedly an hourglass. "So you might need to find them."

"But I don't even know who 'they' are," I tell her exasperated, frustration rising in my voice.

"Sometimes readings just get us to ask ourselves the right questions," Flavia says, half shrugging as if this is something she has come to accept. She pats my hand again, signalling that she's sorry she can't help me further; that the reading i over. She stands and starts to clear the cups away, using a cloth from the edge of the tray to wipe up the spilt tea.

"They're beautiful teacups," I tell her, feeling guilty for the anger that crept into my voice just moments earlier. I'm also desperate to keep the conversation going, as I'm not quite ready to leave the cocoon of scarves and smells.

"I buy them at flea markets," she explains. "So they hold the history of other people's lives and are better at tea patterns. They should always be matching, mind. We need to show some respect for traditions."

With everything piled back onto her tray, she starts to move towards the beaded curtains at the back.

"You can sit there for a while if you like, love," she tells me. "It's not as if they're queuing up outside to take your place. Sipping your tea like that put you into a contemplative, meditative state. You need to find yourself again before you brace those high winds."

I turn to look behind me, to see the scarves by the entrance doing a merry dance to the flurry of wind whisking its way along the seafront. Even from within the relative safety of Flavia's stall I can tell the gusts are strong enough to render my brolly useless at protecting me against the sea mist caught up in its layers.

Even though moments ago I didn't feel ready to leave, as soon as Flavia heads into the back the spell is broken. I decide to decline Flavia's kind offer and head out into the gusts. The effect is not like the drizzle it replaced, but more like the welcome mist that hits your bare flesh when you dance between the fountains in Piccadilly Gardens on a rare hot day in summer. Even though I have no idea who this third point of the triangle is, having something to ponder gives my thoughts a new direction and the mist prickling my skin makes me feel alive.

It makes sense for me to stay in Blackpool rather than heading back to Manchester and risk being spotted by colleagues heading home. Even though the Deli-Delicious shop where I work is pretty tiny, I'm the sort of person who bumps into someone from work on the one day I take a sickie. So I decide to make the most of what is left of my day by walking along the promenade again, mulling the question of who this "hat wearer" – this person from my past who wants to get in touch with me – will be.

The deli is where I first met Beth – and how I found out about her weakness for dares. We'd taken a delivery of superhot chillies and I was too scared to try one. We were offering customers the opportunity to try one for free. I saw the look in her eye when I dared her to bite into a fiery looking red one and I knew she couldn't say "No".

I wander along the pavement between the promenade railing and tram tracks, feeling like a heathen for eating candyfloss out of a bag, but knowing the mist would crystallise the edges before I'd have a chance to enjoy its fluffiness. I am glad Beth isn't there to disapprove, as I know she'd be a puritan candyfloss-on-a-stick person. I consider Abbie and Olivia's candyfloss preferences – this should be easy to work out. I decide that Abbie would go for floss in a bag every time out of practicality, whereas Olivia would probably buy whatever the person she was with would buy – and wouldn't get to eat it otherwise because she'd never head to somewhere like Blackpool by herself.

After my candyfloss, I scoff down a hot dog accompanied by a large helping of fried onions and covered in healthy squirts of tomato ketchup and a somewhat dubious looking orange-coloured mustard. And even though Beth isn't here, I feel I should rustle up some Catholic guilt on her behalf for eating dessert before my main course.

When the heavens open I dash inside a nearby arcade, turn a one-pound coin into two-pence pieces and play on the coin cascade machine until my coins are gone, temporarily winning a few coins back here and there. My hands stink of dirty metal, grease and onions, but I don't mind as I'm hoping if I keep my stomach and hands busy that my mind will work out this triangle puzzle in the background without my help.

I plan to have a mooch round Blackpool Pleasure Beach, but I'm shocked to find that it's closed – I assumed it would be open all year round. It seems wrong that they can close it, even though the rides are on private land, because it's open to the outdoors. I can remember how exciting the place felt as a kid: the flashing lights, the exhilarating clacking sounds of the big rides. It was even more thrilling in autumn because the mixture of dark skies and the lights made the whole place feel like an Aladdin's Cave and I would pretend I was hunting for treasure. My favourite rides were the ones that had trains or boats that followed tunnels inside what looked to my child's eyes like huge papier-mâché mountains. At home I created one round the structure of my Fisher Price garage so my Playmobil characters could hunt for treasure too.

THE TRIP TO BLACKPOOL

Abbie didn't "do" fairgrounds, but had agreed to join Olivia and Beth on a trip to Blackpool for the sake of not feeling like she was missing out while they had a day out without her. This was before they knew Faye and did a lot of things as a three.

On the train up, Beth made them both laugh and feel sad in equal measures with stories from her childhood. She told them of her disappointment when she discovered The Sandcastle wasn't in fact a massive castle made of sand, but a strange blue mirrored building that housed a swimming pool with slides which she and her sisters were never allowed to visit because of the "extortionate prices". She also confessed she was upset when both her younger sisters got swimming costumes with frilly skirts on especially for the holidays when hers was just a simple sports one she had for swimming lessons at school.

And Olivia and Abbie both felt sorry for her until Olivia admitted she didn't go on holiday as a child because her Mum couldn't afford it. And Abbie shared stories of fancy holidays abroad where she was bored from the lack of child-friendly activities and quickly learned to settle for reading a book in the shade, day in, day out.

By the time the train reached Blackpool North station, the three of them had made a pact not to share any more family stories and to enjoy the day as much as possible, so Abbie hid her horror when she found out you had to buy an armband to get into the Pleasure Beach. She was relieved, however, to discover a £6 pass would give her access to the complex and the complex only, not the rides, meaning she couldn't easily be pulled onto one – and she'd have time to run, even in heels, to get away from anyone going to a booth to buy her a ticket.

Olivia found it harder to hide her disappointment that the illuminations weren't on, not realising – like many of Blackpool's visitors – they light up the sky for just 10 weeks in the autumn. Beth managed to cajole her into feeling better by agreeing to go back in the September. But nothing could console Abbie when she discovered that all the Pleasure Beach rides were now sponsored and her lovely teacups ride was in the custody of a creepy life-sized Gaffer character from the Tetley Tea adverts.

FAYE

I while away so many hours in Blackpool that it's dark before I head back to Manchester, getting off the train a stop early at Oxford Road so I can head down to the Lass O'Gowrie, where I drank in my student days, for a cheap pint. The mood of the place has changed since the media types from the BBC building across the road had upped sticks to MediaCity in Salford, but it's still a nice mix of students and suits from nearby offices – plus the odd scruffy person there to bore the bar staff with long tales while they sup on real ale. I find myself a stool to perch on and gulp at my pint of Wells Bombardier – what Jack used to drink – as I fight to keep my tears in my eye ducts, where they belong.

The pub also brings a smile to my face as I remember Jack, Ethan, Amy and the rest of the gang playing drinking games and trying to eat as many pickled eggs as possible. I like mine dumped in a bag of salt'n'vinegar crisps – and I feel the saliva currently lining the sides of my throat welling up just from the memory of the tart taste. If I'm going to have to move on, to leave Jack behind – which seems likely after being dumped by him years ago and shunned by his family today – then finding a space at the back of my mind for memories like this seemed like a good idea.

It reminded me of what Abbie had told me, about compartmentalising your history. When I'd asked her about how she'd managed to move on from one man to another – and one marriage to another – so quickly, she'd said: "Everyone has baggage. It's up to you whether you carry yours round in overflowing 9p Aldi shopping bags or in matching designer luggage from Selfridges." I didn't get it at the time and I'm not sure I fully understand it now, but I have an idea what she was getting at. I can't make my past go away, can't erase it from my mind as Kate Winslet did in *Eternal Sunshine*. But I can deal with it in a way where I looked back on those good times nostalgically one more time before putting my rose-tinted glasses firmly away and getting on with my life.

Now let's see. There was Amy? Erm? Masters – that's it Amy Masters, a small redhead covered in freckles – a mini version of me. For the whole of the first year I wanted to call her Annie, like in the musical and everyone else ingeniously called the two of us "the redheads". And there was Ethan who'd been great when Jack had left. But thinking of him made my eyes cloud over with a frown because Ethan had followed Jack down to London a mere eight months later. After Ethan deserted me I'd decided there wasn't any point in getting close to men – as friends or boyfriends. They end up abandoning you.

Ethan and Jack, Jack and Ethan. I can't decide who I feel more betrayed by: Jack for leaving me even though we were perfect; or Ethan for pretending to give a damn and then following his mate to the party capital when he got bored of me sobbing on his shoulder. To give him some credit, Ethan gave me eight months of soaking his jumper with my tears before he'd had enough. And I was close to eight years later without any real improvement in my mental state, so upping sticks had worked out best for his own sanity.

Then it hit me. Ethan.

The. Third. Point. Of. The. Triangle.

11 teacups

BETH

I can't move my legs. I can't see my legs either. Where are my legs?

12 teaspoons

ABBIE

My closest friend has downed a bottle of Paracetamol and is lying the other side of a locked door that requires a keypad access code. I've been the other side of the keypad though, and it is no easier – although at least you have NHS staff with you when you're that side. I feel I should "do something" instead of just sitting here. I wonder how that praying thing works? I'm starting to wish I'd paid more attention when Beth went on one of her rants about her Catholic upbringing, as at least it would have put me in good stead for knowing what to do right now.

I have positioned myself on the row of plastic seats along the far wall so I can watch the comings and goings through said door without having to strain my neck muscles. But so far every raised chin has been greeted with nothing – no glance in my direction, no calling out "Beth Adam's friend" or "Abbie? Abbie Tomlinson?" repeating your first name as part of a ritual. I listen to the strange names being called out, finding myself adding a second surname to the announcements to make them even.

"Emily? Emily Paterson?"

"Paterson."

"Robert? Robert Samuels?"

"Samuels."

"Gobinda? Gobinda Mudri?"

"Mudri."

I only catch myself doing it when I realise I'm saying them loud enough for the person sitting two seats away to shift further along the row, giving me a worried glance as they go. I want to scream "I'm not mental" at them, but that would make me seem the opposite. And I would also feel very guilty at the inference that there was something wrong with being mental when I'm sitting here waiting for the doctors to save my friend from an overdose. And I'm sure all my little habits and rituals are perfectly normal for someone who's under as much stress at work as I am. I just like things to be even. To be balanced.

I look up at the clock. I've not been here a full half-hour yet and yet I feel as if a day's worth of energy has been drained from me. I'm wondering if the clock is playing tricks on me, so I decide to stare at it and count along with the second hand – this time in my head so the lady a few seats down doesn't feel she needs to move even further away. The full 60 seconds pass, as they should.

"Okay God," I think, "If I can hold my breath and sit completely still for a full 60 seconds, you have to make Beth live."

I wait until the second hand is at 12 and take a deep breath in – probably loud enough to scare the timid lady on my row, but I can't look to check because sitting still is part of the pact. Time feels like it's slowing down as the hand gets to 11. I watch – 56, 57, 58, 59, 60 – and then breathe out. I don't feel like I've accomplished anything worthy of saving a life. Maybe that was just a test pact and now I have to do another one. This might be how prayers work: why you have to say so many of them while you count rosary beads. You start off with a simple one and then build up to more complicated and challenging ones.

I shift on my plastic seat, massaging the ridges the edge has left mid-thigh on both legs. I take a few sips from the now-cold cup of coffee on the table ledge next to me. The temperature makes it no more or less drinkable as it was disgusting from the first mouthful, my brain immediately forgetting just how undrinkable it is, so each sip is a brand new shock to my taste buds. My brain is too busy willing Beth to stay alive to process information like "Stop drinking this coffee because it's ghastly".

I've stretched and taken on more fluids, so I'm ready for my next challenge. Four is my lucky number. So maybe I need to hunt out for things in fours? Four is like your engine number: you breathe in and out; your heart beats up and down. A four-stroke engine. It's this four that powers you, so maybe if I find lots of fours it will be a sign that Beth is going to make it.

Scanning the room I notice four people with touchscreen phones out, ignoring the faded posters rather forlornly telling people to turn their phones off. I'm wondering if they're all iPhones or Samsung, but I might be pushing my luck, so I check for other fours. There are four girls with ponytails. There are four noticeboards. There are four internal doors off the waiting room – if you don't count the toilets. There are four people with rucksack style bags. No, there are five, but one is close to the door and he's put his bag on the floor, while the other rucksacks have been plonked on seats. And he's by the door, organising the content of his bag. I have to resist reaching out and kicking him with my leg to get him to go. C'mon. C'mon. And he's gone. I can breathe again, even though I didn't realise I was holding my breath. I hope it doesn't matter that it wasn't for 60 seconds. Maybe fours don't matter after all, I tell myself. We're now a four – me, Beth, Olivia and Faye – but I preferred us more as a three. Before Faye.

FAT ANKLES

Before Faye and Beth had become friends, there had been "Beth, Olivia and Abbie". A unit of three. Now they were Beth, Faye, Olivia and Abbie – and while Beth loved it, there was a certain uneasiness in Faye's friendship with the other two. It had always been Beth at the centre of the universe with Olivia and Abbie flitting round her, both seeing Beth as their friend and each other as acquaintances brought together by a shared friendship with Beth. But Faye seemed to take a higher plane, to get to sit closer, to be listened more, to be confided in, in a way that they were not. They were both in fear of losing Beth and the only positive outcome this brought for them was a strengthening in the friendship between them as they pitched themselves together against Faye for Beth's attention.

The situation embarrassed Abbie, who wanted to be equals. She'd have pushed for equality a long time ago if she'd realised Beth was willing to hand this out. But she'd left it far too long now – their friendship was over a year old – and she couldn't start demanding more at the very point where she felt her friendship with Beth was at its most fragile. For Olivia, the ordeal was terrifying. Her brain became paralysed with fear when she contemplated life without Beth. So she was ready to keep her head below the parapet as much as she needed to in order to hold onto the friendship.

And Abbie joined her there, even though she wanted to stick her head above it and demand more attention, maybe even firing a few arrows out through the crenels at Faye when Beth wasn't looking.

Abbie's way of coping was to turn up late to Friday drinks occasionally, to show she didn't need the plans as much as the others, to say she could take it or leave it. She would turn up laden down with bags from the exclusive shops lining the street between the Royal Exchange Theatre and the cathedral. Unlike the stereotypical shopaholic, Abbie didn't shop to cheer herself up when she was feeling down. She was much more likely to go on a big spending spree when she's on a high and feels as though the whole world is at her feet.

It's on those occasions she doesn't feel fat and is willing to try stuff on, not minding if the size 16 doesn't fit – as long as the 18 fits well and looks great, people will assume it's a 16. Inside her Bottega Veneta handbag, Abbie carried a pair of Tweezerman nail scissors. Although theoretically designed for nails, this pair was for cutting out the insulting labels before she'd even left the shop.

For Abbie, one of the worst fashion sins was squeezing yourself into something in the belief that wearing the smaller size will make you look skinny.

"We are grown women, we have brains, so there's no excuse why we would think this," she would rant after noticing yet another victim of the trend in the pub.

"Seriously, do blouses bulging open across their breasts and bellies hanging out underneath tight T-shirts ever look good? No. Do we need to see love handles hanging over the edge of hipster jeans? No.

"I've seen women who are physically smaller than me look in worse shape because they're wearing the wrong things. Better to buy the right size in Primark than a size too small in Kenzo or DKNY."

Thankfully, the others were capable of buying the right size in Primark, as they didn't have budgets that stretched any further – except for Beth, who refused to waste good pizza or beer money on clothes she didn't need.

Abbie's number one fat person crime was stuffing fat feet into strappy sandals. She could remember her Mum buying her jelly shoes as a child and watching her feet bulge out of every hole between the plastic strips. For hours after she'd taken them off, her feet would be covered in a criss-cross pattern from them.

"I could be forgiven though – I was a kid and knew no better. But those women who wear Sienna Miller roman sandals should know better."

The worst sandals were the tie-up ones that effectively separated chunks of flab into inch-by-inch squared sections of flesh across the ankle and up onto the calf. Those sandals needed to be worn tight against the skin so they stay up – ruling them out for anyone who didn't have skinny feet, skinny ankles and skinny legs.

"Even skinny girls can have fat ankles, and that's where they get caught out. These girls unwittingly add a stone to their presumed weight just by wearing them because they're so unused to checking if they look fat."

Fat ankles. Swollen ankles. Abbie shudders.

ABBIE

It's amazing what you can tell about a person from their shoes, although an A&E waiting area is never the best place to test the theory as, contrary to what you'd expect, you do not get all walks of life here. Most of the seats are taken by people who seem to think that Reebok Classics have made a comeback, when I'm pretty sure they haven't, especially ones where the rubber trim on the front has mostly worn away and the rest of it ripped off.

The staff here wear smarter looking trainers or strange clogs that squeak as they walk across the tired linoleum. I also see a rare pair of white Crocs. Occasionally the main doors will open and someone wearing smarter shoes will come in, but they will usually be passing through. My smart heels look very out of place for A&E.

All the people with serious illnesses are being seen to – those who are rushed in when their regular lives go awry: when a decision made in a split-second turns their life upside down; or when their body fails or fights against them. It's just the dregs sitting out here – people too uneducated about their health to realise they can pop and see the local pharmacist for most ailments alongside people too drunk to keep themselves out of harm's way.

The main doors open again and a familiar pair of shoes walk cross the threshold with a recognisable gait. I scan up from the slightly scuffed black ballet shoes with tiny star patterns cut into the leather, up the various shades of not-quite-black clothing, to discover Olivia's face at the top.

I forgot to leave a note at Beth's place.

How on earth does Olivia know we're here?

13 teapots

BETH

I look down at where my legs should be and see blue stretched across me like the sea with the white foam of the wave across my chest. Maybe I'm a mermaid washed to shore. The pink dress comes over to me and dips her hands into the edge of the blue sea, lapping her fingers about at the edges of the waves. I still can't see my legs, but now I can feel them. I can't tell if they've formed into a big tail, but where my feet should be, fins point out at strange angles. The pink dress has an ancient mug filled with brown gloop, like gravy but thinner. I'm worried she's going to throw it into the sea to pollute me. But no. She holds the mug to my lips. I take a sip. It's tea. It is not hot enough. I need scaldingly hot tea if I'm going to use it to clean my insides from the thoughts clogging up my system with poison.

I like my tea hot. This tea is cold. It will be stone cold. I remember this day. All of us at the caravan taking too long to eat breakfast and my Mum saying over and over: "The tea will be stone cold." Outside the caravan, I touch the stones.

Their smooth sides, so smooth and rounded that they don't have sides. I wear jelly sandals and sections of skin poke through between the squidgy slats of plastic. They make my feet look like aliens. They're meant to make my feet look fat. I can't remember who told me that. It wasn't Grandma; it was someone else.

The stones near the path between the caravans and the beach are warm from the sun. The ones getting a quick bath from the tide are cold. Stone cold. We're meant to be playing on the beach. Although it isn't a beach: it's where pebbles meet the sea. I wonder if this is a new beach, the stones waiting to be ground down to sand by the waves. Is sand just tiny little pebbles?

But I don't ask – don't risk learning anything new in return for the ridicule. It will be one of those things that Beth says. Then instead of saying "This tea is stone cold" it will be "Remember the time Beth asked about pebbles being turned into sand by the sea" – and they will all laugh. All of them: even the ones too dull to think to ask the question and the ones too young to know the answer.

Reincarnation. I've died and come back as a mermaid. I can remember my skin. The small red spots growing blotchy, covering me with a birthmark stain. That's when I first realised I was being reborn. My new birthmark. I feel hungry but I know it's my body digesting itself, starving enzymes feasting themselves on my organs. The rigour mortis has set in. It's why I can't move my tail yet. The transition has begun but is nowhere near complete.

The pink dress wipes the fluids pouring from my mouth and nose. If I were still alive, I would think I had a cold and my nose was running. Or that I'd been to the dentist for a filling and I was drooling. But I know my body is purging itself, fluids draining from my corpse. Soon these fluids will be too much to be wiped up and they will run into the sea and I will be free.

Afternoon tea

In the 19th century, aristocrats made drinking tea at around 4pm fashionable. It was a way to while away the awkward mid-afternoon hours, filling the gap between lunch and a rather late dinner at around 8pm.

Stopping for a brew has become something of a British habit for all classes, as a way to break up the monotony for the general workforce as well as for the gentility. And as Faye knows, it does not need to be four o'clock in the afternoon to be the perfect time for a time-passing brew.

14 teabags

FAYE

I read every self-help book I can get my hands on. Occasionally I find myself experiencing a momentary connection with the words on the page and glimpse at what it would be like to understand myself. I finally have a copy of *Everything You Need You Have* to read on the train. I ordered a copy from Amazon. I could not face Waterstone's.

I'd spent my life on a loop, visiting and revisiting what Flavia said to me, playing it in my mind again and again, wondering if I should be making anything of it: "Whoever this third person is, they're running out of time to find you. So you might need to find them."

That's what Flavia had said. I knew it word for word as if it had been etched onto my brain. And I knew exactly what it meant. I was no longer on a mission to find Jack; I was on a mission to find his best mate: Ethan.

Ethan. What's. His. Name.

I knew his surname was hidden deeply within one of the chasms of my brain, but it was part of my brain that I'd closed off because it was too painful to visit. I now needed to revisit that as well, to open it up and blow the cobwebs away, clearing my mind of any gossamer traces and giving it a good spring clean. My internal detox of lemon tree syrup and external one of three-minute mud mask were hopefully helping. I could feel the premium grade palm and maple saps cleansing my insides and the skin on my face felt cleaner than it had done in weeks.

I hadn't seen any of the girls since our night out, feigning a cold coming on because I needed some space of my own. I needed the luxury of living inside my head while I searched my memories for clues. I was soon surrounded by the masses of paperwork and half-empty shoeboxes from two weeks ago, only this time I was searching the history I'd packed away looking for a surname. I was deep in thought as I'd searched, not about the past and Jack, but about how I'd needed space away from the girls for the first time since we'd become friends. Even though they were moving forward, it was almost like they were holding me back, keeping my life static, and I had to be away from them to move on. I knew it didn't make sense to feel this way because knowing them is what helped me to start moving on from my past in the first place. Maybe I just needed some time away from everyone and everything else and that just included them. It was either that or I was beginning to outgrow my friendships.

Trying to evoke memories from the items I'd packed away was invigorating, empowering almost. I felt the closest I'd ever been to "ready" to deal with my past head-on, although that didn't stop my hands from shaking and a thin film of cool sweat covering my body, beads settling on my newly-cleansed top lip. My heart stopped as my hands settled upon a picture of Jack and Ethan together, arms over each other's shoulders, faint mud stains on their clothes from a friendly kick-about that turned into a more serious football challenge between them. I wondered if Jack still wore his hair with the floppy fringe he'd grown to replicate the young Tories I'd mocked on the telly: and if Ethan's was still sensibly cropped short.

Suddenly I was back there, taking their photo in Platt Fields park: the rotting smell of the pets corner and the stale, dank water from the manmade lake hanging in the air, mingling with the scents of recently cut grass and pollen-rich flowers. A kick-about that turned into a scoring competition was typical of them. Occasionally, Jack would feign breathlessness and ask to borrow my inhaler – usually when Ethan was taking a killer shot. But most of the time Jack would win because Ethan would get bored of him being so competitive – and concede just so they could go back to being mates again. At the time it made me sure Ethan was the weaker of the two, but with hindsight I now realise he was just being a grown-up, letting Jack win so he wouldn't have a tantrum. While I was with Jack he could do no wrong, but now I was starting to see his everyday behaviour in a negative light and it made my tummy do funny jumps. Was I, just as I was starting to try and find Jack, about to go off him?

There was very little in the way of Ethan in the bric-a-brac and other accoutrements from my former life. I vaguely remembered tearing up almost everything I had about Ethan after he'd followed Jack down to London – the photo of them together obviously slipping through the cracks. Ethan's desertion was far more painful than Jack's. Ethan was the person I'd turned to after Jack left me and to have him leave me too was more than I'd been able to cope with. That's when I'd gone to pieces: my fractured life, my damaged organs, my broken limbs. I'd stayed in bed on the sofa for a mini-eternity, only getting up to go to the loo and make cups of tea, until I was lying in a soup of my own sweat, twitching and shaking from malnutrition. It was my hunger that finally broke the cycle and got me out of bed properly. I was rescued by a tin of Heinz baked beans with sausages that I kept in the cupboard for when I was feeling unwell or homesick. I ate them cold, straight from the tin.

With that food in my belly, for the first time in days I'd felt like showering and, still wrapped in a towel, my wet hair glueing itself to my back in clumps, I'd started to paint again. My work was bigger, uglier and more aggressive than it'd been at University. My lecturers would have been thrilled. They preferred mature students on fine art courses because they said you needed to have lived, to have suffered, in order to be a good artist. If you were straight from sixth form, they insisted you complete the Fine Art foundation year first. The extra year hadn't prepared me for the course any more than the years of my life that preceded it. It was only now I was dying inside, suffering unimaginable pain, that I was able to interpret my life, morphing it into brushstrokes on canvas. My artwork was finally coming alive. I'd managed to sell some of my large work on eBay for over £100 a pop, which made me feel incredibly proud. I'd also sold smaller pieces at craft fairs, had work for sale in a shop in Hebden Bridge, and had postcards of my artwork in an antiques, heritage and interior furnishings shop in Didsbury. As well as my building up my real portfolio, I was also selling other work. My most popular images were butterflies – perched on flowers, captured in jars. I liked how they captured the idea of still living, of being alive and being breathtakingly beautiful, even if you were trapped by your circumstances.

I'd given up my manual search and was giving my brain a break from my mental search, curled up on the sofa watching repeats of *Grand Designs* where various rich couples used exorbitant levels of wealth to turn various structures into white boxes with large windows when the name "Gruger" popped into my head. In my rush to write Ethan's name down, I poured half a cup of cold tea over myself, the cold, wet shock slapping me, the curdled liquid seeping into my clothes. My face and chest were soaked and I almost certainly had a stain down one of my old-but-favourite tops that wasn't going to come out in the wash. But I didn't care. I shook the drips of tea from my trembling hands and picked up my phone. Logging onto Facebook, I typed in "Ethan Gruger".

My heart pounded in time to flashing spokes of the spinning circle on my screen as it searched for results. I'm given the options of "Ethan Kruger" or "Ethan Krugersdorp". No Ethan Gruger. I should have known it wasn't going to be that easy. I'd had the opposite problem when I'd tried to find Jack Williams – there were far too many of them and none with photos that looked like "my" Jack Williams. And I could never face contemplating that his account might be one of the ones with his child as his profile picture. He wasn't allowed to have moved on that much. A search in Google gave me a similarly un-emotive response: "Did you mean: Ethan Kruger" and then listed random articles for various Ethans and Grugers, but no Ethan Grugers. Had the one person I wanted to trace never heard of the Internet?

Where else could I find a trace of him? Surely he would have a landline even if not the Internet, so maybe in a phone book? Or could I find him on land registry records if he owned a house? Or maybe on the electoral register if he'd registered to vote? A quick search of the online BT phone book came up blank, but then he could be ex-directory. And the public search on the land registry site turned out to be useless, as it searched names from addresses, not the other way round. Searching every London address online would be quicker than going physically door-to-door but it would still take me months and I didn't have that much data credit on my phone. But heading down there suddenly felt like the right thing to do. The British Government was down in London, so surely they could help in situations like this as they had records on everyone.

The next morning I call into Deli-Delicious to tell them I'm too ill to come in saying I had the runs (I couldn't bring myself to say the D-word on the phone) – making sure I don't automatically put on an "I'm not well" croaky voice so my boss is more likely to believe me. I'd worked out that if you sounded okay but just exhausted from your illness, you were much less likely to be accused of taking a sickie than if you had a croaky voice. My boss joked about how even stomach pains could give you a sore throat when you phoned in sick, so I'd tried to sound as normal as possible, explaining that I had a dickie tummy and though I felt okay, I couldn't stay off the loo long enough to come into work. You can't work around food when you have diarrhoea, so it was a safe bet. I feel very sorry for people who suffer from nasty colds or recurring chest infections who, without a doctor's note, will always be treated with a certain amount of suspicion. I wonder, as I jump on the bus into town, flashing both my Megarider and a grin at the bemused driver, whether someone like that had to be hooked up to oxygen before they got any sympathy from my boss.

I feel guilty that I've not told the girls about my London mission, but it's as if the idea is so fragile that talking about it would break the spell and heading down there would seem stupid. I don't, however, feel too guilty about calling in sick because they only paid me the minimum wage. My job at Deli-Delicious was a stopgap, paying my bills and keeping a roof over my head, while I painted in my spare time, waiting to be discovered. I didn't have time to search for a new job when the anger and frustration I felt at the way I had been treated had translated into the best work I'd ever done. Jack and Ethan had released a being inside of me that made my painting come alive. I'd since developed a maturity about my work that made me excited to paint as I knew that, with each piece of work, I was getting closer to being the painter I'd always aspired to be.

I had to go to London now – today – before I thought about it too much and decided I was wasting my time. I'd had enough of living what-ifs: I had to know once and for all why Jack had left me and whether or not he regretted it. Even if he were married with three kids, as Beth seemed to suspect, I'd be happier than I was now because I'd know – I'd have closure. I could then move on with my life, no longer the one left behind, but the one going in her own direction. That's what I told myself anyway, hoping that the lie would grow enough for me to believe in it. Deep down I knew that another gust of pain from seeing him with someone else would take my paintings in a new direction – and that the trip would be worth it just for that.

The images of Jack in my memories had distorted and faded so much that I was struggling to produce any strong work in his image except to copy photos I had of him, where he seemed to always be wearing a hint of arrogance on his face that wasn't attractive. If I saw him again, I would have newer memories of him and his face would have aged, which would make it much better subject matter for my work.

I used to fantasise about Jack stumbling across a review of my work somewhere like The Tanks at the Tate Modern.

He'd meander down to see it out of curiosity, only to run out, pushing his way past groups of my fans, to puke in an alleyway, at being confronted by his grotesque image. I would have spotted him and followed him out to check he was okay, safe in the knowledge that my painting had allowed me to be free of him. At one time, the thought that I could make him feel both horrified and guilty drove my work more than wanting to be a respected artist. As my painting improved, my feelings about my art had grown stronger and now I longed to be part of the next "Young British Artists" group – the brat-pack of Britart – and be a household name like Tracey Emin and Damien Hirst.

I was itching to paint Jack again since I'd found the photo of him and Ethan, but I had to push that impulse to the back of my mind so I could focus on finding him in the flesh. I knew that if I found him and had it out with him I could focus on my painting to the extent that I would be a painter first, a loser in love second; that I'd be able to live my dream as an artist uninhibited.

Deep down I'm sure Beth knew becoming a food packaging designer was taking the easy route on purpose because she'd already had her dream of being an Olympic gymnast crash and burn. She'd decided not to risk becoming any kind of famous designer. Abbie and Olivia "just" had jobs – nothing wrong with that if that's the type of person you are, but it wasn't the same as having a dream, of coming alive as you worked. The flip side, of course, was that they were already successes by doing well in their jobs, especially Abbie. I wondered if she felt as sorry for me as a struggling artist as I did for her as someone trapped in the higher layers of the corporate machine, not high enough to do what she wanted but high enough to take the blame if the business did a bowel movement, some serious corporate diarrhoea, the shit hitting the fan and spraying everyone below the CEO with sticky brown faecal matter.

I hadn't taken any sickies since I started working at the deli two years ago, except for the day where I ended up in Blackpool eating candy floss and meeting Flavia. And I was actually sick, I told myself – I was lovesick. I needed to get Jack back or out of my head once and for all, so I could mend my heart and get on with my life. I headed into Piccadilly station and bought a saver return to London Euston. I winced at the price, but it had to be done – it was either that or sitting on a bone-shaking Megabus service which would take the best part of the day and leave me with very little time to play Poirot. I went to get on the very sleek looking Virgin train to London, showing my ticket to the uniformed man by the train. He smiled at me and shook his head.

"Sorry love, you can't use a saver return until the half-nine train."

I must have looked so disheartened because he added: "Look on the bright side love: you showed me your ticket and I told you. If you'd got on they'd be charging you the full fare and it's about three-hundred quid."

"They?"

He pointed to a clear plastic bag full of crisp packets and crushed coffee cups near his feet that I'd failed to notice when I'd walked up to the train.

"I just clear them out between runs."

I had just over an hour-and-a-half to kill, nothing to do and no money to spend. So I headed out the front of the station in search of a scruffy café and cheap brew. A couple of doors down from Greggs was the type of place I was after: it had handmade signs of bargain meals scrawled in the windows. I stepped inside and the heat from the fat hit me.

The place stank of old food. It made me homesick for the deli and a tiny part of me thought maybe that's where I should be, not spending my month's socialising budget chasing stupid ideas. I pushed that thought out of my head as I handed 90p over for a cup of tea – saving myself 30p by not getting coffee. It was a cheap teabag in a polystyrene cup, but sipping it would help pass the time away. I had planned to sit in the café, but the smell drove me away and back to the station. I found myself a bench to sit on – an ergonomic looking metal one that was no more comfortable than a standard wooden one – and people-watched as I hugged my brew.

I let my mind wander and was jolted back to reality when I heard them calling the 9.35 train to London Euston. I looked up at one of the big electronic clocks: 9.30. I had five minutes to find the right platform. In a panic I ran up and down by the platforms rather than checking my train on the triangle of screens.

"Oy, lady, the London one's here."

I recognised the voice and spun round. It was the cleaner pointing to an identikit posh red train. I ran over and hugged him. Blushing he pushed me away.

"Get on then!"

I did – and the doors shut and locked behind me.

Only. Just. Made. It.

15 teacups

OLIVIA

Abbie looks surprised but thrilled to see me. I have no idea why she didn't think I'd come, although I've no idea why she didn't just phone me herself rather than getting the hospital to do it. She's just sitting in the waiting area rather than somewhere within the innards of the hospital holding Beth's hand.

"Oh thank God you're here," Abbie says, hugging me harder than she's ever done before. I've always found her a little distant, but the barriers have come down. I'm aware of how much she reeks of not-so-stale alcohol and her outfit is all-awry. I'd wonder what the hospital staff think of her coming in like this, but she looks no scruffier than everyone else in the waiting room and some of them have clearly gone a few rounds in the ring with Jack Daniels.

"Of course I came," I tell her. "I came as soon as I got the call."

"Call?"

Abbie pulls away from me enough to look me in the eyes,

questioningly. I know she's under a lot of stress, but her confusion is worrying.

"The hospital called me," I spell out to her, "like you asked them to."

"But I didn't. I didn't think to call. Or ask them to call. Or leave a note. I drove round to Beth's when I got your message…"

"Drove?"

"I went slowly down side streets," she replies defensively. "Anyway it's lucky I did because who knows how much worse it could be if I hadn't got there when I did. It could already be too late."

Abbie's eyes fill with tears. I can't help but wonder if they smell of alcohol too, but I quickly brush the thought away and focus back on what she's said.

"Too late for what?"

"Beth's overdose. She took a whole bottle of Paracetamol – I found the tub in the bin. She was spaced out completely, like not blinking and hardly breathing. So I called 999."

"There were two empty bottles in the bin?"

Abbie looks confused: "Why would there be two?"

"Well there was the tub I took the last one out of, and…" I twig. "Beth didn't take an overdose. I gave her one Paracetamol for her headache. They must be pumping her stomach and all sorts because they think she's taken the lot."

I head over to the counter, leaning slightly to align my face with the gaps in the Perspex that shields the staff. I ignore Abbie's witterings that they won't tell me anything and explain what has happened.

"And you are?" the receptionist asks me, nonplussed, as if I've disturbed her evening by talking to her.

"Olivia Banks."

"Ol-liv-eyah B-aa-n-k-s," the receptionist says, stretching out my name as she searches her computer screen.

"Ah, the next of kin. Yes, we called you. I'll get someone from Resus to come out to you."

Next of kin? The air is sucked out of the world and I'm left in a vacuum of bright hospital lights glaring off shiny linoleum floors and Perspex and doors. Next of kin? But what about her parents? What about Charlotte and the other one, the shiny sheep? Or maybe a glittery one? They can't all be made up, can they? No, they can't. Just because Beth's funny turn after Faye's news has made me see Beth in a different light, doesn't mean I need to question everything about her. Anyway, it doesn't matter right now, because right now is about being there for Beth, which is precisely where I'm going to be.

"Olivia, Olivia Banks?"

"Banks."

The first comes from an impossibly young male in green scrubs and strange white clown shoes. The second is muttered by Abbie, who seems to be losing it big style tonight. I nod and walk towards the doors, feeling Abbie hesitate behind me. I usher her to come with me and both of us are directed into a small visitors' room.

"It wasn't an overdose," I explain, stumbling over my words as I rush to get them out. "There was only one Paracetamol in the tub. That's all she had."

"We know. She didn't present like she'd taken an overdose, but we checked her blood levels just in case and it was very low – in line with a dose of just one tablet in fact."

I'm relieved, thrilled in fact. And not ready for Abbie's anger.

"You knew! You knew and you let me sit out there and stew and worry. I have been working out ways to try and save my friend's life knowing I'm completely incapable of doing anything and she wasn't dying anyway."

The doctor looks apologetic, but unapologetic at the same time.

"Patient confidentiality means we can't discuss symptoms and probable causes without the next of kin present."

Abbie turns her anger towards me.

"And you. Why are you the next of kin anyway?"

The doctor puts his arm out to try and calm Abbie down.

"I realise emotions are running high right now, and understandably so. But how about we keep them in check for now so that I can update you and then take you to see Beth."

Abbie sags. She reminds me of the inflatable ring I used to have when I went swimming. At the end of one particular swimming session one of the older kids who'd been taunting me in the pool threw it back in again and it floated forlornly to the centre. One of the lifeguards got a long pole with a hook on the end to fish it out. It was acutely embarrassing, but he gave me a big smile and I thought he'd make the perfect boyfriend because he'd rescued me from getting in trouble with my Mum. I went swimming quite a lot after that, just so I could see him. Looking back now, I feel ill that I've ended up with someone who rescued me. I found out the hard way that doesn't mean someone is suitable boyfriend material.

I have to tear my mind away from half-deflated rings of thick, shiny plastic, from the echoing voices in the thick chlorinated air, to listen to what the doctor is telling us about Beth and her current situation. He seems to be saying that she was physically fine, but suffering mentally. He's trying to prepare us for the worst, I can see that.

The hospital reminds me of Levenshulme Swimming Baths, the strange smells, the onslaught of alien noise. But it's

Beth who makes the perfect sci-fi creature, sitting motionless like some form of stasis. Her inactivity seems all the more surreal because she is surrounded by people wailing and rocking.

The staff on the psych ward take up the story where the child-doctor left off. After her bloods come back clear, Beth was sent for a CT scan to check for a clot or bleed, and that was clear too, as was the EEG. They also ruled out post-epileptic fit and diabetic coma. The diagnosis of a possible catatonic state had been reached by process of elimination, rather than by ticking a number of definitive symptoms off a list. Hearing this, I found the same levels of fury rising in my body that Abbie had displayed. The NHS should know and be able to solve everything medical: they should not have doubts; they should not make mistakes.

I'd noticed that each of the four noticeboards in the A&E waiting room was home to a poster about violence towards staff. I now understood how easily it could happen. I'm also annoyed Beth was taken up to the ward and nobody thought to tell Abbie. When she'd asked for an update, the same rude receptionist had told her the NHS had a four-hour window to admit or discharge and that an-hour-and-15-minutes wasn't that long to have been waiting. Even if they couldn't tell her anything, they could have let her sit by Beth's bedside. I wonder how many of those minutes poor Beth had been up here while Abbie sat in the waiting room, both surrounded by strangers but both utterly alone.

I also feel guilty that I'm the next of kin. I have no idea how to get in touch with her family – or if I should even try. Sitting watching Beth motionless on a mountain of pillows while Abbie quietly sobs beside me makes me feel very inadequate. I have no idea how to help either of them. Thankfully, the nursing staff are more clued up than I am and a few sodden tissues later, Abbie is led away from Beth's bedside. And soon it is my turn to leave. We've been allowed in after visiting hours because she's only just been admitted, but they're keen to usher me away too as my presence is over-exciting some of the more over-excitable patients.

When I get home from the hospital, Matt is on his Xbox again. It's as if he's in a catatonic state too, staring at the screen, only his fingers moving across the controls giving him away. I want to ask him what time he got back from seeing Maggie, what's happening about the funeral, and how he's feeling, but there's no space left in my brain for questions and answers. Beth has caused a mental aneurysm in my mind, its balloon-like bulge clogging my head with blood. I wonder if an aneurysm can cause sensitive skin because I head to bed fully clothed so Matt can't even consider touching my skin with his.

I needn't have worried. He doesn't even come to bed. And a new day brings the same day: Matt comatose in front of the TV where he fell asleep killing aliens; Beth's alien body comatose in a hospital bed, starched, stark white sheets folded neatly below her outstretched arms; and Abbie probably comatose from all the wine she drank – although I haven't been in touch with her to ask. But it's my guess as to why she hasn't made it to today's first visiting session. Sitting in the chair next to Beth feels less of a shock today. Although she's the same as yesterday, the daylight makes the situation more normal. The chair I have today is more comfortable too, padded fake green leather on a wooden frame, not a curved plastic shell. Am I meant to talk to Beth like they say you should do with coma patients? She occasionally sighs or takes a deeper breath than usual and her eyes still blink, but she doesn't seem to be with me at all.

"I've been wondering why I'm next of kin," I say out loud

– more to myself than to Beth. "I mean why not someone in your family? I mean, do they even exist? And why me and not one of the other two? Yes, Faye is flaky, but Abbie is reliable, so long as she's not drinking."

I feel guilty mentioning Abbie's drinking. It's not really up to me to decide if she drinks too much or not. Although the drink driving shocked me. I know I asked her to check on Beth, but she could have called a taxi. It could be her I was visiting in hospital instead of Beth. I know what it's like to rely on drinking though. And the horror that comes with waking the next morning knowing what you can't remember is probably more embarrassing than the memories flooding your brain with shame.

FAIRY GIRL

Olivia was the first one onto the dance floor each time Beth suggested it. She loved dancing in clubs because it was the only time she felt totally free, the boom from the speakers pulsing through her body like an extra heartbeat. She didn't care what type of music it was she was dancing to and loved every club in Manchester except the Birdcage. She'd only been there the once and was very unimpressed the first time they cleared the dance floor for the transvestite show. By the third time, she'd taken to dancing on the tiered section between sets of tables and chairs so she didn't have to stop for each show. She'd even found herself half dancing while standing by Faye and Abbie as they were deep in conversation while Beth went to the ladies. Thankfully tonight they were back in familiar surrounding at Tiger Tiger.

"Hey, it's fairy girl," Olivia heard being shouted in her direction. She turned to see a guy in a gaggle of guys all wearing the same Hawaiian shirt. His outfit also included a ring of fake flowers draped round his neck, the addition to his outfit that singled him out as the stag for the night. With a sinking heart, Olivia realised she knew him. And unless he were currently in the middle of a whirlwind relationship, he'd probably been with his girlfriend when he'd snogged her. It didn't surprise her, after all she'd been with Matt, but it did sicken her a little that she was helping half of another couple cheat.

They'd met in the Birdcage on her one outing there. She'd been nicknamed fairy girl by the stag – Peter – because she apparently looked like she should have been at the top of a Christmas tree, having adorned her dark grey chiffon dress with silver tinsel for her Christmas night out with the girls. She'd caught his attention dancing by the tables he and his mates were lounging round. They seemed nonplussed about the trannie dancers too but for different reasons, shouting comments about not wanting to see cocks squashed into leotards. Peter had seen Olivia dancing and pointed her out to his mates, dragging her down to their tables, feeding her cheap booze and throwing a gaggle of corny chat-up lines at her before singing a tuneless rendition of "Fairy Girl".

"You're making that up as you go along aren't you?"

Peter shook his head at Olivia vehemently: "Fairy on top of a Christmas tree!"

"It should be an angel on top of a Christmas tree, not a fairy."

Peter licked his lips: "You look too dirty-minded to be an angel."

Those licked lips were soon smacking themselves against Olivia's for a full-on snogging session which included a level of fumbling that saw them both getting kicked out of the club. Olivia got a taxi home, too drunk to text her friends and ask them to come out and meet her. She'd been horrified they'd assumed she'd gone back to his.

Now that night was catching up with Olivia.

Peter and his Hawaiian mates motioned blowjobs at her, using their hands in front of open mouths, then laughed raucously. Horrified, she began to walk off, leaving the relative safety of the girls because she didn't want them to twig what was going on. The last thing she needed was for them to believe she did go back with him – which is obviously what he'd told his mates. Peter rushed after Olivia, grabbing her arm to stop her.

"Hey, fairy girl, don't go running off. They're only joining in because they're jealous; I told them you gave me the most amazing blowjob ever," he explained.

Olivia gave him a weak smile, which he took as a green light, grabbing her and pulling her into him and kissing her. That night in December came flooding back to her. He was the guy who kissed like his tongue was the spin cycle of a washing machine. As with that night, his kissing was like an assault on her face and Olivia felt like she couldn't breathe. She pulled herself out of the kiss, gasping for air.

"It hit me too, baby," Peter said.

"Hit you?"

"How powerful the kiss was."

He thought her gasping for air was her being overwhelmed by his kiss, overwhelmed by the worst kiss she'd ever experienced. She let out a giggle, quickly stifling it in horror as she realised she was openly laughing at him. But to her amazement he laughed too and squeezed her towards him. He'd somehow read Olivia's giggle as a good thing. Was there no end to this guy's confidence?

Olivia looked back at where girls had been standing and they were gone. Panicked, she realised she'd have to stay with Peter while she waited for them to reappear – who spent the next hour with his arms around her shoulders or waist, squeezing her and trying to get the occasional snog in. As Olivia scanned the room for any glimpse of her friends, Peter nibbled her ear.

"I wanna make sure everyone sees us together too babe," he told her, mistaking her glances as a compliment.

Beth, Faye and Abbie were nowhere to be seen. She blinked quickly to hold back the tears she could feel forming in her eyes, blurring her vision – she needed to be alert if she was going to spot them in such a crowded club. Being with the stag and his mates was the loneliest place in the world. To stop herself from crying, she was downing shots as fast as the rest of the Hawaiian gathering, the layers of alcohol cushioning her fears and covering her in a blanket of calmness.

She surreptitiously checked the contents of her purse and was relieved to see a sharp, glossy £20 note folded carefully behind her bankcard. Ever since that night at the Birdcage, she'd carried emergency taxi money. Olivia wanted to kiss the £20 note and hold it above her head waving it about, but knew she needed to contain her glee if she had any chance of getting away.

"I need to go to the ladies."

"We're leaving in a minute," he whined. "How about you wait until we get back to mine and you can piss all over me. I love a good golden shower."

Olivia felt like she was going to be sick. Then she was sick. With one retch, sick burst out of her and all over his shirt. As he staggered back she took her chance to escape and legged it to the ladies. The darkened mirrors made it difficult to check, but as far as she could see her sick had completely missed her outfit including her shoes. Cupping her hand under the cold tap, she sucked up the water into her mouth, swilling it round before spitting it out. Her mouth still tasted rank.

Scanning the room she spotted a temporarily discarded glass of wine left by a girl not sensible enough to take her drink into the cubicle with her. She swiftly poured it into her mouth, using the first mouthful as mouthwash, swilling and spitting, before gulping the rest down. Placing the empty glass down she tried to purge herself of guilt at stealing someone else's drink. It occurred to her that she could leave money for whoever it was so they could buy a new one. But she didn't have any way she could break into her £20 and the coppers dancing about in the bottom of her purse would be a bit of an insult – and that's assuming the next person to come through the door didn't steal them. Convinced there was no point, Olivia snapped her purse shut.

Exiting the ladies, Olivia scanned for Hawaiian shirts ready to either punch her or drag her home, but the group had disappeared. Relief washed over her as she headed downstairs ready to put her emergency note to good use. On the ground floor, as she was heading to the main door, something familiar caught Olivia's eye – Abbie's bob. Shuffling past haphazardly deserted empty chairs, Olivia weaved her way across to their table and tentatively sat down next to Abbie, half hoping the others wouldn't notice her so she wouldn't be given the third degree. Sitting at the other end of the curved booth, Faye was the first to spot her. She beamed at Olivia.

"You're back! We thought we'd lost you."

"We noticed the Hawaiian shirts leave and assumed you'd gone with them," Abbie added.

"You're lucky you turned up when you did," Beth said in a stern voice. "We were about to head off ourselves and you'd have been here by yourself."

"He recognised me from Christmas," Olivia explained. "The memories of that night were enough to shake me out of the madness of the situation."

All three of them made "ahh" noises and nodded their heads, now being able to place his face.

"We knew we knew him," Beth said. "To be honest we were worried you'd pulled someone from your work and your behaviour was finally going to catch up with you."

She was smiling as she said it, but her comment hit home.

"I just want to be loved too hun," Abbie told her. "Pathetic, in some ways, I know. But I don't feel whole if I'm not with someone. I'm just like you Olivia."

For Olivia, the world stopped. Everyone else faded into the background. It was just her and Abbie. Abbie understood why she behaved the way she did. Abbie didn't condone it, but she did understand. And she saw similarities between the two of them. For the first time in her life, Olivia realised she had two friends, not just one – Abbie as well as Beth. Olivia felt closer to her friends than she ever had before. And she could finally admit to herself that she was with the wrong man for fear of being alone because Abbie could admit the same thing.

They piled into a taxi back to Beth's house. Everyone felt at home at Beth's and its mix of strong paint choices, unusual art prints and haphazard belongings. Most of the furniture was the result of charity finds being sanded within an inch of their lives before being painted, papered, coated, varnished and whatever else you could to with a piece of furniture. When she got bored of something, which she invariably did, it usually ended up at Olivia's, re-sanded and painted white.

That night at Beth's house, lying on the deflated side of an old sofa bed and trying to take up as little space as possible for Abbie's sake, Olivia slept better than she had done in years. The next morning, the world seemed to be made up in slightly different tones, as if someone had adjusted the contrast and brightness on the internal TV set in her head. Sounds seemed louder and clearer too, as if she experienced the world anew. There also appeared to be a calmness between her and the others that hadn't been there before. Life was like one of Matt's games and she'd made it to the next level: to adulthood.

It wasn't the day Beth decided Olivia would make the perfect family, the perfect next of kin. Beth had decided long before then. At the bus stop, when the sad girl had said "Yes" to a brew.

16 teaspoons

BETH

I'm in the sea. Just above my head and to the left is the side lamp. Too dull to read by, too bright for sleeping. I look down and see my book of nursery rhymes is on my knee. I remember this day. I have been promoted to the top bunk. The nursery rhyme book has a hardcover. All my other books are squidgy and can be rolled up. I get into trouble if I do that, but a circled book has a slanted edge where the edge of the pages flex together. One way is smooth to the touch, but brush your fingers the other way and the pages are scales, like on a fish. I wonder if my legs are covered in books instead of scales. If it's just lots of books weighing me down and not the sea.

On the top bunk I can see the room in a different way. It's like being a tall person. Taller than my Dad because when he comes in the room I can see the top of his head where he doesn't have any hair. I asked him about it – why he had a patch with no hair where he had just pink skin like a blob. He got angry. It wasn't one of those times when Beth says something funny. He didn't tell everyone "Remember the time when Beth noticed the patch of skin on my head and didn't know why there wasn't any hair there?"

I can see the top of the wardrobe where the dust hides. When it's up there it gets to live rather than being eaten by the vacuum cleaner. It looks really thick, like grey snow, and I long to be able to reach over and draw my finger through it, making squiggly snakes. But I can't reach. From here, the top of the wardrobe doesn't look far, but I know it is. When I lie on the ground and stretch out, my tiptoes can just touch the edge of the wardrobe when my fingertips are touching the bottom bunk. But there's no floor to lie on when you're high up and air isn't very strong: if you jump into it you fall straight away.

My nursery rhyme book is my favourite book. I can read it but Grace can't because she doesn't know the words yet. The edge of the hardcover has fallen off – the edge that holds the pages together in one place. The smooth and shiny front with all the rhymes behind it is in one hand; the edge of the book is in the other. The rest of the book now has an ugly grey edge with threads like thin string woven through it. I no longer want this book. I'm angry at the smooth, shiny rhymes.

The book edge that has worked itself free is made up of layer upon layer of thin cardboard and I pick at the edges, peeling it back like the skin round my fingernails. My Mum comes in the room, then my Dad. I'm crying and I didn't realise, and they want to know what's wrong. They are annoyed when they see the tentacles of cardboard strewn across the top of my blankets. My Mum sighs: "Dad could have fixed that if you hadn't ripped it up. He could have made your book good as new." I know this isn't true because the book came from a second-home shop. Where stuff is given away and then new people give those things second homes. So my nursery rhyme book was good as new for someone else. It was only ever good as second-home for me.

I cry more. I know Mum thinks it's because Dad can no longer fix the book because it's broken, but it's not. It's because she said he could make it good as new and it's a lie. Once something is old, it can never be new again, no matter how hard you try. You have to get another one if you want a new one. I know that because when Grace came along I told my Mum I could have been a baby again if she'd wanted a baby that much. She'd laughed and told me that now I was born I would only get older. Things don't get younger; they don't get new again.

Grace was the new baby sister everyone cooed over. So Grandma took me to the second-home shop to treat me to something that's just mine. "Grace won't want a book," she'd told me. "She's too tiny to read. Only big girls can read." And I realised that Grandma still liked me even though I was old now. So I asked her if she could buy me from the shop and I could live with her; that her house could be my second home. She'd laughed and I thought it was going to be one of those things that Beth says, that she'd say "Remember when Beth said…" but then she got upset and hugged me tight and told me her home was always my second home. You get a second home when your parents split up – I know that from someone at school, I think. They call it a second home, but lots of times you don't get to live in both; you live with the parent left behind. Then you change roles and you become like the parent and look after them. I used to know someone who did that. Or I know someone who used to do that.

THE RUBIK'S CUBE

The stickers are fiddly and my nails are too short to take each one off undamaged. But none of them rips and I have them lined up in rows stuck to a plastic bag, ready to re-stick in the right places. The Rubik's Cube looks a lot less interesting when it's all black. It reminds me of a grenade from the book about war that I'm not allowed to take out of the library, or like the bodies of the beetles that live in the sandpit in the corner of the garden. I can still remember digging to the bottom where the sand smelt funny.

Putting the stickers back in the right places takes a lot longer than I thought it would because I'm also thinking about things like sandpits being scary when they shouldn't be. When I've finished, I take it to Dad. He looks shocked and says things about being pleasantly surprised. Which is strange, because what other kinds of surprises are there? But then he notices some of the stickers are peeling where the edges are damaged and then he starts talking about Pete. I don't know who Pete is but Mum hears him and comes in. He tells her about the stickers and she agrees – it's for Pete's sake. I hope Pete likes the Rubik's Cube even though the orange stickers are peeling a little bit. I started on the orange as it's my least favourite colour, so they're the worst ones.

17 teapots

Near the front of the train I find a window seat next to a girl that's close to anorexic. Perfect. Not only will she not spill into my seat, but she won't gorge herself on food while I sit there with nothing to snack on. I'm instantly wracked with guilt – she might actually be ill. My guilt grows as she smiles at me gratefully, obviously as happy with me as a companion as I am with her. Thankfully, she doesn't want to engage in conversation because I'm not able to concentrate on anything other than my master plan – except that I don't have one. I'm not entirely sure how to trace Ethan when I get down there.

I have a small overnight bag with me, but I'm on an early train so I have plenty of time to do some detective work and return empty-handed the same day if necessary. I can't afford to stay over somewhere unless I can find a bunk bed in a dorm. But I don't even care about being so skint to have to drink water at our next girls' night if it means I manage to track him down. While I stare out of the window at the passing fields and towns, I play the *Rocky* theme tune over and over in my head, the image of the "118 118" runners in my head making me smile. I don't know why I'm smiling because the moustached lads were unable to help me – they needed both a surname and address to give me a phone number and wouldn't give out any details, phone number or address, from just a surname. I hum to myself in my head and the tune morphs into *The A-Team*. Oh well, I'm an artist not a musician.

The A-Team was my favourite show when I was a kid, partly because my Mum thought it was too violent for me to watch. I remember being the odd one out in school because I couldn't talk about soaps with the other girls in my year. It had been an epiphany to meet Beth and find she wasn't allowed to watch whatever was on after that boring news show for kids which nobody watched anyway. That's when the rest of us would turn over to ITV. Being allowed to watch TV didn't help Abbie and Olivia fit in though. We were four geeks who, as adults, had discovered each other and formed our own in-crowd. Apparently, we weren't even geeks.

"Only blokes can be geeks," Beth had said, forbidding anyone to disagree with her on the matter. I secretly disagreed with her. I'd reclaimed the word "geek" to mean all the things it used to mean but in a positive way – so people who were geeks could be proud of the fact. Geeks who desperately wanted to fit in weren't actually geeks: they were nerds. Nerds, bless them, were scorned by everyone, even geeks.

My Virgin Pendolino. Pen. Doh. Leee. Nooo. I can't say it in my head without sounding like Loyd Grossman, all elongated vowels. My Virgin Pendolino zooms along at ridiculous speeds one minute only to coast for a while, pick up speed again, then slow to a crawl. We pass slowly through Cheddington, which seems a bit of an indulgent place to have a station as there's only one building within sight. Then Tring, which appears to consist only of a temporary metal two-storey car park structure. And Berkhamsted, which with castle ruins and a canal seems the most promising as somewhere posh enough to sell my postcards or prints.

We finally come to a halt underneath a motorway flyover that, after much neck-craning and squinting, I decide must be the M25. An announcement over the tannoy explains the delays were because of signalling problems at Bushey. The broadcast is met with huffs and tuts from the suited members of the train as if the wait was just to hinder them personally. The disembodied voice says he "apologises for the inconvenience" in a tone that says anything but. We eventually start moving again, through Watford Junction and the despised Bushey, and on through smaller, scruffier stations that are merely thin runs of tarmac or paving proudly displaying orange versions of the iconic London transport sign. I'm reminded of the trip to Marple.

The last few miles into Euston are a cocoon of bridges and buildings. They must be so short of land in the capital. They build closer to the train line here than anywhere else. I stare out at the mismatch of old houses which had seen better days and ugly concrete constructions that could be cramped flats or anonymous office blocks – any company signs giving the game away would be on the other side of the building, where it faced the road. I gawp at a strange multi-storey-car-park-cum-office-block to the left and a stepped concrete prison jutting out over the edge of the tracks to the right. From this view, it is difficult to see why so many people think London architecturally outstanding.

It is already 11.45am when I get off the train. The

morning is gone, I'd only just arrived and I have no idea where to start looking. Thankfully, Euston station has a tube station, so it's where I head when I can't find a tourist information office on the concourse. Beth had once told me the escalators in London moved faster than anywhere else and I thought she was joking. But trying to step on one was a nightmare and I only managed it because I was half-pushed by someone behind me.

I'm pretty sure there's a tourist office in Leicester Square – it sounds like there should be one – so after following the colourful snakes on the tube map with the tip of my finger, I find myself being lightly jerked about by the black line train as it heads south. I almost got on the wrong train because there are two black lines at Euston not just one. Had they really run out of colours? I'd already made a mental note to not get on the green one: it looked far too complicated. I'm secretly incredibly proud of myself for getting this far by myself. A trip to Blackpool was easy, but London was another country.

In what seems like no time at all I'm at my stop. I'm pretty sure it took more time to go up and down escalators and through ticket barriers than it did to travel between Euston and the strangely gloss-bricked station at Leicester Square. I take a closer look at the tiles that look both dirty and freshly cleaned, still and gleaming wet, all at once.

Some people around me are rushing round at a pace far too fast to notice the details, while others are gaggled round maps, too engrossed in the coloured lines version of the world to stop and take in the beauty of the real thing. I am relieved to be street level again and away from the stale smelling air of the tube system. I blow my nose and can't resist a quick peek to see if it is black – and am somewhat put out to see it's the typical green sludge. It must take more than one quick journey on London Underground to change the colour.

I get to the grassy area in the middle of Leicester Square to discover what I thought should be a tourism office is actually a hut selling discounted tickets for the day's theatre performances. Tempting as it is to see *Cats* or *Starlight Express*, I leave empty-handed, the words to *Mr Macavity* going round in my head. I spot a policeman and head towards him with such a look of determination on my face that he must have assumed I'm about to report a serious crime. He looks both disappointed and relieved when I asked him for help, and he soon points me in the direction of Lower Regent Street and the closest Tourist Information Office. Thankfully his instructions are easy enough to follow.

When I get to Lower Regent Street, I stand in the queue as patiently as I can, hopping my weight from one foot to the other while I listen to someone in broken English ask for somewhere that seems to be on the most convoluted and difficult tube and bus journey ever, with each stage of the journey explained three or four times before the lost visitor nods their head in vague comprehension. When it is finally my turn, I stumble over my words to get them out, not making myself any more understandable than the previous individual. But after a few fluffed attempts, I'm able to explain that I need to trace someone living in London.

Rather than looking baffled at my request, the guy the other side of the counter points me in the direction of the British Library at St Pancras, suggesting a search of old phone books and the electoral register. My journey feels like a bit of a wild goose chase because the library is only half a mile from Euston station, but I'm just grateful for somewhere to head. This time I have to brave the lift at Piccadilly Circus station – well it's that or 300-odd steps and I can only do needless exercise when it's somewhere pretty. I can wander for hours in a park, on a beach. But I never feel at home indoors. The stale air infiltrates the lift as we headed deep underground which, apart from being totally gross, reassures me that we won't die from lack of oxygen if the lift gets stuck.

About 10 minutes later, after I fight my way through the crowds and out onto the street, I'm standing in front of the building that might lead me to my destiny. Nervously, I concentrate on the patterns my mind makes with the block paving as I approached the entrance. I had expected something to match the curved elegance of Manchester's Central Library – Olivia's favourite building – or maybe even a gloriously Victorian Gothic structure like that of the John Rylands Library on Deansgate, which I prefer, but I am greeted by a rather ugly red brick building with a sloping roof that looked like the veranda of an overly-authentic Chinese restaurant. In front of the building is a very plain clock tower. Although it's disappointing, it does look industrious enough to hold up-to-date and back copies of all of London's phone directories.

The security guards on the doors seem a bit incongruous, but at least they seem uninterested in me as I passed through the doors and into a vast, sterile hall. There's nobody around to help. It's more art gallery than library: the lack of front desk, the echoing, people wandering round aimlessly, not sure what they're meant to be doing. Nobody ever feels quite at home in an art gallery.

I walk up a set of grand-but-plain steps and then up an escalator and find myself at the café round the back. A coffee and some cake sounded like a good idea. I realise I haven't had anything to eat or drink since the nasty cup of tea at Manchester Piccadilly. I don't see any change from a fiver, but the carrot cake is exceptional and the Peyton and Byrne coffee divine. I make a mental note of the name so I can suggest selling it in the deli. It's a nice place to people-watch too, the library obviously attracting a rich mix of Londonites, from the ankle-flashing long-bearded hipster to the absurd display of pseudo-French the beret and rollneck sweater wearer sitting opposite me was trying to pull off.

Re-energised from my pit-stop, I head back down to the central area and notice the information desk is now manned. I approach eagerly but I'm cut down to size with one sly comment after another.

"Do you have an appointment to view the documents in the Reading Room?"

Reading Room?

"Err, no. I just want the main bit of the library where that information is held."

"Do you even have a Reader Pass?"

I shake my head.

"I didn't think so. This isn't an ordinary library you know. A lot of our information is kept in storage and you have to give us up to 48 hours' notice to view certain information. And that's only when you have a Reader Pass. For that you need two different forms of ID and you need to make an appointment with the Reader Registration Office."

I leave the building with my shoulders so low they bang against my knees. By the time I'm through the door I'm hunched into a crouching position. Once outside I allow myself to sink onto the block paving, hugging my knees.

"Excuse me, lass."

I hear the hint of a Northern accent and look up to see a burly but friendly looking security guard looking over me.

"You alright?"

I nod. He helps me stand upright. Embarrassed that I'm

upset at a library, I tell him about my Reader Pass predicament.

"You want to get yourself over to the Guildhall Library. They've got all the directories there are in there. Specialist library in't-it."

He points out King's Cross station and explains how to get the Northern line to Moorgate and the warren of side streets I'd need to walk down to find myself at an ugly slatted concrete building that looks like a 60s office block, but that I'd know which one it was from the tinted glass porch and the paved square. I feel very sorry for Londoners and their ugly libraries. I want to hug him, but I compose myself, thank him and head off towards the station.

"Got a posh job has he?" he shouts after me.

I shrugged: "Maybe?"

"There's a chance he's not in London then," he explains. "Many folk travel in from all round, commuting like. Get trains in from as far as Brighton some do. You'll need to check more than just London."

His comments warm my belly. Maybe I'd not found him in an online search looking at just London because I'd missed him as he lived further out. I half run, half skip to the station, not even stopping to take in the glory of St Pancras station and hotel – just allowing myself a glimpse – and almost missing the way into the tube underneath it, catching on too late why the tube station is called "King's Cross St Pancras" and not just "King's Cross". I weave my way through the crowds down to the tube platform and the next part of my mission, filled with the warmth of hope once again. Even if this library couldn't help, maybe there'd be another Northern security guard to point me off to somewhere else.

A 60s office block is the perfect description of the

Guildhall Library and also fails it completely. It is exceptional. Standing next to a church and cocooned in a square, I am just a few steps from a busy road but have entered an alternate universe where London is filled with a vacuum: tiny pockets of air that mute all lifeforms. There are no signs of life in any of the buildings on the square and the sounds from the nearby streets are dulled. The porch he'd described is a long glass corridor running the full length of the building, connecting the office-like construction with something far more grand and library-like. It seems less foreboding than the British Library and I cross my fingers about not needing a reading card.

Thankfully, not only do I not need one, but there are also staff keen to help. The lady who takes up the challenge seems disappointed that the person I'm looking for is still alive and that we need to use recent directories, but she digs in with relish all the same, fuelled by the fact that he could be anywhere in the south east. We are soon flicking through a vast collection of phone directories, steering me away from using the electoral register as it's done in ward order and then address order, not alphabetical order – and with no electronic copy to search through quickly, except for ones I'd have to pay to use on the Internet, it could take days for me to go through the full set looking for his name.

She chuckles more to herself than to me as she says he might be in an old directory, but not a new one, from the days before paranoia led to people being ex-directory, and what was the point of having a phone if nobody could get your number? It's evident that she doesn't get much company or many people interested in what she does because she's soon wittering away about phone books dating back to 1880 and how they are all available on a special website. Her wittering is quite soothing but it makes it difficult for me to concentrate as I charge through the "G" section of every directory. Soon she was holding the Hemel Hempstead directory aloft with a grin on her face.

"Gruger," she says victoriously, "I've found him."

She puts the directory down in front of me. And there he is. My heart has stopped and my fingers shake when I try to take my notepad and pen out of my bag – this time I am more prepared than I had been in Preston.

"I'll photocopy the page for you," she says, rushing off with the directory before I can argue. I feel sick. I don't want the directory out of my sight now I've found him. Time freezes while I wait for her to return.

What. If. She. Doesn't. Come. Back?

But she does, with the photocopy as promised, and she's even highlighted his entry.

"The funny thing is that he's in the current directory, so you could have found him at Manchester Central Library. But," she says with a smile, "the important thing is that you've found him."

I run my finger over the highlighted line of tiny text. Berkhamsted. How funny that I'd noticed the place when I'd been coming in on the train, drawn to its prettiness, and now I'd be heading back out there to see Ethan. For the second time today – and almost the third time – I hug a stranger for taking extra time and care to help me. A library worker, a cleaner at Piccadilly station, a security guard. These are the people who make the world work.

I am grateful to be heading back towards Manchester after a long afternoon of feeling out of place and out of my depth. I've found the whole episode very stressful and can't imagine myself meandering along the streets lost in my thoughts as I had in Blackpool. The London Midland train I get on at Euston goes as slowly as the Virgin train had gone, although this seems to be the designated speed for the journey as we arrive at the tiny stations at the times on the platform displays. It's absolutely packed full of tutting and sighing commuters shifting about, trying to find a comfortable place to lean in the vestibules while trying not it invade each other's personal space.

I watch the crowd by the doors from the relative safety of my seat, thankful now that I'd just missed one train and had therefore been one of the first to get on this one. I got on the end carriage because it was closest but I'm now wondering if walking up the platform would have made more sense. The end carriage stays packed until Berkhamsted, which we reach 40 minutes later, whereupon everyone gets up in unison and heads like a mist to the train doors and down the platform steps.

I miss following the larger crowd of passengers into the town centre after a false start of following the first few off the train leftwards, in the direction of the car park. I manage to catch the tail end of the human mist as I rush back through the tunnel section of the station, but am lost once again outside when I see half of the crowd turning left by the parkland and the other half turning right.

I pop back into the station and ask the lady in the coffee shop for the best way. She signals right and I follow the dregs towards the high street. There are no regular shops on the street I walk down. Instead it's posh interior design junk and fancy food shops that make Deli-Delicious look scruffy, interspersed with overly cool bars and restaurants that look anything but inviting. Thankfully there is a pretty florist shop on the corner of the crossroads and the lovely lady at the counter points out where Ethan's road is. I have to walk up a rather steep hill, but catching my breath at the top gives me the opportunity to prepare myself. And here I am, for the third time, standing in front of an uninviting front door, psyching myself up to ring the doorbell. This is ridiculous. On the other side of that door is Ethan.

And. Ethan. Likes. Me.

"Diiiiing-doooong!"

I jump at the rather dramatic and shrill doorbell. After what seems like both a millisecond and eternity, the door opens and standing in front of me is Ethan, who has changed entirely but also hasn't changed one bit at the same time. He wears his hair slightly longer and his face looks slightly weathered and covered with the same smile wrinkles I remember his Dad having. He is wearing a smart shirt and trousers, but the top button and cuffs of his shirt are undone and his tie is nowhere to be seen.

He still has his shoes on, so I make a guess that he was probably on the same train as me, suffering the monotony of heading back on the same train as he did every day, unaware that what awaited him was sitting just a carriage or two away. Or maybe even the same carriage. If I'd only looked up, looked around more, seeking out a familiar face in the mist, perhaps I'd have been saying hello to him 10 minutes ago and not now.

He breaks the stalemate first, stepping towards me and enveloping me in the hugest of hugs. He smells just how I remember, and in my head I am 21 again, recalling how he hugged me to try and stop my sobs when I watched the train to London pull out with Jack on it. Ethan had joined him down in London a few months later, but in those few months I'd felt very alone and Ethan was a rock to me. Since then I'd relied on myself, my art, and then the girls to pull me through. For all their faults and for all the whinging I did in my head, Beth, Abbie and Olivia were often my warmth, my comfort and my sanity. I wish all of them, any one of them, could be standing here with me giving my hand a reassuring squeeze, being the rock that Ethan had once been. Maybe I wasn't outgrowing them after all.

Back in university, I'd committed the biggest relationship crime: deserting my female friends to spend all my time with my boyfriend. It came as no surprise to find they'd all moved on by the time Jack and I split. I spent a good few years with only fair-weather friends before Beth came along. No matter how great my future relationships were, I'd not be doing that to my friends again.

Ethan pulls away from the hug.

"Oh Faye," he sighs. "I'm afraid you're six weeks too late."

18 teabags

BETH

Lift. Lips. Sip. Lift to my lips and sip. The pink dress is at my bedside. I've worked that out now. I'm not in the sea; I'm in bed. I know because they pulled back the sea and I saw it was a blanket with a white sheet underneath. My legs were there, both of them. It was a surprise. Then I remembered to look to see if I had arms and I did. So I'm not sure why the pink dress holds my cup for me.

The pink dress is wearing a brown wig today. She had a blonde wig on before. I have no idea why she wears different wigs but the same dress. Her dress is like the one the dinner ladies wore at school – a pink version of the blue gingham dresses we all wore during the summer at school. But she only does mugs of tea. Maybe she tried out being a dinner lady but wasn't good enough. When it was summer we were off school. Mum would spend the summer saying: "I wish you were back at school. It's ridiculous that you get the whole summer off without any homework."

But we had summer school uniforms; the gingham

dresses. Why did we need summer school uniforms if we spent the whole of summer at home? I didn't understand. I asked my Mum, but this wasn't one of the times she laughed and then said "Remember" to other people. Instead she called me "fishes". She said: "Stop being so fishes." I wanted to ask her what kind of fish I was, but I knew not to. So I asked my Dad and he grinds his teeth.

There's the lady in the pink dress. And there are people in green pyjamas too. It's funny because you never see any of the green pyjamas getting into any of the beds. The beds are full of people wearing mostly what they like, and the people in pyjamas stop at the ends of the beds but never get inside them.

I have a blue blanket over my legs again. It's hydrangea blue and just as lumpy as the puffball flowers my Grandma would grow in the border. Or maybe it was more like the colour and consistency of Elijah Blue – the grass that used to be in pots that were thrown out because plants are "too thrifty" – I used to know someone who did that.

Or maybe it was more like the squidgy blue foam my Mum used to have in a pottery vase. It held an arrangement of silk flowers, their plastic stems pushed into the firm surface. Then pitted finger marks started to appear on the surface, which turned into finger holes, turning the foam into the Emmental cheese kept on the top shelf because it was "just for Dad". And then the holes joined up and the foam turned to powder and all the flowers lay limp on one side.

Mum didn't even bother looking for the evidence of foam dust that I tried to carefully wash from underneath my fingernails. She knew it was me. Because. It always. Maybe if I used nail polish, it would have stopped the dust from being trapped. Not that my Mum looked. But I could have said "Look, no dust" instead of hiding my hands behind my back the way a magician does. Except going to bed without any tea isn't a very good magic trick. But it's paint, not dust, that gets trapped in fingernails. I know some that happened to – it's a very sad story.

Mum knew it was me. Because. It always was. Except for the time there was mould. I squeeze my eyes tight to try and forget the image of the blue fur on the surface of the orange. I remember this day. The air smells funny because of the oranges from Christmas left to go mouldy on the shelf because Grace and Charlotte refuse to eat the ones that Santa left. It's the only time they both get into trouble and I don't. It was very strange watching. I must have been watching wrong because then Mum says: "And you can wipe that look off your face" and suddenly the mouldy oranges are forgotten and I'm the one in the wrong again.

I'm in one of those non-spaces between two sets of double doors. I remember this day. The space is big enough to be a bedroom but there's no bed. It's just a space between the reception area and the hall. My school is full of these capsules of old air like this. No matter whether you take in a big sniff or a small one, the air smells of floor polish and of oranges from Christmas left to go mouldy on the shelf. So I breathe through my mouth so that I'm not sick from the smell. It's not like the other type of polish, the type you use to cover the splits in your nails.

I'm up on the ceiling, like being on the top bunk but my body is still on the floor below me so it's just my eyes up here – and maybe my brain too. Lots of days are like this in my memory. I guess my eyes got used to being up on the top bunk even after Charlotte came along and Grace got the top bunk. Then I got the box room, which is a silly name because it's not made out of boxes and doesn't have any boxes in it. But I'm learning to keep these points to myself because my Mum stores them up to tell people at church and they make my Dad grind his teeth. I've noticed it's still called the box room, even though I have a new bed in there. My old room is now "Grace and Charlotte's" room. There's no room with my name on anymore.

I'm not in the box room now, I'm in the capsule between the swinging doors that don't have handles. Instead they have huge sheets of metal that are shiny but not shiny enough to be mirrors. If you're first to the door, you can see a wobbly version of yourself as you open it. The doors are heavy and swing both ways so it doesn't matter which way you come from, you don't need a handle. It's very clever. When I'm older I'm going to reinvent all doors to be like this.

Both sets of doors are shut and my Mum and the gymnastics coach are there. I'm crying because I don't get to go into the next class and I'm better than some of the other girls who do. I don't understand what I've done wrong. I thought I couldn't get it wrong at gymnastics. I'm crying, but my Mum doesn't even lie and say Dad could fix it if I hadn't messed it up so much. That lie got far too dirty and if it hasn't been washed, it can't be used again. My Mum doesn't know how they get washed either. When I asked if lies go in the washing machine, my Mum looked for the answer on the ceiling. But she's the one who says that lies won't wash with her, so I don't know where they do wash. So how do lies get clean?

WASTING GOOD MONEY

Beth cries as a stressed woman in a faded tracksuit tries to convince her she's being kept in the lower class to help the newer, less experienced gymnasts get better. Beth is distraught as she has no idea what she's done wrong. She doesn't understand it's because her Mum had refused to "waste good money" on a team leotard, never mind a good haircut. Gymnastics is a cruel sport and the coach knows the team will lose points with a gymnast with a home-cut bob. And the coach can't afford to be out of pocket, buying Beth a team leotard, especially when she can't see Beth's parents letting her go on the coach to competitions. So they can't afford to waste a space on the new team on Beth.

What the stressed woman in the faded tracksuit doesn't realise is the truth would have been best. It would be years before Beth realised it was effectively her parents' fault she didn't make the team, not hers. The stressed woman in the faded tracksuit didn't want to be cruel about Beth's family. She doesn't know that Beth would be secretly thrilled that something was her Mum's fault. Because her Mum is never wrong. So Beth looked in the wobbly door-mirror and saw she wasn't as petite as Olga Korbut or as skinny as Mary Lou Retton and realised she'd got it wrong again.

19 teacups

ABBIE

My eyes are glued together. Licking the inside of my index fingers and thumbs, I take my rows of eyelashes between them and rub gingerly, balancing clearing the clumps of tar with saving as many hairs as possible. I have so many eyelash extensions to cover up the bald spots I might as well wear an eyelash wig. I brush my face with my hands, removing blackened flakes of crusted make-up from my cheeks. I need to treat my eyes with more respect. At least it's just my eyelashes suffering this time, not my eyesight.

I'm trying to remember if I need to work today or not. I've been working quite a few Saturdays, but I wasn't woken by my alarm, so I'm guessing not. I'm in no fit state to work today anyway. There's only so much Lemsip a girl can handle, and my boss already thinks I'm unlucky when it comes to catching colds. Now my eyes are open I should check my phone though, just in case.

It's not on my bedside cabinet. Nor on the floor. Nor is my handbag hanging on the back of my door, on the hook

I've carefully padded with a dash of quilt wadding – then wrapped in Cath Kidston "Highgate Ditsy" and finished with ribbon – to ensure it doesn't distort the line of the leather strap. Where the fuck is my bag?

I go from not being able to move to jolting up out of bed. Heat rushes through my body, followed by cold. I feel faint. Maybe I should check for my bag while sitting on the edge of my bed. I scan the room. It's not here. I step over the debris that is bottles and beauty paraphernalia and pull open the bedroom door. I sway down the stairs, very much needing the wall as much as the bannister. Thankfully, Dominic works Saturdays. I'm counting my blessings.

Do I need to re-rub my eyes open? My car is not outside.

Dominic can't drive. And it's rare anybody else would borrow it – especially not without asking. I'm loath to let anyone sit in the passenger seat, let alone drive it, but I'm trying to be less attached to material things by pretending to be. So occasionally someone else will be at the wheel. But not without me running through the checks they need to make, outlining how they must use car parks and not park on the road, and drumming into them the importance of the "no eating in the car EVER" rule.

It's been stolen. My baby has been stolen. And I can't phone the police because I haven't got my fucking phone.

Yes, I can. I have a landline. The landline nobody ever uses because we're all programmed into each other's phones under our names and photos, a string of numbers hidden behind them. Thankfully, 999 is not something easily forgotten. I pick up the walkabout handset and dial. I hear a faint beeping in the background: the dying battery's cry for help. It hasn't been sitting straight in its cradle. I hope there's enough battery for this call.

"Emergency. Which service do you require?"

"Police. My car has been stolen."

God, this feels familiar.

I need to cut down on how much *Law & Order* and *Luther* I watch. I like watching *Luther*. Idris Elba is the first black man I've ever fancied. The only one in fact: I've not liked another since. But it's the first one that counts. I've always worried I was racist, so I'm relieved I'm not. I just fancy successful people – and you just don't get many black people in law firms.

"999 is the emergency line. You need to hang up and redial 101 to speak to someone in your district who can deal with this."

"Does it make any difference if my handbag, mobile and just about everything else that's important to me is in the car?"

"I'm afraid not. You need to hang up and redial 101 to speak to someone in your district who can deal with this."

Am I dealing with artificial intelligence? Or does the man on the other end of the phone get calls like this so often that he's developed a phrase that just runs off his tongue? I can't remember anyone dialling 101 on TV and cars get stolen in those programmes all time. Where else would car chases come from?

I dial 101 while listening to the phone's distress call getting faster. I hope this call is as swift as the one preceding it, but with a better outcome.

THE WARMTH OF ANOTHER

Abbie used to think watching TV was something you did as a duo, half slouched, half intertwined, shouting and laughing at the TV, pointing out when something seemed unrealistic or you'd worked out part of the plot. Now it was very much a solo sport. *Luther* had been watched in four-hourly chunks on Netflix months after it had aired on BBC1, on a weekend when plans had been cancelled last minute, and she'd had to find a way to keep herself entertained.

Paul had introduced her to *Prison Break* and *Dexter*, and she'd watched a lot of American drama shows on box sets after that. Dominic mainly wanted to clog up the screen with "hilarious" programmes on Dave, so she'd taken to sitting in the Acapulco chair in the corner of the lounge, feet up on the coffee table, laptop on her knee, headphones on, watching at her own pace, dreaming of being married to Wentworth Miller or Idris Elba.

She didn't mind as much as she should do though. She never quite got used to the intertwinedness of her life on the sofa with Paul. Her parents had rewarded her and punished her with words only; high praise taking the place of hugs, sharp words instead of smacks – although she will never forget the hiding she got after the perfume incident. There were some days at school where she'd lean into another child in the corridor while waiting to go into class just to feel the warmth of another human on her skin. And although she craved human contact, she also despised it – hating Paul for every hug, cursing him for every caress, because she needed it more than she needed to breathe.

ABBIE

So now I get to sit and wait. I'm not very good at that. But at least the officer on the end of the 101 call was interested in the theft, made the appropriate clucking and soothing noises, and assured me he would "put out an APB for your vehicle" – although admittedly, not in those words. I put the phone back in its cradle, jiggling it to ensure it connects properly to the base this time. The last thing I need is the police not being able to get in touch if they manage to find my car. And until they do, I'm stuck here. I'm can't leave because I'd need my keys… I'd need my keys to get back in… So how did I get in in the first place? Did Dominic let me in? I don't remember.

I sway carefully to the front door and open it. My wedding photo-free keys hang innocently from the lock. My handbag mocks me from the step.

I bought a house with a front alcove so I didn't have to stand in Manchester's incessant rain while digging out my keys, but I now realise it has another use – hiding your keys and handbag from opportunistic thieves. I take the keys out of the door, spin the car fob round in my hand and press to disable the alarm. Nothing.

With my keys firmly in my hand I'm happy to step out onto the path, even though I haven't brushed my hair or looked at myself in the mirror yet, even though I'm unsteady on my feet the way only drunkenness, a hangover or influenza can make you feel. The road is quiet for a Saturday. I hold the fob out in front of me, trying it in various directions, just in case I chose to park down the street rather than on my driveway. Not even the faintest of beeps. Although I've found my keys and bag, my car has definitely been stolen.

As I head back into the house I hear the landline ringing. It's the police.

I'm so angry. How fucking dare she just borrow my car. I was tempted to let the police officer know she'd taken it without asking but decided it made more sense to pretend I was happy for it to be found parked half on, half off the pavement outside Beth's flat. Her appalling parking had alerted a neighbour to the possibility of it being stolen, and in turn she had alerted the police. So the registration details were sitting waiting to be found when the officer searched for it.

As far as I'm concerned, it's up to Beth to return the car. But at the same time, I don't want her touching it again. I might even get a taxi down there and pick it up without telling her – give her a taste of the cold fear I can still feel at the back of my mouth when she thinks it's missing.

Right. Phone. Thankfully, it's still tucked in the side pocket of my bag. I give it a squeeze before taking it out – my lifeline, my extra limb. I feel a jolt looking at the screen. It's covered with the disoriented blinking of messages via SMS, WhatsApp, Facebook and phone. Olivia, Olivia, Olivia, Olivia.

Oh fuck. Beth. The hospital.

That was yesterday. That means today is Sunday. How the fuck did I lose a day?

CLOSE FRIENDS

Why do boyfriends have to come with idiot friends? It's something Abbie seems to ask herself far too often. Paul seemed quite happy to leave his juvenile friends behind shortly after he got serious with Abbie, but she's been less lucky with her choices since then. She finds Dominic's crowd from work rather adolescent – although she only has to compare him to Ebb's tantrum-throwing, attention-seeking toddler of a best friend to put their relatively harmless annoyances into perspective. Olivia, on the other hand, is secretly thrilled when it becomes clear Matt has no close friends to speak of. It means she can have him all to herself.

ABBIE

I need to take a few breaths before calling Olivia. She hates it when I get into "swear mode" and the f-word comes out every fourth word. I realise now it must have been her who'd driven us all to the hospital and then headed back to Beth's afterwards. I'm still annoyed that she parked the car so badly, but I'm sure she would have asked me for permission. I'm just having trouble remembering that particular conversation right now.

She answers after just two rings.

"Thanks for getting back to me," she says. "I wasn't sure if you'd be human enough to call me until this afternoon."

"Oh?"

"You were really quite drunk."

I think about the empty wine bottles I stepped over without thinking this morning, assuming they were old ones. I'm now not so sure. Even with her appalling parking, I have to be grateful Olivia was doing the driving.

"I wasn't," she replies.

"What?"

"Doing the driving. You drove. I asked you to check on Beth. So you drove to her house. You found the empty Paracetamol bottle in her bin. Remember? Called an ambulance?"

Nothing.

"Then I came to the hospital," she explains.

"I called you?"

A pause. Longer than a heartbeat.

"The hospital did. I'm next of kin."

That's the jolt I needed. Beth in bed. Her body too too still. Shaking the Paracetamol tub. It being too too silent.

The Second Cup

The ambulance. The siren. Beth's limp body. Travelling with them. Waiting on a plastic chair. Names being called over and over but none of them the right one. All the different shoes people were wearing. All the scruffy trainers. Then shoes I recognised. Olivia turning up. Sharing a hug. Needing her more than I've ever needed her before. Then the sharp stab of jealousy. Olivia is next of kin, not me.

"Sorry."

I'm not sure if I say that or her. But when I say it – or say it for a second time – I hear her say it too.

"I can't believe I got in the car that drunk. But I didn't know…"

"I should never have assumed you'd be able to go to the hospital. Matt's Nan died. I had to be there for him. I needed someone else to be there for Beth."

"I'm so sorry. Of course I should have been there. It's just Jack, Beth…"

"You and Dominic."

"Matt and his Nan."

I feel the need to catch my breath. To exhale.

I need to do something practical, so I call a taxi. I tell the taxi driver I will tip him £20 if he drives really slowly. I hold up the note so he knows I mean it. I hope driving my car home from Beth's will be easier on my anatomy than sitting in the back of someone else's.

Olivia has ordered me to stay at home. But I need to pick up the car before the police decide to tow it away. And I want to find out what Faye is playing at. I would say "what the fuck" Faye is playing at, but Olivia seems to have knocked all the profanities out of me.

The taxi fare plus £20 lighter, I stare at my car in disbelief. It looks like someone purposefully parked it badly, maybe for a sketch show or sitcom. I'm so embarrassed about having to get into it. I don't care that Beth's neighbourhood isn't as salubrious as mine. Right now I don't want to be judged by anyone – even those twitching at ruched net curtains as opposed to looking out between the slats of restored shutters.

I hold my head up high as I walk over to my car, then shake my head in disbelief at the parking for the benefit of any incidental audience I may have. Yes, I may be getting into this car and driving it away, but let me assure you, I didn't leave it like this in the first place – I say all that with a headshake.

The engine purrs. This is not going to hurt my peristalsis anywhere near as much as the cab did. I gingerly put her into gear and glide off smoothly. I'm aware of the fact that I'm not quite sober. I should probably not be behind the wheel any more than last night. But at least I'm aware of my inebriation this time round. At the end of the road, I hesitate before indicating. Left to Faye's deli, right to go home. I choose left.

I can remember how to get to the deli, albeit via a convoluted route that takes me back out to the dual carriageway and round the outskirts of Didsbury. But today is not the day to be testing my map-reading skills, so the long route it is. The long route pays off. As I pull up outside the deli, I can see the recognisable shape that is Faye behind the counter.

I walk to the shop door, my steps much more steady now than just a few hours ago. Pushing the door open, I wince slightly at the old-fashioned bell tingling above the door. I'm too busy confirming Faye's slight frame and positively fizzing hair to take in the rest of the shop. Is it my hangover, or is she smiling that brightly? I instinctively feel for my DKNYs on the top of my head, forgetting it's not summer.

My mind is full of thoughts the way it is when I've had too much wine the day before. Thoughts slide in and out of focus as Faye comes around to greet me. How can she smile so brightly when Beth is in hospital? Oh, she doesn't know, does she! Do I tell her?

Yes, I'd like to meet Ethan. Oh, it's that Ethan. No, I don't tell her it's that Ethan. An icy "nice to see you again". Yes, you too. Air kisses and polite hugs. Yes, a small world. How funny that you knew Ethan in Manchester and I knew him in London. Jack, no I never met Jack. Oh you mean that Jack. Of course you do. The toddler. How funny that you knew Jack in Manchester and I knew him in London.

Well I must get back to Beth. She's in hospital. She does seem to have taken his death badly. Don't forget to visit her, will you. Maybe she knew him too. Although we shouldn't make such jokes. But it is a small world. Get out of the shop. Breathe. I'm no longer steady on my feet. Not that I was anyway, but I'm now much less so.

A SMALL WORLD

Driving away from the deli, Abbie wonders if she should be looking for Beth's family rather than bothering with Faye. She's so shocked to see Ethan that her brain doesn't process her discomfort in seeing Faye so smiley. It's only when she's driving away, heading to the hospital, that she twigs what the smile is for. She pulls over and manages to shove the car door open before she's promptly sick.

"The world is too fucking small."

Nobody is listening, but it makes her feel better to say it to herself between spits. Thankfully, her trusty bottle of Evian is in the footwell of the passenger seat and she swills her mouth out before taking a few tentative sips.

Her brain is full of too much hangover to process thoughts quickly. So it takes her until she's parking at the hospital to work out that Faye just isn't interested in Beth's precarious condition. It dawns on Abbie that, while Ethan may not be Jack, he's the closest Faye can get to him. And whether it's because of her fragility or her selfishness, Faye isn't going to let Beth's plight spoil her second chance at happiness.

20 teaspoons

OLIVIA

My least favourite part of visiting Beth is the journey to the hospital. The journey on the bus is a slow one and gives me far too much time with my thoughts. I stare out of the window, hoping something or someone would catch my eye and drag my brain away from thinking about everything. The bus stops at a crossing. The guy who saunters across in front of the bus doesn't look familiar, but the lazy way he walks reminds me of David.

We were at sixth-form college together and it took us 18 months of the two years studying there to go from blushing at each other and staring at our feet to going out on our first date. After that, we'd been inseparable. We'd spent nights together at the cinema, but would always watch the film, leaving kissing to when we were in private. We'd walked hand-in-hand in the park, but talking more than snogging. We never went further than a heavy petting session when he felt my breasts through my clothes – I'd panicked when he did, calling him a perv and running off.

We got back together a few days afterwards, but he was never that brave again and my hope of losing my virginity before university slowly slipped away with each month of our last summer together. In the September, David headed down to Leicester and I went to Huddersfield. We wrote to each other occasionally – well I wrote three letters and received one very half-hearted reply – before going our separate ways. I would still have been a virgin when I met Matt if I hadn't been singled out by one of the third-year students as his cherry-picking challenge. I had no idea at the time and thought I must have a magical aura that attracted this older guy.

THE DEED

Once the deed was done, when Owen was no longer interested in Olivia, and his mates laughed about her being his puppy dog, following him round, Joanne, one of Owen's friends, was nice enough to take Olivia to one side to point out what was going on. Olivia was very grateful to her, even though Joanne's motives were not particularly pure. Joanne wasn't one to share the person she saw as her future husband. She was waiting for Owen to finish sowing his oats before making her move but didn't see anything wrong in helping the process along its path.

Olivia was very grateful to Owen too. He'd been warm and caring as well as a good teacher. He saw himself as some kind of Romeo, giving girls the chance to experience his loving. And although Olivia hated to think she was one of many, she was happy her first experience had been such a good one. What mattered more to Olivia though, was that she hadn't realised it was a one-night stand when she'd gone to bed with him. She thought it was more than that – and she knew she'd never be the type to sleep around.

Thankfully, Owen had finished his finals and left at the end of Olivia's first year, so she knew she never had to face him again. But when she should have been starting her second year, she just didn't turn up to campus. She'd spent so much time with him, either being chased by him or trailing round after him, that she hadn't made any friends and the last few months of her first year were really lonely. She wasn't enjoying her course either and realised she was quite happy with her small life and the security of her Mum's cooking.

Nobody in Olivia's family had been to university, and Olivia's Mum thought it gave people ideas above their station, so nobody berated her for dropping out. In fact her Mum was much more proud of her when she got herself a little flat and stood on her own two feet for the first time.

OLIVIA

I'm jolted into reality by the bus taking a sharp left and down a road that isn't on the regular route. I look out of the window and see mangled metal and police tape. My first thought is: "Is it Abbie's car?"

I know I should get off the bus to check, to make sure it isn't. But I can't move. My blood runs cold, freezing me to the seat. My teeth even start chattering. I take deep breaths to calm myself down.

Two stops later and I'm outside the hospital. I walk quickly round the line-drawn path to the main entrance, being passed by two ambulances on my route. Of course – any victims of the crash will be taken here. I run through the main entrance, ignoring the swinging doors up to the wards, and take a sharp left turn, following the red signs to A&E. There's a queue at reception and I try to speed it up by jiggling back and forth from left foot to right to left again.

Someone joins the queue behind me.

"Are you here for an emergency?"

I turn round, ready to defend my spot, and find myself facing a creature from *Splatterhouse* – Matt's favourite Xbox game.

"You were in the crash," I say. I just know.

The girl under the blood nods. She is easily 10 years younger than Abbie. For a split-second I feel an uneasy mix of relief and guilt – before the fear rushes back. The other car. That could be Abbie.

"The other car?" I ask her.

"A Mum and her two kids. I'm here to see if they're okay."

I collapse to my knees, wheezing. The waiting room spins. A nearby staff member in green scrubs helps me to the end seat of a row. I wave them away to let them know I'm okay and they turn their attention to the girl covered in blood. A muffled conversation later and the green scrubs lead the blood girl away.

I know I need to get up and find my way back to the stairs and Beth's ward. I breath in to "One finger, one thumb keep moving", breathe out to "One finger, one thumb keep moving", breath in to "One finger, one thumb keep moving", and out to "We'll all be merry and bright". I'm mumbling the words under my breath – just as Abbie and Beth have been. Maybe we're all moments away from madness.

After retracing myself back to the stairs up to Beth's ward, I decide to get the lift. I need to take it easy for the rest of the day. The doors open and I'm met by my reflection. Except my reflection is first surprised, then happy to see me, walking out of the lift to give me a hug. It's not my reflection; it's Abbie. I just hadn't expected to see someone familiar.

"I thought you were me," I mumble into her hug. "I thought you'd been in an accident. And then, just now, I thought you were me."

Thankfully, Abbie has seen enough craziness over the last week to take it in her stride and leads me to the hospital café. As I explain everything – from coming to the hospital the first time to find her drunk, to Matt's family not paying for a funeral, and from seeing the crash outside the hospital, right up to seeing her in the lift – Abbie squeezes my hand, my arms, my shoulders, hugging different parts of me to tell me to carry on with my story.

"You're not going mad."

She sounds very certain.

"We're all in shock. First Faye thinks she's seen Jack, then finds out Jack is dead. Then Beth collapses and I think she's taken an overdose. I drink drive and think my car has been stolen. Then Matt's Nan, and then his family. And Faye is avoiding all of us and only spending time with her friend Ethan. And, well, her friend Ethan. Well, Ethan…"

Her voice breaks.

"Is Ebbs."

OLIVIA

I shouldn't have let Abbie go. But she said she didn't want to talk. And when I say that I mean it at least 51% of the time. Instead I'm sitting in a chair next to the bed where Beth's body lies. I'm not sure Beth is still inside, although I've been assured by the nurses she's been drinking tea with some gusto. This is the quiet ward, where most patients lie in bed unmoving. The other side of the nurses' station is an orchestra of stomping and banging, or shrieks and whines. I almost wish Beth were one of the noisy ones.

I stand up and stretch. I've been up here over an hour now – I try to stay for at least an hour to make the journey on the bus worth it. I slowly walk up to the far end of the ward, and then meander back down again, keeping to the centre of the ward, between the two rows of eight beds. Only the end seat at the nurses' station can see down the ward and it's empty at the moment, so there's nothing or nobody to stop me wandering up and down. Except that I feel like I'm spying, that I'm invading their private worlds. I don't know if any of them are watching me, even if they can open their eyes voluntarily. Some of them look in my direction, but I'm not sure they see me. To them I'm just a pale skinny girl take timid, quiet steps on the scuffed linoleum.

I reach the end of the ward and start to turn when the person in the end bed catches my eye. For some reason the shape she makes on the pillow looks familiar. She is both puffy and swollen and a skeleton. But there is something about her forehead, the line of her nose, the curve of her chin that makes me know I know her. I daren't get any closer though: her breathing is ragged and I can't risk her waking up and screaming the place down when she finds me standing over her. I've had enough scares for one day. So I take slightly less timid and slightly squeakier steps towards the nurses' station and to the whiteboard above their heads. I count the beds down. One, two, three, four, five, six, seven, eight. Eight. In nurses' scrawl the name below is "S Muhhell". Who? Mutchell? Oh. Mitchell.

S Mitchell. Sophie.

For the second time today I find myself collapsing to my knees, winded. This time it's an auxiliary nurse wearing a pink gingham frock who comes to my rescue, helping me to one of the dark green padded seat that's always far more comfortable than I'm expecting. I slump into it, once again moulded to a seat, though this time I feel the temperature of my blood rising. She crouches down next to the seat, putting herself lower than me, making me feel safe, at ease. I point vaguely in the direction of the ward.

"Sophie," I say. "She's here."

"Your friend? That you came to visit?"

I shake my head.

"No, not a friend. Sophie."

As if the poor nurse is meant to know. But she is used to dealing with people who aren't connecting with the world 100%, so she explains she will get me a cup of tea. Tea is the main medication on this ward.

She returns with a mug just two-thirds full of tea, so I can't easily spill it with my shaking hands. And it's already cool enough to drink straight away, so I can't burn my lips. If only everywhere took such care.

"My friend Beth is here. I'm visiting my friend Beth. But I was walking the length of the ward – to stretch my legs – and recognised the person in Bed Eight. I came to check, saw Sophie's name…"

The nurse looks up. Nods at "S Mitchell".

"She bullied me at work. Made my life hell. She was so mean. So very mean. When Beth first came here and I saw all the people lying in these beds, too damaged to be in the outside world, I wished for all of them to get better. But I don't want Sophie to get better. She's better in here where she can't hurt anyone."

The nurse pats my knee. Sits down next to me. Waits for my breathing to become calm.

"When most people come here, they're visiting someone they love. They ask how this can happen to someone who's lovely, who's so caring, so smart. Then there are others who are going through hell and are grateful for the respite. Think of all the adjectives under the sun – positive and negative – and I've heard them said about the patients in this ward."

She glances down along the beds and I follow her gaze.

"And I say the same thing to them that I'll say to you. That everyone is fighting a battle. And that the ones who end up here have just lost the last round of the fight. I'm usually saying this to people asking why their loved ones are here. But it works the same way for bullies."

OLIVIA

The first time Matt speaks to me is when I wake him up on Wednesday morning to let him know I've ironed his smart trousers and dark blue shirt for the funeral. He's slept on the couch since he got back from the care home, snoozing between games on his Xbox, and giving the occasional grunt in my direction if I bring him food to eat. Crisp packets and Sprite cans are littered round his feet from the times he's fed himself. He recoils when I shake him awake, like he can't bear me touching him. I put it down to him grieving, accepting that I'm going to be the person on the receiving end of his loss and despair.

"I'll see you at the church," he says. "I need to clear my head first."

He then waits for me to turn to leave before starting to put his smart clothes on over days-old undies and I wait for the front door to slam before heading back into the lounge to turn it from a pig sty back into the homely lounge I pretend it usually is.

Once ready, I head down to the chapel myself, sitting in the second row. I don't want to make any assumptions about being a part of Matt's family and I know I could always move to the front row when he turns up. I just don't want to be sitting on the front row by myself when his parents turn up, wanting to know who the hell I am. I guess I'll recognise them from the photos Maggie used to have on her mantelpiece – which ended up on her dressing table when she'd gone into the home. But they don't show. Matt or his parents.

The service itself is as simple and impersonal as you'd expect a council funeral to be. And nobody gets up to say anything about who Maggie was when she was alive. Had other people in the chapel needed it, I would have stood up and said the lovely things I knew about her, but the other people in the chapel sat at the back, giving the impression they were here to respect the dead, rather than Maggie in particular. The building is dull and cold and full of dark wood that has been suffocated by too many coats of cheap varnish. At first glance the cream walls look as if they'd been aged with the cream paint they use in restored pubs. But it was a congealed mixture of age and death that made them look yellowed and grimy. The building feels no more loved than the people who end up here.

After the service, Maggie's coffin is taken to the nearby crematorium. I follow the hearse on foot, desperately wanting to be anywhere else, but never falling more than 20-or-so metres behind because of the traffic. I owe it to Maggie to be there – someone should be there. I'm relieved when it's finally all over and I can head home.

I used to think someone dying alone was the worst thing in the world. But now I know it's worse to have people out there who couldn't be bothered to turn up. You can be widowed or orphaned and have nobody special there for your final days, but still know you were loved and cherished up until that point. But to have a Son and Grandson unwilling to give an hour out of their day was far worse.

Back at home I attend to my grumbling stomach. I hadn't been able to face breakfast before the funeral but now need some comfort food. I make myself a brew and sip it while making some toast. I have two slices, Warburton's with Dairylea cheese, half a triangle per piece of bread. It's something my Gran had made for me when I was a little girl and I wanted to feel closer to her, to feel comforted by her, even though she passed away many years ago.

My thoughts turn to Matt again. I'd half expected his parents not to show, as they'd shown so little interest in Maggie's death or the funeral arrangements the council made. But I know how much his Nan means to him – how could he have missed her funeral?

NOT CONFESSING

Matt was missing for a couple of days before he came home again. He never mentioned where he'd been or why he didn't go to the funeral and Olivia didn't ask. She was too angry he hadn't shown to be able to ask him calmly where he'd been. But worse, she was scared to ask him and for him to open the floodgates. Being there for Beth. Fine. She was a good friend. Being there for Maggie. Fine too. She'd been a good person. But being there for Matt? Olivia was struggling with that one. So she let him carry on living a half existence on the sofa, not returning to work, while she carried on with her life as best as she could, relieved to be heading into work each day and the hospital each evening to escape the claustrophobic air that surrounded him. But she also didn't want to confess.

OLIVIA

It didn't want to have to speak to Matt. The only constructive conversation we'd had since the night at the care home had been about the wording for a headstone. Well, it was more a monologue from Matt, with me making positive, soothing noises in response to his suggestions. The silence between us was uncomfortable, but I knew if we spoke I'd have to tell him Maggie was cremated. And he would get angry and seethe heated words at me before he gave me a chance to explain it wasn't my decision. He wouldn't wait to listen to be told that the council is only required to bury someone for disease control purposes; that everyone who's not diseased gets cremated.

I only found out after the service, when I asked if she had to share a grave or get her own plain headstone. I was hoping for the latter because it would mean we could replace it with a personal one once Matt had decided on the words. If Matt had been there, he would have found from the chapel official the same way I did. But because he didn't turn up, he'd now only find out if he asked me. The official had explained to me cremation was better than the traditional "pauper's funeral", where she would have shared her final resting place with strangers in a shared grave, no headstone to mark out her spot.

So Maggie had been cremated and was sitting in something akin to a Golden Syrup tin or rusted tea caddy at the crematorium, ready to be claimed. Waiting to be claimed. And I'm hoping I won't have to tell him that's the case until some of his anger had dissipated, so I spend as little as time as possible with him. Although he seems to spend as much time as he can in my thoughts.

I'm sitting in the memorial gardens watching an old dear

drink tea from a flask. It's one of those old-fashioned chunky Thermos ones that are half a foot wide but don't even hold two complete mugs of tea. The gardens are quaintly pretty and have a haphazard mix of decorative garden stakes stuck in the soil between plants – a mix of gingerbread from the Christmas Markets and shabby chic signs from Homes section in TKMaxx – each one carrying the name of a person important to someone. The 6ft wall separating the gardens from the main road is covered in a mix of shop-bought mobiles – a fusion of hearts and butterflies. Between the miscellany of glossy wood and sleek wire, I catch glimpses of the occasional homemade wind chime, yet more hearts and butterflies, yet more carved names.

I have achieved very little this week. And the latest thing I haven't achieved is rescuing Maggie's ashes. I'm not allowed. You have to be a family member – and being the girlfriend of her Grandson isn't enough, even though it's my signature on all the forms. I should have lied about who I was. Right from the very start. Nobody would have known because nobody who knew her turned up. I can't get Matt to come here because I haven't told him yet. He still thinks she was buried. And at some point he's going to realise how stupid he was to miss the funeral and ask to see her grave. Although I'm hoping he never asks. So far I've only earned weary grunts, along with the occasional sigh and whatever noise rolled eyes make.

If left just four more days, Maggie's ashes will be scattered here, in the remembrance gardens, with amateur wooden sculptures dangling from strings and tea-drinking ladies for company. It's not the same as scattering her ashes in the sea at Lytham St Anne's where she used to go on holiday, but it's better than a shared grave. She'd be able to have her own sign: much better than no headstone.

The Second Cup

I shrug to myself. There is nothing to be done. I can't magic Maggie's ashes away from here. I can't help her any more than I can help Beth. Any more than I want to help Sophie. I can't reach Matt any more than I can reach Beth. Any more than Faye will let me reach her. Abbie is far too proud to ask for my help. And I'm unable to help myself.

21 teapots

BETH

Lift. Lips. Sip. Lift to my lips and sip. I'm getting good at this. Drinking tea is something I can do well. It's something I've done since as soon as I was allowed. Dad didn't want me to have any because it was hot and I might hurt myself. I told him he was being silly because I got in a hot bath on Sunday nights and it didn't hurt. And that was a whole bath full, and this was just a tiny cup that I couldn't even fit one foot in. This was another one of those times when Beth doesn't say something funny. Dad didn't say: "Remember the time Beth said the mug of hot tea couldn't hurt her because she got in a whole bath of hot water and it didn't hurt." He grinds his teeth instead. It was what he'd started to do when I said the wrong things. So I tried to make it right.

"But the cup is tiny. Teeny-tiny. Even my Sindy wouldn't fit in it and she's a grown-up doll. But that's because she can't bend her legs. Maybe if she could curl up she would fit, but only just. See Daddy," I say, dunking my hand in the mug, "See, look I don't fit."

The Second Cup

It didn't hurt at first. Then my hand felt like it was growing really quickly, ready to burst out of my skin. Mum dragged me to the kitchen taps and put my hand under the water that she made gush from the cold tap. I was half hanging off the kitchen counter, so Dad got the stool so I had something to stand on. My ribs felt sore, but I didn't say anything because I didn't want to get my dress wet if I had to put them under the tap too.

Afterwards, when we were sitting in the hospital waiting room, I thought that maybe I had the wrong words inside my head. Because when I spoke I said things that were funny or things that were naughty. I never said the right things. I thought it was because I was young: even though I wasn't a baby anymore and I was older than Grace, I was still younger than everyone else. That had made Grandma laugh, when I asked her if it meant I was the same age as her now. She told me that when she was with me she felt as young as me, and that was the best thing about me. I thought if it were a good thing she'd tell Mum, so Mum could see I could say the right things. But she didn't – she said: "Let's keep it to ourselves. Your Mum wouldn't understand."

I was shocked. I thought my Mum knew everything. But here was something that she wouldn't understand. I knew my Mum was old before her time because Grandma had said so. So maybe that's why she couldn't know. Maybe Grandma could be as young as me because she'd stolen the years from my Mum. I liked Grandma best and didn't want her to get into trouble, so I agreed we would keep it to ourselves.

It's a trick Grandma can't share though, not even with Grace. Grace is stupid. Now she is older and Mum wants another baby. But Grace is excited. She doesn't realise yet that the baby gets all the attention and soon she'll be saying all the wrong things. I'm scared because I don't want Grace to get Grandma. I got Grandma when I started saying the wrong things. I'm wondering when Grace will start saying them too. Will she need to steal the wrong words from my head? Will I get new words? The right ones? Except Grace doesn't say the wrong words.

And then Grace finally gets her own book. Not nursery rhymes, but about fish. I'm curious as to why it's not mine – I ask Grandma, telling her that I'm the one Mum always calls "fishes". Grandma laughs and says "She calls you facetious" – and once she's stopped laughing enough to speak, she tells me it means that I'm clever and funny. So maybe I do say the right words sometimes.

Lift. Lips. Sip. Lift to my lips and sip. The pink dress is very pleased with me because I've finished the mug of tea. It's stewed by the time it arrives, but I drink it anyway for something to do. My Mum wouldn't cope very well in hospital because all the tea is stewed. But I can do this. I can drink all the tea. The pink dress is really pleased. To show me how pleased she is, she tilts the cup towards the green pyjamas and to show them it's empty.

"Would you like a second cup?" the green pyjamas ask me.

He asks again, like a second cup needs a second question: "Would you like a second cup?"

Silver tip white tea

White tea is a rarity in Britain, where people drink various black teas as everyday teas and green ones for the health benefits.

Made from tender spring buds that are plucked before they open, white tea is the purest and least processed tea, going through just the withering and drying processes before it is infused in hot water and drunk.

Silver tip white tea is the most prized of white teas. It is rare and delicate and needs to be handled with care. Just like Faye.

22 teabags

FAYE

Six weeks too late. I can't believe I'm just six weeks too late. Just 42 days late. Or is it even 42? Maybe it's just 38 or 39 – not six full weeks, but what people like Ethan call six weeks because it's almost there, just missing one day plus a weekend. After days, no months, no years, of wondering, hoping, pining, aching to find out why, find out what had gone wrong between us, finding out I was maybe not even 40 whole days too late was unbearably painful. But without a time machine I had to accept that all hope had been lost.

Jack. Was. Dead.

Jack. Is. Dead.

It's his current state and it's not going to change.

He's dead and I've never felt more alive. My body is wired up to an extra power supply, twitching at my nerves and making my legs jiggle at my knees. Ethan holds onto me. He thinks he's helping but all his hug does is remind me of how different hugging Jack was, that the tiny crevices and pockets of air that formed between our bodies were the right ones and the ones Ethan and I formed were jagged and misshapen, like the edge of a rusted Yale key.

I'd also managed, by some tragic misfortune, to end up on Ted and Sylvie's doorstep the day of Jack's funeral. I can't help but feel that Jack was calling out to me somehow, that his presence was strong and I knew I could no longer wait. I wonder if, as I'd stumbled away from their house, poor Sylvie had stumbled over to the closest armchair so she could sink herself down into its protective folds of fabric, and poor Ted had stumbled over to the phone to call Ethan and warn him I was probably on my way?

So. Much. Stumbling.

Nobody was wearing moon boots that day.

With Ethan holding me, I realise I am as angry at that maybe-39 days not knowing as I am about the years not knowing. I wish I'd known Jack wanted to split up with me. I wish I'd found out after our second year. I could have thrown myself into my studies and come away with something better than a 2:2. Or I could have attempted to enjoy my university years the same way other single people did, by getting drunk and sleeping around. I hadn't worked hard because I knew Jack was the clever, more successful one and I would be the proud wife throwing dinner parties. I look back now and realise I wasn't living in the real world. We'd have both needed jobs if we'd moved down to London together just to afford something bigger than a matchbox. And exactly when did I expect to become this amazing cook in order to throw dinner parties? Or had I thought that takeaway pizza or Chinese would cut it? I'd loved the idea of little Jacks and Fayes running around, but in my fantasy there were no dirty nappies, just lovely kids playing in the garden in the sunshine. Yes, sunshine. None of this clouds and rain nonsense in my perfect life.

I didn't want to be a Mum though. Not really. Not the reality of it. And I didn't want to be a domestic goddess either. I'd actually wanted our lives to stay pretty much as they were, with us going to work instead of going to university. I was looking forward to no exams and no 3am coursework sessions. Looking back I realise that although I'd fitted Jack's student lifestyle, I was never going to fit his London life. If I'd given myself a chance to understand that at the time, maybe I wouldn't have wasted so much of my life pining after someone who was a chameleon – someone who never truly existed as I saw them because I only saw one side. Jack was enjoying his university years because he planned to buckle down and live a serious life once he'd graduated: a life I couldn't see him living, but one that he wanted all the same. Thankfully Ethan is ready to talk me through this all over again because he's been waiting for me to turn up. After a frantic call off Ted, with Sylvie wailing in the background, he's been expecting me to get in touch.

"Because you'd tracked them down, they assumed it was just a matter of time before you turned up on my doorstep," he explains.

As soon as the words "tracked them down" have left his mouth, he sees my face and regrets it. It confirms my fears that they still blame me for Jack moving so far away: that it was somehow my fault he died because it wouldn't have happened if he'd been nearby.

"So it's still my fault?" I ask. "All of it? Even him dying when I haven't seen him for years?"

"I think a little, yes," he says, hesitantly, realising he has to come clean, that I want the truth, but at the same time still trying to protect me from it all. "That doesn't mean she's right to though. She blames you because she actually blames herself and wants someone to share the guilt with. The way he died…"

The. Way. He. Died.

And what way was that? There's something not quite right about how Ethan stumbles over these words the way the rest of us stumbled over our feet six weeks before. He won't look me in the eye.

Ethan composes himself, starts again: "The way he died, you can understand why she's looking for answers, for reasons why. Then you turn up and Sylvie started to wonder if you were back in his life and that was the reason why: the missing link to understanding her Son's life – and this death. I told her you weren't."

I am grateful but also gutted as for a minute it is as if I had been back in his life – his missing link – if only just in Sylvie's mind. Thankfully, the gratefulness dilutes my anger for being blamed. And as the anger didn't really take hold of me, it seeps away, leaving me somewhat unscathed. So that's why Ted and Sylvie (mostly Sylvie) weren't happy to see me.

Ethan tries to make it okay by wrapping me up in one of the comforting, soothing hugs I remember from the months after Jack headed down south. We no longer felt like a rusty key. He's changed his aftershave to something more subtle, but he still smells like Ethan underneath and it is like being cocooned, being pulled back into the womb. I feel so incredibly safe, like I'm back where I belong.

That night Ethan and I sit up drinking tea (followed by rather a lot of wine) while we fill each other in on our lives over the last seven years. (Was it only seven years? It seemed a different lifetime.) We talk about my life and Ethan's life as well as Jack's. Well, we obviously talk about my life in relation to Jack's at the very beginning, but we got onto Ethan's life when I pull the photo of the two of them out of my bag. As I show the photo to Ethan I see a faraway look on his face, as if he is back there that day, just as my mind had done to me when I first laid eyes on the photo again just days ago.

"You took that photo. I remember your hair was blowing in your face and pissing you off, so you bought one those headband things…"

"Deely Boppers"

"…Deely Boppers, with pompom-type things on, to hold your hair back. You were wearing them when you took the photo and you kept saying 'smile for the aliens'. That was the sensible photo you took…"

Ethan's voice drifts off as he distracts himself, searching through drawers, muttering to himself about knowing where it was.

"Ah-ha!" he exclaims, taking two photos out of the third drawer down of the left-hand side of his rather beautiful but quite badly beaten bureau. It reminds me of the shabby chic furniture sold in some of the posher shops in Didsbury, except they have been painstakingly decorated to look old. This one was just old, and seriously well loved and well used.

He hands the first photo to me and for a second time I am back in that park. The boys are in front of the camera and I am shouting at them in a pretend stern voice to 'smile at the aliens', giggling so much as I take the photo that the image is slightly blurred from my shaking hands. I couldn't tell that at the time though: only when I went to get them developed – because the photos were taken with a cheap 35mm film inside a cheap plastic camera from Argos, and not with anything as sophisticated as the new-fangled digital camera everyone carries around in their smartphones without even thinking about it.

The second photo is of Ethan wearing the Deely Boppers and looking very proud of himself. His arm was in the foreground as he'd held the camera out in front of him to take the picture himself – a selfie, although there wasn't a name for them back then.

"I don't remember that photo."

"That's because you were busy snogging Jack when I took it."

I vaguely remembered Jack trying to wrestle my Deely Boppers off me, but it was Ethan who ended up with them – and the camera – when our play fight turned into a long kiss. I was suddenly aware of what that must have felt like for Ethan, going from a friend to the third wheel at a moment's notice. I threw him an embarrassed look, which he shrugged off.

"You two did that all the time, so I got used to it."

"Why on earth did you put up with us?" I ask him, but this time the shrug he gives as an answer is not accompanied by any words.

Feeling slightly awkward, I let the moment go and stare down at the two photos in my hands, trying to view the world from Ethan's perspective of never being able to spend any time with his best mate without the girlfriend – me – tagging along.

"I must have made life so difficult for you," I say. "I'm sorry. It never occurred to me to leave the two of you to it."

When I am met with another shrug, I feel something inside me about to snap. I need Ethan now just as much as I'd ever needed him. He'd turned into a flaky friend once and I wasn't going to let him do it again.

"I'm sorry, okay. I was head-over-heels in love with him to the point of being obsessed and it never occurred to me to leave the two of you alone because it never occurred to me that he'd want time without me. And although it didn't work out, looking back I don't think he did, not back at that point."

"He didn't," Ethan almost whispers. "He was making the most of his time with you so he had loads of memories to take with him."

"He was planning memories?"

A look on Ethan's face that I don't recognise – except I do: I'd seen it once before, when he'd hesitated.

"The way he died. What is it about the way he died? What's going on here Ethan?"

BORN FAULTY

The day Jack met Faye, he'd felt dizzy and light-headed. He'd felt faint during an induction session for his course. He'd gone along to the walk-in centre only after he felt a strange pounding in his chest. The doctor thought it was probably a panic attack – common in new students away from home for the first time – or possibly asthma. He'd been given an inhaler and told to take things easy. But it wasn't a panic attack and he didn't have asthma. Jack had Romano-Ward syndrome.

Jack had been born faulty. The irony wasn't lost on him. He had a genetic heart condition that could kill him – and one that neither of his parents had. Which meant only one thing: he was adopted. It had never occurred to him because he superficially looked quite like his Dad – although now he looked closer he only saw the differences. He wondered whether, if he told them about his diagnosis, they'd come clean. But he didn't want to tell them because it wasn't up to him to push the truth out of them. So he carried on knowing without them knowing he knew. And every day he knew, it ate away at him, until he realised he never wanted to share anything in his life with them again.

He also wondered if his biological parents knew he'd

been born faulty, if that's why he'd been given up. But he suspected he was a fault in their lives in other ways.

FAYE

"You knew he was collecting memories, using people, and you let him?"

Ethan looks horrified: "God no. I didn't know about that until recently. Jack's life has followed a destructive path and I called him on it recently. He got angry and I finally got the truth."

Ethan pauses. He looks at me with that look that says he's desperate for me to believe him. I nod that I do.

"Jack was pretty sure his condition would kill him," Ethan explained.

"Did it?" I ask.

Ethan shrugs uncomfortably: "I don't know."

TRAPPED

Ethan is trapped by this knowledge – the knowledge he's had about Jack's health and his adoption since he and Jack were at university together. The knowledge he's just lied to Faye about knowing until recently. He's trapped by it, and he knows it. As soon as he heard about the accident, he waited for the autopsy, waited to hear if it was definitely suicide. But the answer doesn't come. And nobody else knows to look for the question. If Ethan tells Ted and Sylvia now, they will want to know why Jack kept his illness from them. They will want to know why he, Ethan, the one they trusted, kept it from them – even though it wasn't his place to say. So he has to carry on lying to them by not saying anything. And the longer he leaves it, the more impossible it is to say anything.

FAYE

"I never got over him. I was holding onto something pure – something too pure. It wasn't real, was it? How could anybody compete with that?"

"Tell me about it," Ethan half-muttered under his breath.

"What?" I asked. He didn't answer. So I pushed him, asking him again. "What?"

"Well no guy stood a chance, did they?" he said. "And I've been on the receiving end of that."

"Really?" My ears perked up, grateful to get the conversation away from me and Jack. "So your time in London has been about unrequited love?"

Ethan sighed.

"You don't get it, do you?" he asked.

I half-shrugged and shook my head. He took the silence that followed as an opportunity to pick up the empty bottle of pinot grigio in front of us and head to the kitchen for a replacement. But I wasn't letting him off the hook that easily. I followed him, cornered him by the fridge.

"Come on, spill the beans. We've talked about how Jack ended up with some married woman, about how I never managed to replace him, and now it's your turn."

Ethan looked me straight in the eye.

"It's you. Okay?"

"Me?" I whispered.

"Yes, you. It was always you," he said, thumping his chest with his fist.

"I gave you a shoulder to cry on and I waited and waited. And then I left on the pretence that I was following him down to London because I couldn't bear to be with you and to not have you."

I looked at him dumbfounded. Jack had always joked

about Ethan having a soft spot for me, but I never realised he meant anything more than just being friends. I was aware of Jack's jealous streak but I'd never tested it out on Ethan because I loved Ethan far too much – I hadn't been willing to use Ethan to get to Jack. And God was I grateful for that now, knowing how he'd felt.

"By the end of your relationship I hated Jack. The way he treated you was treacherous. But now I understand why. He wanted a beautiful experience, the memories to hold onto, in case…"

"I had no idea, sorry."

"Sorry? You're sorry? Why, would it have made any difference?"

I tried to think back to those months when I thought I'd die because my heart was breaking so much. I shook my head.

"No. Well, yes. But to me, not to you. I didn't understand why you'd deserted me after Jack. One minute you were on my side and the next you wanted to be his mate again. It was like a slap in the face. It would have been easier for me if I'd understood why you left. After you'd gone I felt like I had nothing left."

He gave me a weak smile: "At least I meant something to you."

"Something? Are you mad? You were my rock. You kept me from crumbling long after everyone else was bored by me. And even before, while I was still with Jack, I loved you to bits. In some ways, my love for you was more real than mine for Jack because that was about striving for a perfect relationship whereas with you it was about accepting each other warts and all, like good friends do. After you'd gone, I looked round me and realised so had all my other friends: I'd driven them away. I went for years without any proper friends because I'd destroyed what I'd had at university. I was like a hollow person."

He pulled me into another hug; his strong arms wrapped around me like a warm blanket. He stayed like that just long enough to repair some of the aching inside me that had been there for a very long time. I felt a rush of love for him and squeezed him tightly. As we pulled out of our hug, the world fell into slow motion. I could hear his breath and mine making a pattern, like the irregular ticking of two clocks slightly out of kilter with each other. I was aware of how close his lips were to mine, of how much I hungered for his touch. I tilted my head – and it was all the encouragement he needed. It was the soft, moist and tingly kiss, the kiss you expected kisses to be like when you've never kissed a boy before.

COLLECTING MEMORIES

Ethan and Jack were accidental friends in the same university halls. Ethan was the one who went with Jack to the hospital, who'd stop playing footy whenever Jack struggled. He'd known all about Jack's illness: Jack's need to collect memories. Ethan had understood why, and he'd gone along with it without much cajoling. But now he had to lie to his precious Faye about it. He'd been sworn to secrecy. And he'd agreed.

He'd agreed in an attempt to appease some of the guilt he felt for knowing he was waiting for Jack to die so that it would be his turn with Faye. He knew he couldn't compete with Jack, but he had always been ready to pick up the pieces. But Jack didn't die; he just moved one. And once Ethan had filled his arms with pieces of Faye and found yet more discarded scraps of her that he could not manage, he had followed Jack down to London. If he couldn't fix Faye, he couldn't bear to be around her.

But now he was older, stronger. He knew he could hold her together this time. So when Ted had phoned to tell him about Faye arriving on their doorstep, he wanted to be all four operatic voices in *Bohemian Rhapsody*, from the deep baritone to the soaring falsetto, calling out her name. He willed her not to stop looking, to find him. It was perfect timing. It was too late for her to find Jack. And she could finally be his.

23 teacups

ABBIE

I pick up the bundle of post that I've been ignoring and take it with me into the kitchen. I flick on the kettle, going through the post idly as I wait for the kettle to boil, opening the different envelopes haphazardly as I get together the necessary tools for making myself a decent coffee. The normality of the tasks – after the hellishness of the last week – doesn't go unnoticed and I relish every part of fussing over coffee and faffing about with my post.

I leave the A4 envelope until last, sorting through the bills and random insurance, credit card and mobile phone offers first. It has the stamp of a solicitor's firm on so I know it's from Dominic. I'm not sure I have the strength to read it. He'd moved out within a few days of slamming the front door quietly and I'd been so focused on Beth that I didn't notice him go. A few things I considered "mine" had disappeared, but nothing of any sentimental value, so I was prepared to let them go.

When I phoned my solicitor to give her his new address,

she sounded very relieved to be sending the papers elsewhere. The never-ending trail of paperwork between us would now begin. I knew from experience that even a quickie divorce took forever, but at least Dominic was out of my life now, even though I didn't have the decree nisi yet, never mind the decree absolute. I knew I needed to read the letter so I'd feel prepared when my solicitor phoned to speak to me about it. I also knew from experience that the weight of every letter is far heavier than the paper it's written on.

But wait. What was this? My heart runs cold. There, in size 10 Times New Roman font – such little letters, such colossal damage – was what I hadn't feared because it had never occurred to me. Dominic wanted to fight me for half the house. I feel sick. I'd made the assumption that my marriage would be the only part of my life that was falling apart, and that I would be able to hold it together because I still had my job and my house. I reread the letter. It talked about taking our ancillary financial proceedings to court if I didn't agree to a 50/50 split. If I didn't agree? So that meant I could contest it? I know I have to get onto my solicitor. I root around in my bag for my phone, find my solicitor in my recent numbers and press to dial.

"Come on, come on," I mutter under my breath as the phone rings.

The dialling tone cuts out.

"Welcome to Wetherall Associates. Our offices are currently closed. We are open Mondays to Thursdays from 8.30am to 5.30pm and Fridays from…"

I cut the message short. Sunday bloody Sunday. I throw my phone down on the sofa where it bounces and ends up on the floor. That will be another iPhone screen cracked then. I retrieve it and sure enough there is a spider's web of thin cracks in the glass from the bottom left corner. I press the menu button: it's still working. In a few swift movements, I'm dialling Beth before catching myself out. I cut the call. Finding Olivia in my contacts takes slightly longer as I guiltily acknowledge her absence from my favourite numbers.

She answers straight away: "Calling for an update on Beth?"

I swallow, ignoring the guilt gurgling up from my stomach.

"That and to rant about Dominic," I admit. "I stupidly thought I was going to get away with divorcing Dominic scot-free and I've realised I'm not. He's after half the house."

The row of expletives that come out of Olivia's mouth as a response is so creative and expressive I have to laugh. It's my first laugh in a very long time.

ABBIE

Simple is only a five-minute walk from the Blue Pig, but it feels like a different continent. The Blue Pig represents the perfect end to every hectic week, but Simple is just another bar in the Northern Quarter – which is just too scruffy to be my favourite part of town. And I know I'll never meet work colleagues wining and dining clients on a corporate night out here. I don't feel totally at home here – like visiting your friend's house as a teenager and knowing their parents' rules are not going to match yours: the shock of watching your friend put her feet up on the coffee table while still in her school shoes and half wanting to join her while half recoiling at the thought of the mud and outside germs infesting the edge of the table.

"You go first" – that's what her nod means. I was ready to say "No, you", but something stopped me. Olivia was wearing her hair up in a high ponytail, her cheekbones catching and reflecting the morning light almost as much as the café bar windows did. So Olivia quietly sips her Blueberry Breakfast shake through her straw while she listens to me talk about how I'd bought the house by myself, how he'd only lived there eleven months, how although he'd paid half the mortgage during that time, he'd paid it as a regular lump sum along with an extra mini lump to cover bills and council tax. Everything was still in my name and even though we'd married, it'd felt like he was simply paying rent. Just a lodger in my life. I finish off by digging the solicitor's letter out of my bag and reading it to her.

"He's threatening me with a consent order," I said, reiterating the main message of the letter. "He wants half the house because of eleven measly months."

I looked at her wondering if she was going to reward me with another string of swear words, but instead when she spoke, she sounded calmer.

"It's not always a case of 50/50 in these situations. Faye's Mum didn't have to move out of the house while Faye was still young – the details matter."

"But we haven't got kids."

"It's not just kids though," Olivia explained, her eyes flickering back and forth slightly as she searched her head for the information she wanted.

"If your name is the only one on the deeds and your marriage has been short, it's very likely a judge would rule he's entitled to much less. Why else would he threaten you with court other than if he wasn't automatically entitled?"

"But how...?"

Olivia sighed and gave me a look that said she expected me to work it out for myself.

"Cruthers, of course," I said, remembering the small firm

of solicitors she worked for. I started to blush. "I've gone with one of your rivals."

Olivia gasped and we both crack up. Laughing seems to be a skill I'm regaining.

Olivia reaches for her empty milkshake glass and slurps the dregs up with her straw. The noise catches the attention of the barman-cum-waiter who comes over to see if we wanted another round. I nod emphatically and ask to see the drinks menu, a thirst for something stronger rising in my throat. I catch a flash of concern on Olivia's face, think about the car crash she saw, how she thought it might be me. I search out the shakes on the menu.

"How does an Oreo Cookie Crunch sound?" I ask Olivia. I'm rewarded with a big grin.

"Two of those then?" the barman asks. I match Olivia's grin, nod and hand the menu back, feeling very proud of myself.

BAND-AID BABY

Abbie wondered if she could get divorced from Dominic without having to tell her parents. Specifically her mother. Trapped in a loveless marriage to Abbie's father, she tried to fix it with a bulging bundle of flesh – a "Band-Aid baby". And when it didn't make her husband love her any more or spend any less time at work and more time at home, she found herself doubly trapped, with a baby she never wanted for herself.

Once Abbie had managed to piece this together, to understand the reason behind the levels of disdain she received from one parent, the levels of indifference from the other, she made a pact with herself that she would never stay in an unhappy marriage. It was only when Paul chose to end theirs that she realised how easily she could accept the same fate, and she started to understand the path her mother had taken. You didn't need love in a marriage for it to feel like a safe haven, especially if it came with the material comforts Abbie's father was able to offer.

So many years on, Abbie realised her mother no longer loved her father, and for that she was grateful. It meant her father was less capable of hurting her mother with his apathetic view of their union. But her mother had standards – and a lack of mutual insight into her Daughter's life – and there was no way she would see a second divorce in Abbie's life as anything other than a failure.

ABBIE

Although I hadn't wanted my parents' marriage, I'd been seeking it, undermining my relationship with Paul searching out the things that didn't matter. Paul stayed faithful to who he was, but once I was earning more I wanted to reward myself with the luxuries I'd seen in my childhood – the outward display of marital success my mother had clung to. At the time I was still angry with my Mum and I wanted to show her I could have those things too – and that I didn't need to live a life like hers to get them.

It's when I also started to treat myself to expensive bottles of wine – bottles that Paul was rarely interested in trying, so I'd drink the lion's share myself. I'd never explained to Paul just how isolating my childhood had been and how scarred I was on the inside from knowing that neither of my parents had wanted me. So all he saw was the person he loved changing into someone he didn't recognise. And his lack of support for my situation made me angry – made me push him away. I'd accepted that I was becoming my mother after all, that I deserved to lose Paul.

When I ended up with Dominic I initially thought I was getting a second chance at life, but after it turned sour my heart had sunk with the realisation that I was stuck in another version of my parents' marriage – a union between two people who couldn't begin to understand each other. And in between them there was Ebbs. And the less said about that, the better – although I knew I'd have to tell Olivia something.

And sure enough, another nod from Olivia. This one meant "Tell me about Ebbs".

"Faye always felt familiar and I didn't know why."

Another nod, telling me to go on.

"I recognised her but didn't know her. I realise now it's from the photos dotted about Ebb's flat. He had collections of them from university in multi-frames – him and the same two people, one girl, one boy. The boy I met, Jack, he was so self-absorbed. Ebbs just gave him all the time in the world and he never appreciated it."

"You met Jack? The Jack?"

"Yes," I say slowly, hoping Olivia picks up on the fact that I don't want to talk about him.

She does, and instead asks: "So why the name Ebbs?"

"He used to talk about 'going with the flow'. That's what he'd say every time I raised any issues about Jack. It felt he was cutting Jack some slack for a reason he couldn't share. I found it infuriating, so I nicknamed them Ebb and Flow. I knew the girl in the picture was something between them: often wondered if she were the reason Ebbs gave Jack so many chances, but they never talked about her. I guess I spent quite a bit of time staring at those photos, trying to work out the love triangle. I got to know her face – Faye's face."

"And now that we know Jack is dead?"

I shrug. I'm not sure what's going on between them. Is Ebbs just offering Faye a shoulder to cry on or is there something more? It certainly felt like "something more" back in the shop. Seeing him again had been more than a tad awkward, a disjointed jolt from a section of my life that wasn't me anymore – I wanted to get out of there, rather than stick around asking questions.

"Well it has brought them back together again. I'm just not sure what type of 'together' it is."

Olivia is quiet for a moment and I appreciate it. My mind is more spinning wheels than whirring cogs, free movement, no coordination between thoughts. Whenever I try to conjure up an image of Ebbs in my head, it's Paul's face I see.

"Hmm?" Olivia questions.

"Did I speak?"

"No, but I can almost hear your thoughts," she replies.

Olivia smiles and I understand with the full force of love why Beth chose to be friends with this fragile sparrow of a girl. She is one of those genuine human beings. Yes, some parts of her life are a mess. But she's open to forgiving the mess in anyone else's.

"Paul," I say.

"Yes. Life comes full circle."

Ebbs, Paul, Dominic. I did most of the talking, while Olivia filled me in about work and Beth's tea marathon in between our shake breaks. I drank my body weight in creamy gloop, but it had felt like a strange form of detox – clearing my mind of the thoughts of the men in my life while I replaced every last drop of alcohol in my system with lactose. So a few days later, when Olivia insists on me meeting her at Sinclair's Oyster Bar, a venue that sounds far more salubrious than the working-class, tattooed rugby boy hangout that it was, I agree.

Olivia isn't one to be impressed with the latest city centre construction of concrete, steel and glass. She is more likely to be found in a slapdash venue like Simple with mismatching furniture that predates the hipster craze for it. Sinclair's Oyster Bar was a rather more beautiful structure which now took pride of place alongside another old pub and Manchester Cathedral. I'd only known its current home, but I'd heard the stories from Beth about how it used to be hidden behind McDonald's and by a badly paved stretch of ground aptly named Shambles Square.

"Meet me upstairs," Olivia had said – and I realised I'd forgotten Sinclair's had an upstairs. I find myself searching through old memories in my head that appear with the renewed freshness of a photograph appearing like magic on a seemingly empty sheet of Polaroid film. I'd also forgotten there wasn't much to the downstairs, other than the space for the bar and enough floor for people to queue up two-deep.

Thankfully it isn't too busy and I'm able to find a space at the bar to stare at the selection in front of me, not recognising a single drink named on any of the pumps. It feels a bit like being back at Odd Bar or Trof, with their strange bottled beers, and the weird and wonderful flavours Beth likes to work her way through. After a minute of staring uncertainly at the bar, my brain twigs that I'm in a brewery pub. I'd never grasped the different concepts behind the standard pint – and only vaguely knew of the differences because of discussions between the suits at work about the superiority of real ales and craft beers over other pints. Thankfully, there's a collection of identical wine bottles in the corner. I don't need choice; I just needed wine.

"White wine," I ask the friendly-looking barman who catches my eye "– and lemonade please" I add. He smiles as he hunts down a glass for me. I feel the tension start to drain from my shoulders and realised I'd subconsciously been worrying they wouldn't even have anything I could drink as if it were the arse-end of civilisation, rather than a few hundred yards out of my comfort zone. I take a big gulp before heading upstairs, but stop myself before taking a second. The lemonade is hardly going to help if it has to compete with Olympic standard guzzling.

The upstairs is as small as it is empty: bigger than the downstairs but fewer people. There's a bar by the top of the stairs with its shutter down – they obviously expect people to head down for each round. "Maybe that's why Olivia said upstairs," I think to myself...

I'm halfway across the pub floor when I see a familiar face. But it's not Olivia. I try to move my legs, but they don't want to work, as if my feet were trapped in quick-drying cement. My mind flashes to Beth in hospital, to her only being able to move her legs when the covers are pulled back – as if they're not there when they're covered. It sounded bizarre when Olivia told me but makes perfect sense now. Who is totally in control of their whole body?

On the beach, when I was about 11 or 12, while other kids constructed castles with moats, I'd press my hands into patches of smoothed out sand pretending to leave handprints behind like the big stars did outside Grauman's Chinese Theatre on Hollywood Boulevard. My Mum would laugh – although she hadn't seen the funny side when I tried to put my hands in the cement of our next-door neighbour's newly laid front garden path. So she put the fear of God into me by telling me a horror story of someone who got stuck in quick-drying cement and died before anyone could rescue them. Looking back, the story now sounded extremely unlikely, but on the off chance of it being true, I was pretty sure that right now I knew exactly how that victim must have felt.

The familiar face staring back at me is attached to a body with working legs. Legs that get him up out of his seat and walk him over to my spot. I can't believe the face I see staring back at me.

"What on earth are you doing here?" I stammer.

24 teaspoons

OLIVIA

"This is Siobhan Riley, this is Liam Reeves, and this is Paul Casey."

Toby is introducing me to the team of lawyers we'll be joining now Cruthers is going to be Thricks & Cruthers, explaining how I'm the cornerstone of the office. My eyes follow a ripple of smiling – maybe slightly patronising – faces as I'm introduced to each one, Toby taking great care to make sure I'm introduced to everyone, knowing I'm the person most likely to be overwhelmed.

Paul Casey. Are life's discoveries really that easy? When Faye searched for Jack and Ethan, did she just pick their names out of a hat? He hadn't changed at all, except for his eyes being slightly craggy and his curls now wearing a respectable tinge of grey. I'd never met him but had seen his pictures in the photo album Abbie felt she had to keep in the boot of her car, even though Dominic said he was okay about her keeping it in the house. Her house.

OLIVIA

I need to tell someone about my serendipitous happenstance, so I start up a conversation about Abbie when I next visit Beth.

"I'm obsessing a little over her house situation. I'm not sure why. I think maybe if I focus on other people's problems, I don't have to think about mine."

I look at my companion for glimpses of awareness, for even the occasional weary sigh – glimpses of the progress I wanted to insist to the nursing staff she surely must be making. Nothing. I noticed her staring when I unzipped my right ankle boot to pull my rogue sock back up, but I've been told she responds to noises. I've left the zip unzipped because I can't bear another one of her synthetic stares, her empty eyes seemingly blind to anything around her.

When I first visited Beth in hospital, I longed for Beth to get well to the point where I could ask her the niggling question. Why she'd reacted so badly to the news of Jack killing himself. Now I just longed for her to acknowledge my existence. So far the only reaction the staff had seen in Beth was when a particular doctor had spoken to her. They believe he must sound similar to someone important in her life because what he said to her was innocuous – asking her if she'd like another brew. Since he'd spoken to her, she seemed to have been awakened to noises around her, like my boot zip, but didn't seem to respond to anyone else talking to her.

Each day, during the evening brew round, I would watch them put a mug of tea slightly out of her eye line. The first day they did it, I moved it in front of her – if she was going to attempt to pick it up, they should at least make it easy for her, surely? But I was scolded for my actions. And their strange game paid off. When the mug was directly in front of it, she ignored it. But on the edge of her peripheral and Beth would reach out, as if on autopilot, and picked it up. The first time I saw it, I had no idea I could get such enjoyment from watching someone drink a mug of tea.

"Hopefully, Abbie now has a new lawyer now who will stop Dominic in his tracks."

Nothing. No head tilt and eyebrow rising at the microscopic pause before I said "new lawyer" – something Beth would usually home in on like a hawk. I often stumble over my words, trying to hide any hint of anything unusual, but Beth would be able to read this too.

I miss her.

OLIVIA

I wonder if this is what undercover spies feel like. It's a bit like being back in the pit, watching the moves of everyone, getting a feel for when I can move without being pounced on by prey. But instead of assessing when it's safe to go to the ladies, I'm trying to work out when to pretend to be thirsty.

And there he is, Paul Casey, all 6ft 3in of him striding towards the kitchen area. His actions seem purposeful. Is he slowing down enough to use the kitchen? Or walking past to head to the gents or meet a guest at reception? He's slowing. Excellent. The perfect time to top up my glass of water. I quickly down the dregs, count to five to calm myself, and head to the kitchen.

I place my glass under the blue nozzle on the water cooler. There's a white nozzle too and I have no idea what the difference is, but I've noticed most people use the blue one, and I like to try to fit in.

"Do you know anything about housing law?"

Musing something to himself while choosing which pod to load into the Nespresso machine, it takes him a second to realise someone is talking to him. As he turns towards the direction of the voice he's heard, towards me, I hold my breath. If he does that frown thing that lawyers do when someone unimportant has pulled them from their thoughts, I'm going to struggle to like him. He doesn't.

"Sorry?" he asks pleasantly.

"Housing law? Do you know anything about it?"

He looks pained. I'm not sure if it's because I've asked him a work question in one of the few breaks he'll get today or if it's because he has to say "No". I know he's going to say "No". I already know he knows fuck all about housing law.

"I'm afraid that's not my area of specialism. You could…"

"Oh that's a shame." I cut him off before he can tell me who to talk to. He's so shocked he reacts physically as if I've stepped into his personal space. I try to channel Beth's thick skin.

"My friend Abbie is getting divorced. Her second husband is making moves on the house even though they've been together just 11 months. I was hoping to reassure her that he can't take half. I don't suppose you know her do you? Abbie?" I take a deep breath. "Abigail Rachel Tomlinson?"

And yes he does.

His body is a choir of atoms inside his expensive but understated suit and they sing in harmony at the sound of her name. Excellent.

"Abigail… Tomlinson?"

"Works for Schmitt Thomas Smith," I add, helping him along, reassuring him that, yes, this was the right Abigail Rachel Tomlinson.

"What a strange coincidence."

"Oh really?" I ask, trying not to look smug, trying not to blurt out "Not really, as I've already figured out you're her first husband and I've already sneaked a look at your HR file to check you're not remarried".

He looks at me sheepishly as if he's going to confess to something.

"I didn't realise she'd remarried. You see," he pauses – I see a glimpse of "Am I going to say this?" flash across his face – "I'm her first husband."

The surprise on my face is real. Not because I didn't know, but because I'm shocked this is so easy.

"Oh. Oh I see. You're that Paul Casey. Wow."

I then shut up and leave the air free for him to fill. It takes a few seconds of awkward silence for his Britishness to kick in, but soon he is filling me in on how they met, how long they were together, anything to fill the potentially uncomfortable pause in our conversation, to stop it from swallowing us both whole.

A LESSON IN NONCHALANCE

Olivia had hoped Paul would end the conversation with the admission that he'd love to see Abbie again. But she wasn't perturbed when it didn't happen. She just channelled more of her "internal Beth" as she liked to think of it, painstakingly waiting for a couple of hours to pass before emailing him, nonchalantly asking him to join her and Abbie for a quick drink after work one evening. Paul didn't have her two-hour willpower, emailing back just five minutes later, suggesting Sinclair's Oyster Bar "maybe tomorrow night". One pushy phone call to Abbie later, and it was all set up.

OLIVIA

"I want to know where my Nan is buried."

I knew I wouldn't be able to share my little victory with Matt. But I had hoped to enjoy it myself this evening, to cuddle it inside my head. Paul was expecting to see Abbie, but for some reason I'd chosen not to tell her, to let her think she was meeting me. I'd behaved more like Beth and I knew, in this instance, I needed Abbie to be like Faye. Only she wouldn't be. She would think of a million reasons why she couldn't go to the pub, why seeing Paul again was wrong, even though whenever she talked about him the whole world surged with a rose hue.

"I don't know where your Nan is," I said – leaving off the word "buried". It's true. I didn't know exactly where she was: still in a tin waiting to be collected because the staff at the crematorium had fallen behind on their sprinkling duties, or dust collecting in piles round the stems of flowers and the bases of homemade memorials to those who'd had their tins shaken out there months or years before her? I didn't want to think about it. I wanted to remember Maggie as the warm and caring person she'd always tried to be – that I'd only seen slip when she talked about her Son.

"I tried to explain to you on the day of her funeral that they can't tell me anything because I'm not family. They were expecting you or your Dad to…"

He storms out of the lounge and out of the flat. The front door slams behind him. After a millisecond of worrying, I realise I no longer care. A sense of peace descends me, and my flat, for the first time in months.

I'm channelling Beth again. Beth is reaching into the cupboard under the sink and digging around for the roll of black bin bags. Then she's pulling them off the roll one at a time, filling them haphazardly with clothes and DVDs, wrapping bulky jumpers round the X-box in an attempt to protect it – although maybe that bit is me channelling myself because I can't bring myself to drop it into the black bag from a great height in the hope that it breaks. Am I being kind? Or do I just want to make sure he keeps busy enough with his games not to miss me? I don't stop until all of his stuff is in bags, knotted at the top, piled in the hall. Then I clean. Everything. Scrubbing him out of my life forever.

I'm awake seven minutes before my alarm is due to go off. I have a heightened sense of the day beginning. I didn't hear any banging or swearing last night, so I'm assuming Matt didn't come back to the flat. A peek through the gap in my bedroom door reveals black bin bags innocently staring back at me from where I neatly piled them the day before. He's not here.

What would Beth do? I have no idea. But while I mull it over, I get myself ready for work, eating a decent breakfast for the first time in weeks. I usually struggle with more than a piece of toast in the mornings, but I'm ravenous. I pick up the Dairylea box from the bottom shelf of the fridge, but it's so light I know it's empty before I open it. Why put it back in the fridge empty?

I open the cupboard by the cooker and reach for the peanut butter – my toast-topping back-up. Thankfully, there's enough caked on the inside of the glass to thinly cover two pieces of toast. And after wolfing them down I eat the rest of a packet of chocolate digestives except for the two at the top that felt slightly mushy. I make myself a strong coffee. Today is the kind of day that needs a bitter kick of caffeine.

What would Beth do? As I hesitantly sip my disgusting coffee, I wander round my little flat, taking in how it feels alien and more like home at the same time without Matt's stuff coating every surface. I walk into the hallway and stare at the front door of the flat, worried that Matt will come through it any moment. I stare at the distressed-effect coat hooks that now hold just my summer jacket, winter coat and a couple of forlorn scarfs. I notice the stains round the lock from where hands have been too many times – a patch I missed when I cleaned the flat. Doors. Skirting boards. What else did I miss? My eyes gaze down to the second lock. The deadlock. The lock to which Matt has no key.

I don't need to know what Beth would do: I know what I would do – what I will do. I'm back in the kitchen, I throw the rest of the coffee down the sink, and then dive into the mess that is the draw above the pan cupboard, the one filled with all the rejected and anonymous items of life, the ones too important to throw away, but meaningless or pointless in everyday life. I feel around through the assault course of paperclips and rubber bands, push aside the stockpile of batteries and the fluff-coated depleted roll of electrical tape. And there it is. The key to my freedom.

I take out my posh writing set from the next drawer and write Matt a note, telling him about the funeral, the cremation, Maggie's ashes waiting to be picked up. I fold it, put it in an envelope, wincing at the taste as I lick the envelope to seal it.

I open the front door and pile the black bin bags in a heap outside, then place the envelope addressed to Matt on top. Then I take my coat down off the pegs and quickly shrug my arms into the sleeves, grab my bag, and pull the door shut behind me. I put the freedom key in the lock and use all my force to try and lock it. It locks first time.

The Tea Moth

The *Parametriotes theae* – otherwise known as the Tea Moth – is the enemy of the tea bush.

The Tea Moth lays up to 70 eggs on the tea plant in a season, the larvae boring into the heart of the plant, gnawing their way into the cortex, eating through the stems, making tunnels throughout the plant and emerging from the shrub when mature.

As the tea plant is destroyed from the inside, with few visible signs of infestation, the damage is usually discovered too late to save the bush. This is how Beth used to feel. But she doesn't feel that way now.

25 teapots

BETH

I squeeze my fists together, my fingers merging into a single mass. I look down at them half expecting them to be dissolving into my palms, as if I were losing my skeleton, my bone turning into a gloopy, pulpous mess: for my skin to become a hard pupa and cocoon my whole body, to ready me for my metamorphosis into a faded grey moth. Ready to fly away from here.

Not a butterfly. Faye would be a butterfly. She would dress up as a magnificent creature, pale wings decorated with huge eyes. She would flap around you in an attempt to get your attention, all colours and swirls, as she had done that evening with her tales of NOT-Jack. And Olivia. Olivia would be a butterfly, tentatively flitting about, landing on each person, before flitting away again just as fast. And Abbie would be a butterfly too. An elegant body eclipsed by strong curved wings.

No, this was no magnificent, resplendent transformation. I was merely a small, insignificant creature stumbling blindly to the next stage in my ordinary life, fumbling towards the obvious conclusion of spending my days head-butting light bulbs with reckless abandon. And that's okay. I don't need to be a butterfly. Moths can still flap their wings and fly.

I know I'm not actually flying. I'm not mad. This is not the mermaid episode all over again. I know I'm lying in a hospital bed surrounded by people who seem to be a heady cocktail of lost, helpless and angry. I don't know if I am like them. I think I feel lost and helpless and angry on the inside. But my outside is broken. I've forgotten how to translate myself to my limbs. I no longer talk my body's language. My tongue no longer forms English.

I've been mulling over the things happening in the outside world while I've been trapped here in this bed, trapped in my head. Faye losing Jack, Faye finding Ethan, Ethan hating Jack, Abbie recognising Ethan, Abbie still loving Paul, Olivia tricking Paul, Olivia tricking Matt. Out there – in what they call the real world – is no less messy than this psych ward. The only difference is that people out there are still trying, still functioning: people in here have given up, and not necessarily of their own volition. But I'm ready to try again – to fly again – because the girl Olivia hates has gone.

At first I was too wrapped up in the creamy-grey brain mush inside my skull to realise anything was going on. But then I'd notice the sideways glances Olivia made to the dark-haired girl in the nearby bed, her face so distorted by the shapes and angles it formed that she no longer looked like Olivia. At first I couldn't work out what it was I was seeing, and it's because I'd never seen it on Olivia's face before. It was hatred. Hatred and fear. Whoever The Girl was in the bed near me, Livvy didn't want to see her ever again. I became fixated on her, watching her erratic behaviour.

Sometimes she would strip down to her knickers and twirl around the room, singing and giggling. Other times she would sit on the floor – usually not wearing very much – moaning and rocking. No matter if she were twirling or rocking, a staff member would come and wrap The Girl in a blanket, hush her back to her bed and give her something to help her sleep.

It was early evening, after visiting hours were over, when nurses and doctors collected at the side of The Girl's bed. The Girl did not respond to the nurse's call to sit up and take her drugs – insubordination of the highest level on this ward. The nurse shook her shoulder. Then touched her neck. Then they called for the doctor and he did the same. Notes were looked at. Paperwork was filled in. The curtains were drawn round her bed.

The rest of us waited a long time for our drugs that evening. But even the most detached and unstable on the ward knew it wasn't the time to play up. So we all behaved and waited for the tiny circles of humanity to be handed out for us to swallow. You'd almost think we didn't need them.

It was much later, when most of the rest of us were either sleeping or in a drug-induced slumber, when they came back, drew back the curtains, pulled the sheet over The Girl's head, covering all but a few rebellious curls of dark hair, and wheeled her bed quietly off the ward. By the morning, an empty bed stood innocently in the space where she had been. And The Girl's name had been wiped off the board above the nurses' station. And I knew I had to get myself better because I couldn't die in the place where The Girl had. The Girl may be gone, Jack may be gone too, but I now had something to live for.

ELIZABETH ZEBRA

With a surname like "Adams" Beth got used to being first from a very young age, especially when it came to dreaded events such as childhood jabs. Beth could distinctly remember standing in a corridor by a set of swinging doors – not unlike the ones where the gymnastics coach talked to her Mum, but this was before that had happened, so Beth doesn't notice the coincidence until she's reliving both events in her memories. She makes a mental note to only stand near doors with proper handles from now on.

Beth was at the front of a queue waiting to see the school nurse, the left sleeve of her school jumper and school shirt haphazardly rolled up together into a makeshift armband just below her shoulder. Beth clenched and re-clenched her fists as if preparing herself, her arm already aching in anticipation.

She could remember one of the nicer teachers standing next to her, telling her in a hoarse whisper that she had to be brave or she'd scare the rest of the kids in the line behind her. She remembers the power she felt in that moment, as if the fate of her fellow pupils rested in her hands.

When she told the nurse what the teacher has said, the nurse told her she was lucky to get it over and done with. "The fear of an injection is far worse than the needle ever is in reality," she explained. She also said Beth should be glad her surname didn't begin with Z, and Beth spent the rest of the day wondering what it would be like to be called Elizabeth Zebra.

If she'd been Elizabeth Zebra she would have sat at the back of the classroom during Friday afternoon maths tests. The teacher gave out the papers at the front first, turned upside down, and worked her way to the back of the class.

Beth would stare at the piece of A4 paper on her desk, willing her eyes to see through it and give her a head start on any hard sums. Friday playtime was always spent with gaggles of girls in her class stressing about the Friday afternoon maths test, some repeatedly saying how they were going to fail.

Beth would feel worry build up inside her like bubbles from drinking ice-cold lemonade too fast. She would line up first at her classroom door, be first in her seat, and be the first to have the tortuous piece of paper on her desk. But then they would be given permission to turn the paper over, and Beth would see a row of easy sums the same as the ones they'd done in maths class that very week. Beth usually got 100%.

Getting 100% on tests didn't mean you could decide what you had for dinner though. Even at Christmas.

Sprouts. They were a new addition this year because there was a feature in the free Tesco magazine covering how getting them right was the key to a perfect Christmas dinner. Beth had never eaten them, but she was fearful of them because of Charlotte's near hysterics at having three put on her plate. Christmas was meant to be about good things, including being allowed to drink fizzy pop out of a can, so the presence of three round green brains on her plate greatly concerned her.

She drank her lemonade slowly, making sure it didn't bubble up inside her and making sure she still had some to wash down the balls of evil on her plate. She watched Charlotte soak her green brains in gravy, mash them up and mix them with potato. For once, her sister seemed to have an excellent idea. So she started to copy her until her Dad told her off for "Playing with her food".

"But Charlotte…"

"Just because she has, doesn't mean you should copy her."

"But you didn't tell her off."

"I'm telling her off now."

"No you're not" – which Beth mumbled so quietly she might have just said it in her head. Angry, Beth stabbed a sprout with her fork and bit into it. And her thoughts turn to how boring it is as a food. She had no idea what Charlotte was making a fuss about – and why she was wasting perfectly good boiled potatoes, best enjoyed sliced, by mashing them.

Charlotte had been given a perfect school report, which was far more important than getting 100% on your maths test every week. The reward for a perfect report was being allowed to drink her lemonade out of one of the posh glasses, her ice cubes making chinking noises each time she picked up her glass. Beth didn't care for the glass or the ice cubes, but she was jealous of the bendy straw Charlotte got in her drink. There weren't meant to be any straws, they were wasteful, but Charlotte didn't like the way the ice cubes hit against her top lip when she drank. And even though they were just frozen chunks of water, Mum said she wasn't allowed to waste them by putting them in the sink.

So Mum sighed and fished out one of the bendy straws left over from Grace's birthday party three months ago. And Mum made it clear you only got a bendy straw if you drank from a glass with ice cubes. But you also get on if you're called Grace and Charlotte gives you hers when you cry. Beth closed her eyes tightly and remembered that she liked drinking out of a can best – that was one of the special things about Christmas. So she drank her lemonade resolutely from its can every year, even when she was easily old enough to be trusted with a glass without the perfect school report.

BETH

The fear of the taste is far worse than the food. The fear of the test is far worse than the questions. The fear of the injection is far worse than any needle. The fear, the waiting, that's the worst bit. So I'm not waiting any longer. I need to get on with life. I'm ready to reach out. Ready to get things said – get them over and done with. So I sit upright in bed, waiting my last wait. And with almost immaculate timing – at the start of visiting hours just 37 minutes later – Olivia walks in.

"The Girl," I say to her, my words slow, my tongue thick. "The Girl has gone."

Livvy looks at the empty bed and then back at me.

"And the motorbike," I add. "It was the motorbike."

26 teabags

FAYE

The. Penny. Drops.

I'm back in a library. This time the one at Manchester University, sweet-talking the security guard into letting me through without the library card I don't have. Outside the building is an ugly brick bunker. I'm getting used to libraries not looking like libraries. Inside it feels more futuristic but still very much for students. It reminds me of those 24-hour gyms that aliens who look like humans use. Metal and glass and bold colours. Purple. I'm assuming that's the university's colour. I don't remember them having colours when I was a student.

I've discovered a book on Romano-Ward syndrome. It's also purple. *Childhood Disorders Diagnostic Desk Reference*. It covers Romano-Ward in a way I don't understand, talking of long QT, which just makes me think of Q-tips – the name my mother used for cotton buds. I remember her sitting on top of the toilet seat, me kneeling on the bathroom floor, my head turned sideways on her knee. Her using the same cotton bud over and again to clean my ears, it feeling cold to my skin from the second delve onwards. It used to make me cough, which annoyed her as if I coughed on purpose. Afterwards, she would bend the used ones in half, as if the orange gloop on the ends wasn't enough to warn people they weren't new ones. I now have my own such habits. Like twisting my curls round a biro when I think. And cleaning the nails on one hand using the thumbnail of the other. Is that what we become? A long list of quirky behaviours that we mistake for fully formed human adults?

The older I get, the more questions I have – and the fewer answers there are. Thankfully, I have learned something from my purple book – how Jack was able to keep any heart surgery scars from me. He didn't have any. No. He'd have been treated with beta blockers, to decrease the electrical stimulation of his heart. Does that mean loving me made him more sick? He was always so healthy. Went to the university gym – back when gyms were scruffy and sweaty and didn't look like this library. He always ate well, took his vitamins.

They. Weren't. Vitamins.

COFFEE TAMING

Faye watches Ethan's morning routine with feigned interest. In his house in Berkhamsted, his routine comforted her: now it irritates her. So many things have to be done a particular way before they can leave her flat. The flat she shares with two other artists she has always loved. Bohemian. Full of light. Except now it is impractical, messy. From where she's sitting now, watching him, swinging her legs, Ethan reminds Faye of Abbie. She is not surprised they found each other, even in a city as big as London. They both have patterns. Routines. Habits like bent Q-tips or curled hair wrapped round pens but for every moment of every day.

Ethan's mood had shifted since he saw Abbie. It's why Faye hasn't gone to her to find out if she got the chance to meet Jack, of what she thought about him. She realises she doesn't want to know what happened when Abbie was around. This wasn't a stone Faye would just leave unturned. She planned to plant the heel of her moon boots on top of this stone and firmly twist it into the sticky mud of life. Stamping and twisting until all that was left on the surface was a swirl of disturbed dirt.

Faye is sitting on a stool at the makeshift breakfast bar, a narrow section of kitchen countertop supported by the wall and two unrealistically skinny metal poles. It's too narrow to fit under properly, so she has always eaten her breakfast while sitting sideways, her spoon-free arm resting haphazardly on the surface. But this wonkiness makes Ethan stiffen, so she tries to sit up straight as she eats her Shreddies. Even her choice of cereal is questioned.

The first morning in her flat, Ethan even turned down a mug of Nescafe Blend 37 – an expensive everyday choice for someone on a deli salary. Instead he chose to get a croissant and coffee from Starbucks. Faye watched him eat and drink absentmindedly as he crossed Piccadilly Gardens without looking, not appreciating the sustenance that has cost him a small fortune, not noticing the small details of the world around him. He reminds Faye of Subway-coffee-drinking-NOT-Jack. She had wished for him not to be a person in a suit. Then she had wished for him to be a better version of a person in a suit - an Illy-coffee-drinking-suit. She doesn't know how to feel about a Starbucks-drinking-suit. The fact he's wearing smart jeans during his time off work doesn't matter.

In the deli they have four different beans to choose from

and all customers have their favourite. Faye has managed to tame the Elektra Barlume better than anyone else on staff, people popping in for an extra coffee whenever they see her behind the till. The Barlume reminds Faye of the art deco cinema in Stretford – forlornly left to rot while the soulless shopping mall diagonally opposite is lavished with money in an ode to consumerism – or the front fender of a mercury street rod, like the "greased lightning" ones from *Grease*.

This morning Ethan is brewing Taylors' Rich Italian in a hastily bought cafetiere. As a small act of rebellion, Faye has chosen to drink tea. Sitting upright at the breakfast bar, Faye jiggles her knees anxiously. Ethan stares at them, annoyed. Faye uses every inch of willpower to stop them. It has been too long since she bounced along in her moon boots – every step with Ethan is measured. She needs to escape. To jump on a train. To be anywhere but here.

FAYE

I'm back in Blackpool, but this time there's a storm. Rain is pouring down inside my skull and a naughty child is stomping through the clear puddles of my mind in bright red wellington boots, rippling my thoughts until they are as distorted as my reflections. I'm back in Blackpool, but this time I'm deep inside the maze that is the hall of mirrors, different versions of me staring back at me no matter which way I look. I seek out my true reflection, but I have no idea who I am anymore.

Maybe all of these reflections are me: perhaps I've become a fragmented version of myself which will forever bend and bow. There is the "me" that still wants Jack after all this time, even though I now know it wasn't real. There is the "me" that wants Ethan because he is the one pure thing still left from my past. But dancing in the mirror behind tha me is another "me" who mocks me for even thinking this is the case. The mocking me thinks I want Ethan simply to be close to Jack again and to attempt to live the life I feel was cruelly ripped away from me even though it was never meant for me in the first place. The image in the warped sheets of silvered glass isn't just looking back at me: it is also looking back at my past and finding it wanting.

The hall of mirrors at Blackpool Pleasure Beach is part of the "Impossible" experience. That's how my life feels – impossible to navigate. The mirrors are like an echo of my existence, fading as they get farther away from the real me, the first voice. I call out a "Hello" and it fades into "oh-oh–oh–oh" before turning into cackling laughter. It isn't just my warped, convulsing reflections staring back at me in this hellish fairground experience. I am also surrounded by laughing clowns too, their garish clothes and vacant faces glaring back at me from behind their glass boxes as they jolt and sway with frenzied, almost maniacal laughter.

I wake up startled by the vibrancy of my dream. Ethan's hot body is inches from mine, but I choose not to hug him as he seems cold and unwelcoming. I feel dizzy.

"The dizziness. It wasn't migraines, was it?"

I can hear the accusatory tone in my voice, but I can't help it. I've been lied to all this time – seven years of carrying a lie round because nobody corrected it with the truth – and the only person who can clear it up didn't seek me out to tell me. I had to find him. And now he is right in front of me, I want to know everything.

Every. Last. Detail.

"Was it?"

Ethan wearily shakes head and I realise he's gone through similar trains of thought himself, working out what was the truth, and what was Jack covering up his illness.

"So? Did he kill himself?"

Ethan shrugs again. This time it's a pitiful effort, a struggle, held down by the weight of the pain of his silence. Silence that he can only break with me. He can never admit this to anyone else. We are bound together forever because of it. We will never know if Jack killed himself or not. And I realise that Ethan will never leave me because of this. He needs to keep me close; keep me complicit. So he may not be Jack, but with Ethan, I now have a NOT-Jack forever. Whatever train I jump on, I'll have Ethan at my side.

I. Will. Never. Be. Alone.

27 teacups

ABBIE

In the taxi back to mine, I scrunch my toes up in my shoes, left then right, then left then right, marking out how many buildings I passed. If I reach home on an even number, things will work out for me and Paul. If it's uneven, I'll spend the evening feeling wonky, unable to right myself.

Paul squeezes my hand. I glance up at him and smile, losing where I am with the buildings on my side of the road. I now won't know when I get home if it's odds or evens. I'm hoping it doesn't matter. When we get outside my house, I squeeze both sets of toes as tightly as I can inside my shoes. I want to feel as even as possible. I want this to work out.

I manage to keep them clenched as I get out of the taxi and hobble to the door, knowing Paul will blame the height of the heels I'm wearing – he shakes his head at me fondly. But better that than me relaxing my toes and risking the wrath of fate.

The next morning, my toes ache. I think I must have slept with them scrunched up for good luck. I unfurl myself from Paul and from the duvet and push one leg out from under the warmth of the covers. My foot stares unassumingly back at me. My toes are slightly pink, but my ankles look fine. Not swollen at all. That was the first sign.

SWOLLEN ANKLES

Abbie had known there was something awry with her body the way only a pregnant person can. And it wasn't just the swollen ankles, swollen abdomen and swollen breasts. The tiredness and the backache that she'd put down to too many long days and too many late nights had reached the heights where they could no longer be ignored as symptoms of something bigger.

The pregnancy test was a mere formality: a wand to wave magician-like at Ebbs in a "look what we've made" kind of way. Except that she didn't want to wave anything at Ebbs, except maybe a hand to shoo him away. She had a little person growing inside of her and it was half Ebbs and she didn't know if she wanted it. And until she knew, she wasn't going to be able to tell him.

The secrets and the waiting and the decisions. They all became nothing when the pain came. It didn't just rip her in two: she'd felt hung, drawn and quartered, her mind flitting back to history lessons at school, to the horrors of the centuries gone by where people who betrayed the crown were subject to a slow and humiliating torturous death. Abbie felt like she was suffering a similar agonising fate, but all she could think of was the little person inside of her, that they were probably dying in her place.

Ebbs rushed her to A&E, knowing something was terribly wrong, but having no idea of the cause. At that point Ebbs simply cared about Abbie – and she realised she could have told him. But it's too late for confessions, so she must speak in whispers with the hospital staff. A positive pregnancy test confirms what she tells them in hushed tones. An ultrasound scan confirms the worst. Nothing in her uterus.

An explosion in her right fallopian tube. The worst type of ectopic pregnancy. A medical emergency. Abbie rushed into theatre, crying for herself, for her dead baby, for anything to make the pain go away. She cried out – the sounds began to form the name "Paul" – and she quietens herself with her fist in case Ebbs is near.

Later, after a straightforward laparoscopy, she was moved to the recovery ward, her ruptured fallopian tube removed. Her baby removed. The part of her and Ebbs that she didn't know if she wanted she now so desperately craved. She knew it was the hormones pulsating round her body, but that knowledge didn't stop her womb from aching for the life that never was.

Later still, she was at home with Ebbs, the two of them coming to terms with the pregnancy neither of them supposedly knew about. He thinks it is easier that way: that they never got to know the idea of having a baby before it was taken away. She agreed, nodding, trying to hide the waves of grief for the baby she'd known about for three weeks. And along with that grief, she needed to come to terms with a diagnosis of pelvic inflammatory disease causing damage to her fallopian tubes. The reason her baby didn't make it to her womb. The potential damage it may have caused to her other fallopian tube. The problems she may face conceiving safely in the future.

She comforts herself with "at least" – the motto she has come to live her life by – that at least they didn't have a Band-Aid baby. So Abbie knew she needed to be grateful alongside her grieving. To not be trapped by a baby like her mother was.

And then later still, none of it matters. Shortness of breath, followed by feeling faint, followed by yet more pain. Another hurried journey to A&E. Another visit to theatre. A nasty infection. Another tube removed. Just isolated ovaries swimming around inside her, with no connection to her womb. No way to make any more babies, Band-Aid or not.

And then later still, Abbie and Ebbs are no longer together. The doctor checked Abbie's scars and told her she had healed well. She looked down at her abdomen and agreed. Physically she had healed very well. The little cream lines near her belly button sat in the natural folds of her skin and could easily be mistaken for chicken pox scars. Yes. Physically she had healed very well.

And then later still, came an extra glass of wine to ease the pain, to keep her company, an attempt to fill the hole. And then later still came Dominic. But the hole was too big for him to fill too.

ABBIE

There's a florist outside the hospital, a makeshift tent-like structure that shelters the flowers from a rather chilled wind. From the weathered look of the owner, the stall is a somewhat more permanent structure than first glance would have you believe. I buy a sunshine mix of oranges and yellows, not sure what to get Beth, so choosing what seems safe. Olivia says she sometimes talks now, so she's on the road to recovery, but I have no idea what to expect. The flowers will give me something to hide behind. I am ready to be adamant about searching for a vase – and taking the whole of the visiting period to find one – if the Beth emerging isn't a person I recognise. I almost wish she was still catatonic – at least then I knew to expect nothing.

We get to share the lift up to the second floor with an old

man on a trolley, his pale, skinny shoulders and head supported by a thousand pillows, his torso and legs creating the smallest ripples in the blanket. He is singing to himself, conducting with one hand. The duo of orderlies in charge of his bed-on-wheels seem disinterested in their travelling patient. They talk to each other in short, sharp sentences in what I suspect is Polish. The patient doesn't seem to care that he's in a world of his own. I wonder if that's how Beth has felt – why she hides inside herself.

I feel far more nervous going up to her ward this time than I did on my other visits. Partly because she's now awake; partly because Paul is with me; partly because I'm sober. I usually face difficult times with wine. At least I have a protective bouquet in one hand and Paul's hand in the other. I can do this.

Beth looks completely normal and very ill at the same time. Her eyes are Manga-wide, the look of surprise on her face when she sees me also hints at cartoonish exaggeration. But underneath the out of sync facial expression I can sense Beth's presence. I hover by the foot of her bed until a nurse comes to rescue me, fussing over how gorgeous the flowers are and suggesting I sit down by the bed. Beth shakes her head and we all hesitate.

"Hug." She stretches out her arms. I fall into them. I have missed her so much.

She looks at the flowers the nurse has found a vase for: "Not a potted plant."

Paul starts laughing. I'd forgotten he was here. I'm embarrassed that something so irrelevant from our past has been dragged up. It's obvious her comment is about him – that it's something I've dragged with me from my past.

"So you've talked about me then?" he asks graciously, gently nudging my shoulder.

Beth looks from me to Paul and back to me. She may still seem to be surrounded by fog, but she's registering who he is.

"Beth, meet Paul, my, err, ex-husband…"

"And new boyfriend," he adds, smiling.

Beth holds out her arms again and gives Paul one of her famous bear hugs.

THE PERFUME INCIDENT

A hug. That's what Abbie craved from her Mummy. She stood in the doorway of the living room, broken sobs heaving from her chest, congealed blood and caked mud on her knees. She ached to be cuddled, to be soothed.

"Don't you dare come in here without cleaning yourself up first. I do not want that mess on my carpet."

With renewed sobs, Abbie dragged herself upstairs to the bathroom to clean her knees. Her feet heavy on the stairs, she found comfort in the pattern of creaks the stairs always made. The terry-towelling facecloth was hard and abrasive against her grazed skin, but she persevered and soon she had two too-pink knees, the skin in broken strings collecting around the sides of the wounds. She carefully peeled the strings off to make her knees look neater. Then she cried for the mess she had made on the floor and on the cloth, knowing both the splashes of water and the stains would be more reasons not to hug her.

Days later, Abbie had impressive scabs on her knees to show off at school. She told everyone she came off her bike at 100mph, even though she knew it wasn't that fast. Even the boys were impressed. The teacher gave her a quick squeeze of a cuddle and she felt the warmth of another human being surge through her arms and her chest. It took all her strength not to start crying again.

Abbie's epidermis healed quickly, as it was expected to do. As the main layer of protection between organs and the outside world, the top layer of human skin was designed to rapidly replicate, to heal itself by producing more skin to replace the damaged cells. Unfortunately for Abbie, the mental and emotional damage was not so easy to heal. She didn't even understand damage was being done – she's too young. She just knew she was not pretty enough or clever enough to be loved in the same way her friends were loved.

She sniffed at her skin, wondering if she was not huggable because she smelled funny. She couldn't smell anything, so she breathed on her skin and then sniffed it again. She recognised the scent of the swimming baths from three days ago, even though she has had more than one wash since. She realised she was not clean enough to love.

That evening, she spent over an hour in the bathroom, washing herself with the hottest water she could manage, scrubbing at her skin with a fresh facecloth until it felt pink and raw. She scrubbed everywhere hard except for her knees because they were still scabbed over. She sniffed at her knees again. They smelled metallic. She stood on the toilet seat, one foot at either side to steady herself, and reached up to the top shelf of the cabinet for Mummy's perfume. She managed to just get hold of the curved glass bottle without dropping it. Then she sat herself down on the toilet seat and pulled her knees up together in front of her. She didn't know if she was meant to shake the perfume bottle first, so she gave it a good wiggle, just in case. Then she took the lid off, pointed the tiny hole in the top at her knees, and pressed down on the top. A fine mist escaped the bottle and lands on her arms, her face, her knees. The stinging on her knees was equalled only by the burning in her eyes. She couldn't see.

She dropped the perfume bottle – which glided down the

edge of the bath like an experienced skier. But Abbie cared less about the hiding she'd get about a broken bottle. She was blind – and she was too young to know the affliction was temporary. She desperately put her hands out to find anything that can help her. Her left hand found her damp facecloth and she brought it desperately to her eyes, squeezing the water out onto them, blinking the soothing drops in. A few more blinks and her sight started to return, blurry at first, but then clearer as she grew more confident in her squeezing and blinking. She climbed down off the toilet seat, turned on the cold tap and cupped water in her hands, throwing it onto her face. The person she could now see clearly in the mirror looked like they'd been crying at 100mph. But at least she could see. At least.

She bent down and sniffed her knees. They smelled sweet. Abbie knew she was now worth hugging. She just needed to convince her Mummy. But Mummy was more interested in why Abbie smelled of her perfume, of why the perfume bottle was in the bath, all but smashed.

"But it's not broken Mummy," is all Abbie could say over and over.

But Mummy is angry, shouting about how the bottle could have smashed, how it would have been expensive perfume down the drain – literally. How Abbie couldn't be trusted with important things. How Abbie shouldn't climb up on the toilet seat because it's not for climbing. How she'd made a mess of water splashes all over the floor that mark the tiles and how Mummy would have to mop an extra time before Daddy got home.

"But it's not broken Mummy."

And her Mummy strikes her across the face and sends her to her room to "think about what she's done". Abbie was so shocked about being hit that the tears did not arrive until she was in her room. But she didn't mind because at least they soothed her eyes a bit more. And Abbie didn't get her hug. But at least her knees smelled nice.

As an adult, Abbie spends a lot of time wondering how many people go weeks, months, without hugs. Those who are single, who are not close to their parents, who don't have friends who are tactile. It's no wonder people crave being in a relationship, any relationship, just for the warmth of contact, just to hear the heartbeat of another human being. Without Paul, Ebbs, Dominic, Beth, she would have died of thirst a long time ago. How do people so disconnected from the humans around them survive without drinking in human contact?

After they leave Beth's bedside – 15 minutes after visiting hours are over, when they are quietly but firmly escorted out by one of the nurses – Abbie and Paul embrace as if they had not just been hugged by Beth, as if they had not had human contact for years. They cling to each other.

"Life is so fragile." Paul says it as Abbie thinks it.

And then he utters the words that break her heart: "Let's try for a baby."

ABBIE

What am I meant to say to him? That at least we have each other? That at least we can adopt? How do I explain to him that my body failed me when I was with someone else, making babies by accident? My life is an "at least" yet again. But I have to tell him. I've been cold towards him three days now and he has no idea what he's done "wrong". I'm punishing him for wanting something he always thought we both wanted together all those years ago.

It's breakfast. I'm sitting at the breakfast bar in his

kitchen on an achingly trendy stool made from reclaimed wood, the seat covered in faded denim. I know I shouldn't judge him for it, especially as it's a rented flat, and I'm thankful it's comfier than it looks. Paul is the other side of the high-gloss work surface, concentrating on frying eggs without breaking the yolks. The bacon is spitting from inside the grill. The beans spinning in a mug in the microwave. It's all perfectly normal. Calm. And I have the work surface to protect my mental space.

"I can't have kids," I tell him.

I watch his face awash with emotions – pain, fear, empathy, anger, more pain – each rippling quickly across his face to make way for the next. He loses concentration and the spatula dips into one of the eggs, breaking the yolk.

"Oh damn," he says. "I wanted your eggs to be perfect."

He then gasps at the unintentional cruelty of his comment.

"Oh God, sorry."

"It's okay," I say. I try to rush to comfort him, but he comes to me while I awkwardly climb off the too-high stool. He hugs me. And it's okay again.

"It was an accidental pregnancy," I tell his chest, talking into his soft pyjama top. "Ectopic. I lost both tubes through infection."

He pulls back slightly so he can look me in the eye, his hands holding firm on my upper arms.

"Accidental? So you didn't meet someone else you wanted to have kids with?"

"No."

"Oh thank God."

He pulls me close again, a hug to triumph over all other hugs. He holds me so tightly I can feel his sobs convulse against me. Smoke fills my nostrils.

"The bacon!"

He lets me go and pulls the grill pan out. Thin strips of black charred cardboard sit where healthy strips of bacon used to be. He starts laughing.

"I've got you back," he says. "I was stupid and selfish and short-sighted and I left you. And now I've got you back. I don't care about having kids if I can't have them with you. I was so scared you'd found someone else you wanted kids with because I never met anyone else. Nobody who could replace you."

This time it's me pulling him into a hug, squeezing him tightly to say I was never able to replace him either.

"But at least we can adopt."

"At least we can adopt?" Paul repeats. "At least? What have I told you about 'at least'?"

I shrug my shoulders. I'd just been trying to find a way to make things okay.

"That's not an 'at least' – that's perfect. We can rescue someone who never got hugs from their parents, show them what real love is about. That's not 'at least': that's everything."

The humble teabag

The teabag is seen as the poor man's version of tea — although it's now more the common man's, as few people bother with the routine of tea leaves on a daily basis.

Loose leaf or teabag, whether the leaves get to float freely inside a teapot or just inside their perforated paper home, they still have the same job to do — the metamorphosis from leaf into infusion.

The old way of doing things — the supposed right way of doing things — doesn't always make the most sense.

Olivia knows that teabags make perfectly good tea. And that sometimes perfectly good tea is all that's needed. Surely the quality of the company you share it with is the most important element of a good cup of tea?

28 teaspoons

OLIVIA

I'm sorting through boxes of stuff. Not boxes of Matt's stuff. He has already been to collect his belongings from outside the flat. Well, that or somebody has stolen them all. I was careful to wrap anything of worth up in his scruffy clothes in the hope that if someone else in the building did go through them, they'd be very disappointed very quickly. Not boxes of Beth's stuff either. Her flat is untouched except for me binning the perishable items from her fridge, many of which were already beyond being fit for consumption before she went into hospital. No. I'm sorting through boxes of Faye's stuff.

She and Ethan are back in just-north-of-London and she's not coming back. She's asked me to clear out all of her belongings, giving anything of any worth to a local charity shop – of which, as in every wealthy-but-achingly-cool area, there are many. I'm surprised at all the stuff she's left behind. It looks like she's taken clothes and very little else. There are patterns in the dust on her chest of drawers that suggest key beauty or jewellery items were taken. But the room feels very much like a mausoleum for a life discarded.

It's difficult to decide what to throw away in someone else's life, but not wanting to carry a dozen loads to the charity shop is enough for me to be practical about it. I have a roll of black bin bags ready to play both bin and carrier of charity goods, plus a couple of Faye's plastic tubs that I'm using as recycling. I've also got a cardboard folder to put any useful paperwork in which I plan to post down to her once I'm done.

The folder is mustard yellow, faded where it must have sat in direct sunlight for some time. The name "Faye Simmons" has been written, crossed out, and rewritten numerous times – an older Faye rejecting the handwriting of her younger self. Occasionally, the name is "Faye Astley" or "Faye Schofield". These versions are accompanied with love hearts. It takes me a second to twig that these are probably childhood crushes – Rick Astley and Phillip Schofield. Calm, friendly, dependable – far more like Ethan than like Jack.

Sorting out the books is easy. There aren't many of them and some are so dog-eared or watermarked that a charity wouldn't take them, so they go in the recycling. Faye hasn't left many clothes behind and except for a couple of rather beautiful cardigans, everything else is for the textiles bin, along with the bedding. I greatly suspect the almost threadbare My Little Pony bedding is a charity find of Faye's. When I think of Ethan's large frame squeezing into a single bed with Faye, lying underneath this bedding, I have to stifle a snigger. It does seem perfect for Faye though. I wonder what, if anything, that means.

I leave the bare duvet folded neatly on the end of the bed, bare pillows on top, in case they belong to the landlord. I leave the curtains hanging in the windows – the jacquard/floral mix is 100% not Faye. Not even ironically.

Under the bed is a tomb to a life left behind. Boxes and boxes of random notes, half-hearted attempts at poetry, pencil drawings, and lots and lots of photographs. The ones of Faye, Ethan and Jack intrigue me the most – not what's in them, but the fact they are here at all. I assumed they would be treasured items that Faye would have taken with her. In all the photos, Faye has a carefree look that I don't recognise, which makes me sad. There's something beautiful about her when she looks like she has everything she needs. Jack's face isn't as easy to read. He's carrying something – pain maybe, a secret. It's hard to tell. My favourite photo is of the two of them looking at each other with that look I've seen other people give each other: that I've never had someone give to me. What a silly thing for Jack to throw away. What a silly photo for Faye to leave behind.

There are no photos of any motorbike, so I'm guessing that came along later – an expensive hobby the average university student couldn't afford. I wonder if their inherent danger draws people like Jack and Beth in; if they ride because they know how quickly, how messily it could end. I never met Jack and I will never know what drove him to do it. But then, I've known Beth for years and I doubt I will understand what made her even consider it. And then there's Sophie. The idea that her behaviour towards me was driven by demons in her mind so terrible they bullied her too? That's easy for me to comprehend – I'm my own worst bully too. In some ways, it would have been nice to sit down and explain to her the damage she did to me. But seeing her again in hospital had been so traumatising, I'm just glad I know I'll never bump into her again.

I take the best photos of Jack and Faye together and put them in the mustard folder. Not to send to her now, but to keep, just in case. With them sit a pile of papers that look important – all typed and addressed to Faye. If she had any personal correspondence, any notebooks, any diary, she took them all with her. Except for the items from her childhood and teenage years, there are very few personal items here.

With her room cleared out and the bin bags stuffed in the wheelie bins outside or lining the pavement outside the closest charity shop, I head to the shared rooms to see if there's anything so clearly Faye's that I should take it. Nothing screams at me as being hers, which suggests to me that she lived in her bedroom, hiding away – not typical actions of the Faye I thought she was, but very much like the Faye I'm realising she is. Her attitude, her extroversion, the forced jollity behind her diving onto the sofa at The Blue Pig – it was her hair to hide behind.

It feels strange leaving a note for the two flatmates of Faye's that I've never met.

I've made a snap decision to move to London and have cleared out my room. If I've left anything in the shared space, please claim it or bin it, as I won't be coming back for anything else.

Wishing you all the best,
Faye x

I have no idea if they've seen her handwriting – I certainly haven't. Well, not a recent version anyway: just the scrawls of her name through the years. Even without seeing its most recent iteration, I'm positive it won't be anything like mine. But that will be something for her former flatmates to ponder over. I quite like the idea they might suspect foul play and get the police involved. But in reality I could do with some normality, some quiet time. So I hope they don't give the note a second thought.

There's something quite satisfying about vacuuming Faye's room and turning it into an anonymous space. I like the idea that it's easy to walk away from something when you've had enough, as I have with Matt. With him gone, my flat smells different; the rotting, festering odour has gone. My lounge has grown in size and the rooms are brighter now the curtains aren't permanently closed. It feels like it's back to being my flat again. I've even turned the mattress. The level of cleaning I put into my place is far higher than I bother with at Faye's. But from the state of her room, I know what I've done will amaze her landlord and her flatmates. They will all have seen the mess and dust she was living in.

MAYBE IT'S KARMA

Olivia wants to squeeze in a visit to the memorial gardens before she spends the rest of the afternoon at the hospital. She's all but certain Maggie's ashes have been scattered there now. She likes to visit because she thinks it's important to remember the unsung people who've made a difference to people's lives in lots of tiny ways.

In her visits to the hospital, she's slowly pulling more syllables out of Beth, watching her rejoin the conversation a few words at a time. Beth needed to tell Olivia about Sophie – it was bursting out of her – and it meant she reached out, she spoke. Olivia realises it means she has something to be grateful for Sophie for. And even though she doesn't believe in any of that karma nonsense that Faye likes to spout… maybe it is karma.

OLIVIA

I know before I see him that it's Matt. I hear a kerfuffle out in reception, the scraping of a chair as Noah, the security guard, hastily stands up to try and stop the intruder making their way into our office. I know it is him because a calmness has descended over my life in the past few days that I very much want. And I know he will know this and will try to ruin it for me. Thankfully, the Siobhan Rileys and Liam Reeveses are not in the main office today, but secured away upstairs in the boardroom for a strategy meeting over the lunch I ordered from Browns, so the audience is going to be far smaller than Matt is hoping for. Noah reaches Matt just as Matt flings the double doors open and calls out: "Olivia!"

The few sets of eyes that are there are on me, then on Matt, then on me again. I know I need to contain this as best as possible, so I nod at Noah and follow the two of them out to reception, Matt going willingly when he realises I'm ready to follow. Toby is seconds behind me, stopping only to ensure the doors to the office are fully closed to give us as much privacy as possible.

"Where the fuck is Maggie?"

Matt is confused, wide-eyed, and I can't help but feel sorry for him. It takes all my strength not to hug him, but I have to remember that this is the person who didn't even turn up to her funeral.

"Did you not read my letter? I told you that you had until the end of last week to sign for her ashes or they would scatter them in the gardens at the cemetery. Whether or not they've done that yet or whether it was an empty threat to get you to collect them, I don't know. As I said in the letter, they won't tell me anything because I'm not a relative."

Matt slumps slightly in Noah's arms and Noah's grip turns into more of a protective hug. I have a feeling Matt angrily threw my letter away without reading it. Or read it and thought he could turn up to hear a different version of events.

I compose myself. When I speak again, my voice is calmer, but I'm still as firm: "I'm no more responsible for Maggie's ashes than I am for you. How could you not come to the chapel? Maggie loved you and yet you just didn't turn up. It made me realise that you've not been turning up for me either."

The confusion grows on his thick-headed face. I'm going to have to spell it out for him. Which is okay: I probably need to hear myself say it too.

"Yes you were there in the flat, but physically, not mentally. You checked out of our relationship months, maybe even years, ago. I've carried you and all your worries for so long, with so little in return. It's what Maggie did for you too, but I always thought you'd give back when you could, so it was okay. And when she needed you and you didn't…"

I stop speaking. I've said as much as needs saying. The resignation in Matt's shoulders is clear. Feeling Matt's acceptance, Noah carefully guides him towards the front entrance. I don't know if there's going to be a repeat of today, either here at work, or maybe outside the flat, but I know I'm going to be strong enough to deal with it if it does. And I know I'm strong enough to deal with any of the fallout at work that Matt turning up today brings.

I catch Toby looking at me.

"You're amazing," he says.

It's not what I expect him to say. I was expecting comments about bringing personal problems to work, maybe an off-hand joke about my choice of boyfriend, as Matt was looking particularly unkempt. At best I was expecting a hurried "Are you okay?" accompanied by an arm movement signalling us back into the office.

"You are. You're amazing."

Toby realises I need to hear it twice.

He has a look on his face I've only ever seen other people give to other people. It's my first time. And I know I have the same look on my face too. So I say I need a drink to calm my nerves and ask him if he'd like to join me. And he says "Yes", an arm stretched out to guide me back into the office to get my coat and bag. He's not giving me the chance to change my mind. And we head out to the pub together like two people who go to the pub together all the time.

All this time I thought I was channelling Beth. I've been channelling me.

29 teapots

BETH

They are letting me go home. Not because I'm better in its truest sense as in being well, but because I'm better than I was, the relative situation I'm in from where I've come from. They also need the bed for someone who needs it more than me. The Girl's bed has already been taken by someone who just sleeps.

I'm not actually going home though. I'm going to stay at Olivia's. She has taken a week off work and we are going to attempt to feel normal about things like reading, eating, watching TV, even though there will never really be a normal for me again. I'm waiting for Olivia to turn up. She's bringing a suitcase for my things, the ones that turned up sporadically as I needed them, usually brought by Olivia, occasionally by Abbie. Someone in the hospital team has already squeezed my things into large, dark green plastic bags. The ones that people leave here with when they leave alive. But Olivia is insisting on a suitcase. Apparently, Abbie says the luggage you use to carry your crap around with you is important. Faye didn't bring any of my things. And not a single visit. The only thing linked to Faye is the postcard – not clever, artistic or cool, so probably hastily bought – with an address in Hertfordshire on it. It's where Ethan lives and now it's where Faye lives. At least for the moment anyway. Olivia and Abbie are concerned, but they have tried to hide this from me, as they see my predicament as far worse than the one Faye is in. I think they should be worrying more about Faye. I have a whole team of trained and experienced NHS staff looking out for me. Faye just has us three.

I'm not sure I can ever admit to anyone that I'm getting myself better because I watched the end of someone who didn't. Those curls sticking out from under the sheet. Those were curls that had not been seen for a long time; when she'd arrived they were smoothed and straightened, temporarily tamed. But here you are the most base version of yourself. Only a few bother with the outside world luxuries of make-up and proper clothes. I'm wearing proper clothes today. They are mine but they do not fit. They hang off me, my narrower shoulders creating longer sleeves that half cover my hands. My mental health has eaten away at my reserves, consumed calories I couldn't afford to lose. I've seen myself in the mirror a few times in the last few days. My face doesn't look as drained or as haggard as I expected. Instead there is something missing – it reminds me of how Olivia used to look. I'm like a Rubik's Cube with all the stickers removed.

As Olivia walks in to collect me, I see her glance up at the whiteboard of names for slightly longer than necessary, double-checking for the name that she knows is no longer there. If I can ever admit to anyone that I'm getting myself better because I watched the end of someone who didn't, I'm not sure the person I admit it to can be Olivia. I've not really started talking again yet, but my thinking is up to scratch. And I don't think she needs the guilt she will inevitably feel from feeling doubly glad that her nemesis is dead.

MUM'S THE WORD

In her first days in hospital, Beth would cry out for her mother. But it wasn't the cry of someone who wanted to be comforted in the way she was as a child. It was the pain of someone who never felt truly loved. The nurses would come over and hush her, give her something to help her sleep – just as they did with Sophie. In those early days, "Mum" was the only word Beth managed to speak. For the rest of the time she was quiet. And the nurses soothed her and were patient.

Some patients, like Beth, wake up from their mental nightmare. And some, like Sophie, do not. The difference is: Beth found a reason to want to.

30 teabags

THE VOICE FROM BEFORE

Today's the day. I'm going to do this.

That's what I say to myself over and over in my head as I pull on my leathers, fasten the straps on my boots, and pull on my crash helmet and adjust the chin strap. Actually, I'm mumbling to myself, saying it out loud: "Today's the day. Today's the day." I take a quick look round to make sure there's nobody around to hear me. Not that it would make much difference. I'm so focused on today I have no space in my thoughts for other people.

I walk up to my bike. She's a beauty. I think bikes are female, as ships are. There's something enslaving about her curves, the way she calls me. I'm addicted to the buzz I get when I ride her. I don't even need to be going quickly. I like to think she responds to my every move, but I'm also conscious of the sliver of fear I get whenever I twitch the throttle and her engine growls.

I put the key in the ignition, climb over her, then put my gloves on, taking time to pull my jacket sleeves over the edges. There's nothing quite like the pain you feel deep in your bones from riding a bike in the cold when you've got a draught between your layers. I've got a patch of skin on my lower back that I believe has been damaged from my early days of riding when my trousers and jacket didn't zip together. The nerve endings on a 10in-by-2in stretch of skin have never fully recovered, not even after hour upon hour of hot baths.

Kicking up the stand, turning the key, pulling in the clutch, putting her in first, I'm a conductor in front of an orchestra playing his favourite piece of music, I know every move. I pull down my visor, my final move before I pull off from the kerb and join the living.

"Today's the day."

THE KEY INTO THE IGNITION

Jack throws his leg over the bike, settles down into the seat, right foot on the ground. He pulls on his gloves and then gives the key a sharp, short clockwise turn. A split-second pause before the lights on the dashboard engage. Jack double-checks the neutral light out of habit. His left foot kicks up the bike stand and takes to the gear pedal in one motion. He's done this so many times it's as instinctive as breathing, as swallowing. Hands grip. Levers in, buttons pressed, gear pedal down one notch. Then a slow twist with one hand while the other releases the lever and his bike purrs into action.

Like breathing. Like swallowing. Jack swallows hard, forcing his nerves back down into his stomach where they morph into butterflies. Or moths. Once he has made a decision, it is made, but that doesn't mean the steps to take him there are any easier: they are simply decided on.

Jack heads out through parts of London he's never seen before. It has been his home for years, but it's a corner of the city that's not his. He's already left what he knows behind. The A40 turns into the M40: the 1960s Westway cocooning the road in concrete, 1940s semi-detached conformity, the jaded art deco sophistication of the Hoover building, all of it gives way to green. A flat, alien land without buildings, with only other vehicles, mostly lorries, for company. The angular road sign arches and skinny streetlight posts are no competition for the occasional majestic pylon rising up out of the green, some with their six arms straight, others with them bent down at the elbow. Finally trees and the normality of motorways.

The M40 to the M6 – a road he knows well from sitting in the back of his parents' car, the kid so used to his Dad's slow and careful driving that he didn't bother asking "Are we nearly there yet?". Weaving in and out of traffic, Jack is not slow or careful, relying on his reflexes to keep him safe. Tiring and exhilarating in equal measures, Jack stops only to refuel – Mars bar for him, petrol for his bike. Head lowered, shoulders curved, knees tucked in, he shapes himself round his bike to offer the least resistance to the flow of air around him. Finally onto the M60 then the M602. The tarmac yawns out ahead of the clock display, ahead of the handlebars, and ahead of the spinning rubber that Jack knows is beneath him, even though he can't see it. You sometimes have to believe in things you can't see.

The hints of rooftops give into shaggy bushes and forgotten fences that blend into the hubbub. At some point the road starts to dip and Jack finds himself at ground floor level. Then the concrete oppression starts. Tyrannical walls jutting upwards from the hard shoulder. The raw, unpainted untreated surface is the closest man has come to achieving urban nature. Manchester's Westway. The road dips down further and the houses are now floating above the road, walkways with metal railings breaking up the monotony of the granite embankment.

Signs for Trafford Park, Eccles, Salford. The poorer cousins of the "Capital of the North" or "Northern Powerhouse" or whatever name the latest horde of politicians felt fit to name it, to pretend that life outside of London mattered to any of them. Jack preferred Madchester or Gaychester or any name that reflected the exciting and free place it was to him before he got confirmation of who he was – of the burden he had to carry.

Leaving Eccles behind, there are flashes of green again, then ridged concrete, then green, and so few signs of civilisation just a few miles out from the city. It is a straight road, unbroken, undeviating, its concrete companion uninterrupted. Jack's bike is crow-flying, taking the straightest route into the city. No reasons to turn. So why is the disc of rubber that Jack cannot see – the one he has to believe is still beneath him – why is it twisting to the left?

The rest of the bike follows, prisoner to the front wheel. There are no sounds of braking.

JACK

Today's the day I end it all. I've been waiting for this moment for a long time. I've lived a life trying to create perfect memories and I've ended up not living at all. I'm sick of existing with the cruelty of this disease and the knowledge that each day could be my last. So I'm taking back control the only way I can – by choosing for myself when the end comes.

I'd chosen the A40 Westway, to paintball myself into an

anonymous stretch of a concrete castle, but for some reason I just kept on riding. Recklessly weaving in and out of the traffic on the M6, I was fully expecting to come to a gristly, grisly end by misjudging a gap, but by the time I reach the M602 I realise my reactions, my instincts, are too good. If I'm going to end it, I'm going to have to do it myself. I'm breathing in great gulps of air, the oxygen mixed with nitrogen dioxide and other airborne chemicals making me high. So much oxygen my hands and arms start to feel numb.

I know what I had always known: that I'm already dead. The numbness spreads through me. I'm going over 80mph. I turn the handlebars. I don't brake.

ALSO JACK

Today's the day I find Faye. I've lived a life trying to create perfect memories and I've ended up moving on from things too quickly, too ready to make the next memories, not holding on to the ones that count. After yet another failed relationship, another person who couldn't match up to Faye, I knew I had to seek her out.

I'm hoping she is exactly how and where I left her – in Manchester, and just as beautiful, fragile, fluid, brave, strong. I can't weave in and out of the traffic on the M60 quickly enough. The longer I'm on my bike, the longer the journey seemed to take. I'm achingly tired, but don't want to stop. By the time I reach the M602, my arms are feeling numb.

Just as I'm questioning whether or not the vibrations through the handlebars could make my hands and arms feel quite this bad, the pains in my chest hit. I start to buckle under the weight of the pain, leaning in towards my left to instinctively protect myself. Inadvertently leaning harder on the right handlebar. Turning the front wheel towards the wall of concrete to my left. My right hand accidentally pulling down on the throttle, my bike accelerating towards the wall.

I realise what is happening too late. I have no time to apply the brakes.

The point is that it doesn't matter which version of events is true. Each person has their own truth and it's the beliefs of the people I've left behind that matter now, not what actually happened. My parents never knew I was ill, so they will never have the "reasonable doubt" Ethan has that I didn't kill myself. And I think that is a just punishment for them not being honest with me. I had to face my illness alone because they never told me I was adopted. Now they will always assume I killed myself, always wonder whether it was nature/nurture, whether they could have done more.

Ethan having to live with that "reasonable doubt" – and never being able to tell my parents – seems a fair price to pay for loving Faye and never being able to admit it to me, to his best friend. He couldn't respect me enough to be honest with me about it because I was ill. I'm not sure at what point he admitted to himself that he was waiting for me to die so he could step in, be the hero, the shoulder to cry on, the one who stood by Faye. On the outside he looks like the good guy, but on the inside he's just as selfish as I was.

I found myself surrounded by people who couldn't be honest with me. And the only person who was? She was the person I threw away. Faye.

Your teacup

Drink up!

– The End –

Interview with Beth

So how has life been treating you?

When I first left hospital, I assumed I'd be on the mend, so when I had another mental crash it was a huge shock to me. I was lucky in that I got to see an NHS psychiatrist quite quickly – I was already on the referral waiting list from my time in hospital.

The biggest shock was being diagnosed with ADHD. When my psychiatrist first suggested it, I thought she was having a mental blip of her own! I didn't know anything about the emotional hypersensitivity or impulsiveness symptoms. I think the disorder needs a new name.

When you hear someone has ADHD, you think of a six-year-old boy terrorising his classmates, rather than a neurodevelopmental disorder that affects people into their adult years. I didn't realise that the hyperactivity the name refers to is in internal – and that not everyone has external manifestations of this.

I thought I'd been coping all those years, but actually I'd been treading water – and making myself more and more unhappy, ill and stressed. If Jack's death hadn't been the trigger it would have been something else.

Now I understand why I ask questions when everyone else is able to hold back, why my mind drifts off when I'm struck by an idea, and why I can be floored by intense emotions. I have a dopamine deficiency.

I'm currently trying out medication that helps raise my dopamine levels, but it's too early to say if it will work for me. Caffeine also increases dopamine levels, so it looks like I've been self-medicating with strong brews all these years. Yet another reason to have a second cup!

Are you still in touch with the others?

Livvy and I now rent a flat together. We've decided it makes sense to have "another person" there – and we're very good at giving each other strength. Not everything has changed though. I'm still working as a designer, she's still working in administration, we still go to the pub on Fridays. Some things are best left as they are.

I see less of Abbie now that she's back with Paul. She was always happy to escape Dominic's company, so it's a good change – it means she's with the right person. I'd like to see more of her, but she's also cut down on how much she's drinking, so I don't pressure her to come out.

I've not seen Faye at all since she moved down to London. I've still not come to terms with what happened there. I thought we had a really special friendship, but it looks like I was just meeting emotional needs that are now being met by someone else. So I think it's best that we've not kept in touch.

I was going to ask you how you take your tea...

Ha ha ha! Strong brews for me. I'm happy with bog standard teabags. In fact I could do with one now.

Interview with Abbie

So how has life been treating you?

Very well, thanks. Paul and I are taking things slowly because we got it wrong the first time round and we want to make sure we don't make the same mistakes. We're living separately and stay at each other's places on the weekends. We also try to have at least one date night a week, but we're both busy workwise, so that doesn't always work out!

Beth mentioned that you're drinking less?

Did she? Hmm. She's become very conscious of how drugs can affect our mental state since her diagnosis, so I guess it's playing on her mind a little. The drink driving was the wake-up call for me. I'd always told myself that I could get blotto as often as I wanted because it was only me it affected. But now I know that's not true.

I tried to have a dry month and that didn't go so well – I managed nine days! So instead I've decided to have a longer-term plan of having four alcohol-free days each week. I've noticed that on the days I do drink I seem to be drinking less although it can easily creep up.

I'm no longer buying cases of wine and having them delivered; I now buy one bottle at a time from the local off licence. So if I get through a whole bottle in an evening and I'm craving for another glass, it's tough – there isn't any! So I'm being more self-aware about my drinking. I don't believe I'm an alcoholic though.

We know you're still in touch with Beth – what about Olivia and Faye?

Olivia and I have become much closer since the night in the hospital waiting to hear about Beth. Livvy was also there for me when Dominic said he wanted to fight for half the house – which he didn't get. We're very different people, but we've developed a mutual respect for each other that I don't think was there before.

I've not seen Faye at all. I get the occasional message from her, but contact is sporadic and she's not very good at responding to questions! I think it was easy for us to be social friends when we were both in Manchester, but the distance has made us both more aware of how different we are.

Beth mentioned that she and Faye are no longer in touch...

I can understand why Beth feels she was deserted. But I'm not very good at conflict and I'm often the first out the door when trouble is brewing, so I can see Faye's standpoint too. I think Faye's head was very much wrapped up in Jack's death and finding out Ethan was in love with her and she just didn't have the space left to support Beth. I'm not saying that's okay, but I do understand it.

Last question: how do you take your tea?

I've started drinking green tea with jasmine. It's part of the whole detox thing now I'm cutting down on drinking. It's quite pleasant as long as you drink it hot. I spend half my time reheating mugs of the stuff in the microwave!

Interview with Olivia

So how has life been treating you?

To be honest, I feel like a new person. I'd depended on Beth for so much I saw her as my oxygen supply, always fearing it would be cut off. It never occurred to me that she would need to rely on me one day – and that I'd be able to deliver. Obviously, what Beth has been through is just awful, and I'm not saying I'm glad it happened – although she is, as it happens, because it means she got diagnosed. I think she feels like a new person too.

So... Matt? Toby?

Toby is just lovely. I think the fact he's older helps: he's more cautious about rushing into anything. He also organised it so that I'm now the PA for a pool of three lawyers at the firm, so I no longer work directly for him. It's the sort of thoughtfulness that I adore him for. I can remember thinking I didn't see him as boyfriend material and now I don't understand why I'd ever think that.

Matt has finally left me alone – hopefully! Although it's

partly because he doesn't know my new address. I also think the chances of bumping into Beth has maybe stopped him trying too hard to follow me home from work.

He's stopped turning up at work now Noah on reception knows him and has threatened to call the police if he comes back again. Noah has even gone out to him and asked him to move on when he's seen Matt loitering outside. I'm hoping not to have to get the police involved, so I'm hoping he's given up.

In his last visit to my old flat, before I moved, he asked me if there was anything he could do to win me back. It was heart-breaking but I had to be firm and say "No". He explained he couldn't go to Maggie's funeral because he wasn't ready to say goodbye to her – and thanked me for going in his place. He also said he'd asked for her ashes to be sprinkled in the remembrance garden so I could still visit her there. I can't go though, which is a shame – it's too secluded a place to risk bumping into Matt and I'm too scared that he'd tried to orchestrate it.

So, you're sharing a flat with Beth, and Abbie says you're now closer?

Sharing with Beth made sense for both of us. She's infuriating to have around because she has piles of things everywhere that you can't move as they're part of her "system". I thought she was joking at first, but she seems to operate her whole life that way. She could never do my job!

Abbie and I are definitely closer, which is lovely. I don't see her as much as I used to, but I think the time we spend together is better quality time. Simple, the bar, has now closed, so we can't have any more milkshake marathons, but I look back at that day as the turning point in our friendship.

She and Paul are so sweet together – I hope they make things work. Paul has since moved firms, but he was at Thricks & Cruthers for about six months before he left, so I got to know him quite well, which was an added bonus.

And Faye?

I never felt completely comfortable in Faye's company: I felt as if she'd prefer me not to be there. I don't know if this is my paranoia talking, but she's not made any effort to keep in touch since I sent that folder of paperwork to her. I think now she's not in Manchester anymore that it's easier to let things lie.

Last question: how do you take your tea?

My favourite is still Darjeeling!

Interview with Faye

So how has life been treating you?

Things are much better for me now I'm no longer in Manchester. I had no idea just how much Jack was casting a shadow across my life. But now I live somewhere where I don't have any memories of him, my vision seems clearer.

And Ethan?

We're no longer together. I initially moved into his place in Berkhamsted, but it was very clear to me very quickly that the Faye he'd fallen in love with was no more real than the Jack I'd fallen for.

I think we can know 50% of someone and we construct the other 50% to be just how we'd like them to be. So the half we actually know lives up to what we expect – and the half we don't know, well, that just leads to disappointments.

Ethan feels disappointed in me, which is a shame, but in the end he was simply the third point in the triangle. He couldn't be anything more.

Beth and Olivia both mentioned they're no longer in touch...

Beth's demands on me were totally unfair. I'd just found out Jack had died and suddenly she wanted everything to be about her. I was waiting until she came out of hospital to see her because I hate hospitals. But then she was in longer than I expected and already I'd moved down south before she got out, so...

Olivia is a lovely girl, really lovely. And I do appreciate her going round to my flat and sorting out my things. But we never really connected, and I think that's a key element to any friendship.

What about Abbie?

She chased me for Ethan's address so Olivia could send me some stuff – apparently Olivia had messaged me and I'd ignored it. I'd given the address to Beth, but I'm guessing that postcard ended up in the bin.

After I sent Abbie the address she asked if I was accepting visitors, so I said "Oh we must organise something soon" – in the way that you do when you want to say "No" but don't want to be so blunt.

So I feel obligated to message her at the moment, but I'm responding less and less frequently, waiting for her messages to die out. I just want to leave that part of my life in the past – along with Jack, Ethan, all of it.

Last question: how do you take your tea?

I know the British are meant to be obsessed with tea, but I think there's a point where you have to stop and say: "It's just a drink!"

I'm much more of a coffee fan myself. There's a gorgeous artisan coffee house near my new place in Hackney. I try to pop in at least twice a week.

It's. Just. Perfect.

About the Author

Sarah Marie Graye was born in Manchester, United Kingdom, in 1975, to English Catholic parents. One of five daughters, to the outside world Sarah Marie's childhood followed a relatively typical Manchester upbringing... until aged nine, when she was diagnosed with depression.

It's a diagnosis that has stayed with Graye over three decades, and something she believes has coloured every life decision, including the one to write a novel. Graye wrote *The Second Cup* as part of an MA Creative Writing practice as research degree at London South Bank University – where she was the vice-chancellor's scholarship holder.

First published in July 2017, *The Second Cup* was longlisted for the Book Viral 2017 Millennium Book Award and was included in Read Freely's Top 50 Indie Books 2017.

A NOTE FROM THE AUTHOR

In *The Second Cup*, Beth's story doesn't have a resolution – she just decides to try and get better. It's something I did after suffering from depression for a long time, and I even fooled myself into thinking it had worked.

Shortly after *The Second Cup* was published, I had a breakdown and have since been diagnosed with ADHD. I have dedicated this edition of my novel to Dr Helen Read, the psychiatrist who diagnosed me.

I now realise I'd accidentally given Beth the same condition, and I wanted to give her the chance to get a diagnosis too – hence the character interviews.

I want to **thank you** for taking time to read *The Second Cup*. If you enjoyed it, please consider telling your friends or posting a short review on Amazon. A recommendation is the best present you can give to an indie author.

FIND THE AUTHOR ONLINE

Website:	sarahmariegraye.com
Twitter:	twitter.com/SarahMarieGraye
Facebook:	facebook.com/sarahmariegraye
Instagram:	instagram.com/sarahmariegraye

28878471R00176

Printed in Great Britain
by Amazon

Linda's

Flat Stomach Secrets

Linda Lazarides

WATERFALL 2000

London

Other works by Linda Lazarides

Principles of Nutritional Therapy
The Nutritional Health Bible
The Waterfall Diet
The HIV Self-Help Manual
Treat Yourself with Nutritional Therapy
The Amino Acid Report
The Big Healthy Soup Diet
A Textbook of Modern Naturopathy

About the Author

Linda Lazarides is a naturopathic nutritionist and founder of the British Association for Nutritional Therapy and Applied Nutrition. She has worked in general practice for the British National Health Service and is best known for her work on water retention, described in her book *The Waterfall Diet* (Piatkus Books, UK bestseller, September 1999).

©Linda Lazarides 2010
Published by Waterfall2000
BCM Waterfall
London WC1N 3XX
United Kingdom
www.health-diets.net

Linda Lazarides asserts the moral right to be identified as the author of this work.

Disclaimer
This book is not intended as a substitute for proper medical advice. All persistent symptoms should be reported to a doctor.

Printed and bound by CPI Group (UK) Ltd, Croydon, CR0 4YY

CONTENTS

Can You See Your Toes?

In this book you will find out some startling and astonishing facts that few people know. Some of the secrets you will learn include:

- The difference between 'belly bulge' and 'belly flab'.
- You have a natural internal corset of muscles which you can strengthen while you're walking, driving or sitting at a desk.
- There is one common food ingredient which adds to your bulge more rapidly than anything else.
- Obsessive food cravings can come from a nasty type of fat that grows deep inside your tummy.
- Women who are most susceptible to stress have the biggest waistlines.
- Why consuming 'diet' products may make you *gain* weight.
- What causes bloating and gas and how to get rid of them.
- How eating a very low-calorie diet can give you a swollen tummy.

Everybody wants a flat tummy. Most of us look longingly at pictures of men with six-packs and models in bikinis with wonderfully toned midriffs. We sigh and shake our heads at the amount of work it takes to achieve such physical perfection. If only we had the time, energy, willpower and so on.

If you're anything like me, you might get motivated from time to time. Going on a diet, running, cycling or swimming or a subscription at the gym. Maybe the pounds start dropping off the rest of your body. But months later, when your willpower is mostly exhausted, more often than not your tummy is still nearly as large as ever, your toes are still invisible unless you pull your tummy in, and powerful control garments seem like the only remaining option. If only it was just a matter of losing a few pounds and doing a few sit-ups!

An episode from my past

In fact, getting a flat stomach could be easier than you think. I was inspired to write this book after recalling an episode in my life when my stomach became flat and I could see my toes with no problem at all. This happened when I was 20 years old, on a student trip in Romania. There were about 200 of us from many different countries, living in a large hall of residence, and all eating the same meals. It was a hot summer, and the inevitable struck—mass gastroenteritis. After two days of running to the lavatory six times a day, I suddenly noticed that my stomach was flat. Completely and wonderfully flat as never before!

Sadly, as soon as I recovered, my tummy went back to its normal bulging self. For the next 30 years I wondered how I could get my tummy flat again. I tried every kind of 'colon cleanse' routine, and even resorted to colonic irrigation—having my colon washed out with water twice a week for six weeks. Some people believe this approach works like magic. Not in my case! Nothing really seemed to help.

Finally, two years ago, after some self-experimentation, I created my Internal Cleansing Routine. After following it for three months, I could finally see my toes. The details of this routine are being published for the very first time in this book.

Easy, three-pronged approach

This guide would not be complete if all I did was give you my internal cleansing routine. It worked for me, but it's not the only solution. So I extended my quest to discover *all* the reasons why a tummy bulge can be so hard to lose. On my journey I found some extraordinary, sometimes horrifying, information which I'm sharing with you in this book.

After putting all this information together, I have designed a three-pronged approach to tackle the four main causes of tummy bulge. I believe it will massively improve your prospects of getting a lean and beautiful silhouette. My Flat Stomach Programme is designed for individuals who:

- Don't want to spend hours in the gym every week
- Have already spent hours exercising and still have a problem
- Don't want to starve themselves to lose weight
- Have a problem with bloating.

The three-pronged formula consists of:

- Exercises you can do while you sit or walk
- My Flat Stomach Diet
- My three-month Internal Cleansing Routine

Go ahead and get a beautiful body. Let me know how you get on!

Linda Lazarides

Success is a journey,
not a destination.
Focus on the process.

Chapter 1

The way you walk can make you fat

Nothing reveals your personality and hang-ups more than your posture and the way you move your body: the way you sit, stand and walk. Most of us don't walk very well. We waddle, slouch, march or strut. Dominant people stride purposefully, lead with the chin, or even seem to stamp as they walk. Less confident people drag their feet or shuffle along.

Many of us walk around leaning forward and partly

collapsed at the waist. Not only does this give you terrible posture, it makes your tummy look much larger than it really is, it makes you look older and it sets you up for back problems in later life. Try observing people as they walk. See if you can recognise your own gait or way of walking. By habitually using the wrong muscles when they walk, many people develop unshapely legs, or foot or back pain in later life.